GALLOWS HILL
The Investigative Paranormal Society
Book 2

Charles F. French

Gallows Hill: The Investigative Paranormal Society
(Book 2)

Copyright © Charles F. French 2018

Edition 2018

ISBN-13: 9781980290919

Editor: Lisa Lewis

Cover design: Judy Bullard
www.customebookcovers.com

To my closest friend, Rich,
whom I have known my entire life.
You are my friend, my true brother.

ACKNOWLEDGEMENTS

As with my first novel, there are many people to thank for their help and encouragement. Lisa Lewis, thank you for being an excellent editor. John Roccaro, Richard Loeb, and Edward Haas, who have always given their support; thank you for your constant friendship. The gang from the writers group was patient and kind in their encouragement: Mike Humes, Joshua Fisher, Delia Marrero, Marc Valle, Dean Ziegler, and Janice Frey. To all of you, thanks! To David Dowdall for his kind assistance in formatting, thank you. Karen Demers Dowdall is a great beta reader, true friend, and talented fellow author who always gives her time to help others. I thank you so much.

Finally, thank you to my wonderful wife, Liz, who has been there for me every step of the way. Thank you for your kindness, patience, and love.

"We are such stuff
As dreams are made on, and our little life
Is rounded with a sleep."

(Shakespeare, The Tempest, Act 4. Scene 1. Lines 156-
158)

"Success is not final, failure is not fatal: it is the courage
to continue that counts."

Winston Churchill

PROLOGUE Two Years Earlier

The old mill was shuttered and at night looked like something out of Dante's Inferno, but without the fire and brimstone. Only coldness remained as if in the deepest layer of hell. Once this had been a small, but thriving, steel mill, even having a single coke oven where slag and ore was mined into steel.

In World War II, it had been converted to making parts for airplanes, and women worked there, mainly as welders. Then in the post war boom, it continued to put out steel for autos and building, although not on the level of the famed Bethlehem Steel just to the south. Then jobs and steel-making began to be outsourced, and the owners never put the profits back into the factory, instead opting for large yearly bonuses.

Order after order was lost, and soon layoffs began. The mill shuffled along but at a shadow of the burgeoning business it had been years before. Then finally in the recession of the early 1980s, the business closed forever, and the mill shut down.

For a while, there were rumors that other businesses might buy the property, even other small steel firms, but nothing ever came of it.

The owner of a development company that built small strip malls considered the property, but then he decided complete razing of the buildings and construction there would be too costly. As a result, he ignored the site.

Slowly decay set in, and walls collapsed without any upkeep. Nature began to intrude with grass and weeds shooting up through the cracked and broken concrete floors.

After several decades, the old steel site was largely forgotten by most people in the Bethberg, PA area. It was for most, no more than an eyesore, a potential distraction from the pretty touristy spot they were building their town into.

Not everyone though, ignored the old facility.

It came to be a gathering place of teenagers looking for a spot away from parents and police to party. Occasionally the Bethberg Police would drive by, but most of the time, the teenagers were skillful at hiding from them.

The buildings with falling walls and ceilings and exposed girders formed a maze that few would want to venture into at night. Danger lurked in rust and debris and rotten floors. For the most part, the partiers were able to hide away.

But they were not the only ones who found use in that place. Drug dealers also went there. It was a convenient and relatively secret place for them to conduct their business. They knew the police would rarely catch them there, and their meth dealing was a prosperous activity.

They had the advantage of being on what was now an older road with relatively little traffic, and the Bethberg Police rarely came this way.

Also, the State Police typically only drove about two times a day. So, if the dealers and their customers parked back out of the way so their cars couldn't be seen from the road, they would be safe.

This evening five partiers made their way to the old steel mill.

They had waited all week—they intended to light it up tonight.

"Over here, man. Follow me," the leader of the small and scraggly group said and laughed. He looked around at the steel beams that were still standing in this section like the skeleton of a forgotten and rotting dinosaur. "Fuck, man. Some serious shit here."

Jimmy, the Monster, as he styled his street name, liked being the leader of this little band of partiers. He had dropped out of high school ten years before, had a few jobs, and got fired from all of them. Then he found work as a small-time runner for the local drug network, and that was something he proved to be fairly good at doing. He did have a few hiccups along the way with two arrests, but he did very little time and kept his mouth shut, which impressed his employers.

A few years ago, he convinced them that he could move stuff on his own, and he began selling, first a bit of weed, but then he moved onto to meth, and he was hoping to branch out into heroin. He had plans to be a big timer. "Man, I'll be getting the fuck out of this town," he told his crew one day as they sat around getting high. "You'll see. I got big fuckin' plans."

"Hey, Monster, you sure about this? It looks fuckin' creepy here tonight, man. The little guy shuddered.

Lizard hated anything that looked like it came out of horror films, and Monster knew it. That was one of the reasons he brought them here, because he knew it would scare the shit out of Lizard. Monster loved tormenting him.

Jessi, the girl with Lizard, laughed. "My big hero. You're supposed to protect me. Keep going like this, and I'll be carrying your sorry ass out of here."

Finding the image of her carrying her boyfriend as he shook in fear hilarious, she doubled over in laughter. Lizard pouted, but she kissed him and led him on.

The other two were two kids from the high school—being primed by Monster to be customers and distributors of product to other students. Monster was certain this was a good career move, and he wanted to be sure he could trust these two, not that they were going to win any academic awards, but they acted like they wanted to make some money. He would watch them and see if they knew how to keep their mouths shut. First though, he would make sure they were, at the very least, good customers. *Got to keep the pipeline flowing,* he thought, priding himself now on acting like a real businessman.

Monster chuckled at the way he pictured himself, wearing a three piece suit and having a real haircut, and driving a fucking hot car, maybe something German. That was it. He would look so fucking good in a Porsche. *Fuckin' damn,* he thought. *I'm on the way up and out of this fuckin' nothing piece of shit town.*

"C'mon, fuckers. Keep up with me. Don't want to trip over anything and get lost."

They scurried along the best they could as he led them through the maze of rusting and collapsing steel and concrete.

"Hey Monster, can we get another hit now?" Lizard needed some to calm his nerves. *Fuck,* he thought. *This is fucking nuts. Should just leave now.*

"Ok, Lizard. But just this for now." He handed the shaking man a joint. "We'll do the rock when we get where we're going."

They all took a hit from the joint and then followed Monster again. Monster was so fucking happy—everything was going to be just as he wanted.

He could see it now. He would be king of this asshole town, and that would be just the beginning. *Gonna be bigger than that loser Max ever was. That fucking detective Sadlowski busted Max, and I hate him, but he's retired now, so fuck that fat pig. Max is fucking away forever, so no worries about him. Both of those assholes are out of my way now.*

He smiled. *First, I'm gonna scare the shit out of these assholes. Man, it'll be fucking hilarious.* This place had the reputation of being haunted, and they would all be paranoid now, so he could really have some fun with them. Man, if he could scare the shit out of Lizard, he could get with Jessi. Wouldn't take much to get the little asshole to shit his pants and run away.

He turned and stopped them. "Got to be real quiet now. Don't want to disturb anything here."

"Anything? Don't you mean anyone?" Melissa, the high school girl asked.

"No, smartass. I mean anything. More's here than people, bitch. And I ain't talking about no animals or that shit. So be real quiet." He smiled as he watched them all go silent. *Fuck,* he thought. *Stupid shits are falling for it. This is great.*

They moved along slowly, no longer saying anything. He moved carefully—not because he was worried about spirits—he didn't believe in them, but he knew there was a lot of scrap metal and debris that could easily be tripped on. Getting attacked by a ghost wasn't going to happen, but, falling and getting hurt here—that could really happen.

"Almost there," he said to them quietly. The night was cloudy, so the moon, which was half-full moved out sporadically and cast light on the gothic scene.

When it did, the shadows metamorphosed from murky to sharp, like the lighting from a 1920's German horror film. Then Monster stopped them again and pointed to a small clearing, set amid a section of the western wall and gridded walkway that somehow still stood. It looked wrong, like somehow the laws of nature weren't being followed, and the section still was there, despite appearing like it would topple over any moment.

"This is the place. Right here. I knew I could find it," Monster said in a solemn tone.

"What are you talking about, Monster?" Lizard asked.

"Man, don't you know anything about your history, shithead? Probably weren't paying attention in school, were you?" Monster loved feeling smarter than them. He'd show them all.

"Hey, I know," the kid from high school said. "It's ... uh...uh...I can't remember." Then he and the girl with him started laughing.

"Well, sit down, shitheads, and I'll tell you. Before they built the mills here, man, this is the place they hung people."

"No way, man." Lizard sounded like a little boy and moved closer to Jessi.

"Yeah, that's right. They called it Gallows Hill. Used to be where they strung up the prisoners and hung them till they were dead."

"Oh man, oh man, oh man," Lizard kept repeating. "That is so fucked up. Man, we' gotta smoke that rock now." He shuddered and looked at Monster like he some kind of lost puppy.

"Yeah, no problem, man. Sure." Monster got the rock out and gave it to Lizard.

Soon they were all smoking, and the meth hit them hard. "Fucking A-right," Monster said. "Right there." And he pointed up to where one level of walkway still existed. "That would be about the height of the scaffold. Bring them motherfuckers up there. Have their heads covered, then put the noose around them, and BANG!

Drop that floor below, them, and they danced till they died!" Monster started laughing, like he had just heard the funniest joke ever told.

Soon, the two high school students were also laughing. But Lizard was close to crying. He hated this shit.

Monster stood up and walked to the stairs leading to the platform. "Maybe the ghosts of the assholes they offed are still around. Gonna find out." He started climbing the stairs, which wobbled a bit as he did.

"Man, are you crazy? What the fuck are you doing?" Jessi was enjoying this, but she wasn't so far gone that she couldn't see the steps moving under him.

Monster was giggling now—he was enjoying this. He walked onto the platform and addressed them like he was an official. "Ladies and gentlefuckingmen, we are here today to preside over the execution of …. of …oh, I don't know, some fucking asshole from back in the day."

Monster mimed putting a hood over someone and leading them to a place on the platform.

"We have found you guilty of…some shit or other…," he said and laughed. Then he gathered himself and continued with the previous serious tone. "You are sentenced to death by hanging, by the order of the court!"

He walked to the edge as if he were leading the condemned man to the hanging spot. Then he reached for an imaginary lever and yanked it suddenly.

"Boom!" he shouted, and the others jumped. "Yeah, and all the spirits of these executed fuckers—they're still here, just waiting to somehow get out of jail!" He threw back his head like he was going to howl at the moon; instead, he laughed and then bent over giggling.

"Man, you are seriously fucked up, you know that?" Jessi looked up at him, shaking her head, but still laughing.

Monster saw her reaction and smiled. She was the one he really hoped to impress. He was looking down on Lizard and thinking *What a fucking loser. I'm gonna have Jessi tonight. Watch and see.*

He started to dance and twirl and continued to laugh.

"What the fuck?" Jessi shoved Lizard to get his attention. Instead of getting freaked out, he was slowly fading out and looking like he might fall asleep. "Look, what the hell is that?" she said and pointed.

The two high school kids had decided they didn't like this story, so they moved quietly to another spot nearby.

"Let's get the hell out of here," the girl said, and the boy shook his head in agreement.

"This is all too fucking weird," the boy whispered back. They moved quietly to her car, got in, and drove away. They were stoned, but they hoped they could make it home without being pulled over. Even so, that was better than staying at the ruins.

Now it was only Lizard and Jessi. And they saw something behind the spastically dancing Monster, who now was oblivious to anything not in the world of his mind.

Something was behind Monster, and it looked almost like a human being, but the clothes were wrong.

It was, it seemed to Lizard's fogged brain, like someone would have worn from the History books he hated have to read for school—when he went.

"Fuuuuck," Jessi said in a very quiet voice. "This ain't right."

It moved closer to Monster, and he still didn't notice.

Lizard was trying to speak, but he couldn't get anything to come out of his mouth other than a croak. Instead he waved as hard as he could to Monster, who laughed more.

Jessi started whispering a Hail Mary, something she hadn't said in a very long time. "Hail Mary, full of grace, the Lord is with thee." She hadn't been to church in over five years, but it came right back to her.

Monster stood tall to take a bow, loving the reception he was getting. He started to speak, but the thing behind him gripped him hard, and Lizard and Jessi saw a noose go around his neck. Monster's hands were jerked behind him, and he moved suddenly, like he had been shoved from behind.

Monster fell off the walkway and then his body jerked to a sudden stop, with his neck snapping and he hung in the air. Jessi and Lizard could only stare. They wanted to run, to move, but they were frozen in fear.

Then Monster's dead body fell to the ground.

Lizard and Jess stood. Then they felt something grab them and pull them to the platform.

Shortly, the world went black to them.

Chapter 1

June 26, The Present

Flames roared around him. Red glare and black smoke filled the bedroom.

Sam's house was burning. He woke and looked towards the closed bedroom door. He could feel the heat coming from beyond it, and he could hear the sound of wood snapping in the flames. Smoke was seeping under the door and moving into his bedroom. Flames were coming through the walls.

Wearing only boxers and a tee shirt, Sam jumped out of bed and ran to the door. He put his hands against the wood, and he could feel the heat from outside his door.

Through the noise of the fire, he could hear screaming coming from down the hall. "Help me, Pop. Help Me."

Josh! It's Josh. I have to get out of here, he thought. *I have to get to Josh.*

He grabbed his robe, put it on, and dropped to his knees.

Then, he inhaled as much air as he could and gripped the door handle and screamed. He could feel the heat blistering his hand. He grabbed a shirt that was on the floor and wrapped it around his hand.

Then once more he took hold of the hot handle and opened the door.

The flames seemed to be everywhere. But if he could move along the ground, he might find a way to Josh's room.

The room should have been down the hall. Instead a second hallway appeared at the end of the first.

Now he had to crawl down this hall, where he could hear Josh coughing and screaming in fear.

"Help me, Daddy, help me!" Josh was only five, and he was terrified.

Sam was desperate. He stood and wrapped the robe around his face to keep the flames away. He could feel them licking at his arms.

He screamed.

He tried to open the door to Josh's room, but it was locked shut somehow.

"Josh, I'm here. I'll find a way to get to you!"

As he tried to get to the door, he was suddenly being held back by two large firefighters. "You can't go into the house, sir. It's an inferno in there."

"But my boy, my boy is in there. He needs me!"

"You can't go in there. This whole place is about to go down."

Sam struggled to get inside. He was coughing and trying his hardest, but the two men held him and dragged him back from the burning home.

"It's about to go down! Everyone back!" the Fire chief yelled through a megaphone.

Sam gaped at the flames pouring out of the building. Then there was an explosion as loud as any he heard during his tours in Vietnam.

It was as if a bomb had detonated inside the house. The roof was lifted off, and flames jutted out the windows like they were being spewed from the mouths of giant dragons.

"Daddy, help me!"

Sam kept hearing Josh screaming for him from inside the blistering inferno.

"NOOOOOOOOOO!" he screamed. "Let me go, you bastards. I have to get to my boy. I have to get to him."

Then Sam was sitting up in bed, gasping for air. His entire body was matted in sweat. At first, he could still see the glare of the fire, but then it faded, and he was once again in his own bed.

Sam groaned and shoved his hands over his eyes as tears poured down his face.

Once more in a dream that was occurring far too often, he had failed to save his son. The dreams were always different, sometimes drowning, sometimes falling, but always Josh was in peril of his life, and always, Sam failed to save him.

Sam wept.

Chapter 2

1870

Ebeneezer Schwarznacht loved his work. At the age of 40 he had reached the pinnacle of his chosen profession in the eastern and northeastern Pennsylvania area. He had become, after nearly 20 years in the field, the most important executioner in the area.

Ebeneezer was a completely ordinary looking man—average height and weight, mousy brown hair, and with a completely plain face, the kind of man who was often passed by and not noticed. He had a small home north of Bethberg, PA, and he traveled by horseback to wherever he was needed, keeping a careful schedule of executions. Occasionally, if the distance was too great, he would journey by carriage or train. Every few weeks he traveled to the local courthouses, where he was given the itineraries of the scheduled capital offenders and their punishments.

As a young teenager, in 1844, he had been apprenticed to a hangman, and he learned his craft quickly and well. His father did not have much money, and the likelihood that Ebeneezer would find any kind of good apprenticeship seemed limited, so when this opportunity arose, his father took it immediately.

While stopping one evening in a local tavern, James Schwarznacht entered into a conversation with a lean, dark man whom others were avoiding.

The other man, Stanley Martin, was the official executioner for the area, and that is why so many avoided him. For Schwarznacht, the lure of several free drinks overcame any fear he might have otherwise had.

"Here is the problem I have," Martin said as he paid for another ale for Schwarznacht. "I'm getting older, and I need to find a boy to be my apprentice. You happen to know anyone?"

Schwarznacht smiled. "I can fix your problem for you. I got a boy of 14...needs to find an apprenticeship, but I have had a devil of a time trying to find anyone who will take him on."

Martin could see this man was a drunken sot, and that probably drove other tradesmen away from him. They probably thought, like father, like son. *I can at least give his boy a try, and if he works out, then I have the apprentice I need.*

James Schwarznacht and Stanley Martin agreed on the terms, and the next week, Ebeneezer was sent to live with the hangman.

At first, Ebeneezer was frightened because he had never been away from home, but then he realized he was safe with his master, and he had more food to eat than ever before. He had a small room at the top of the large house the hangman owned, next to a servant's room. It was the first time in his life he had his own room and privacy.

Many people might have tried to move into something else, even run away from the apprenticeship, but Ebeneezer, from the first time he assisted with an execution, felt like he had found his calling in life. He knew he had discovered his life's purpose. He now felt like he belonged somewhere and was doing something important.

He was still 14 when he helped with his first execution. It was on a sweltering day in July. A man had been condemned for the murder of his wife and sentenced to hang until dead. Ebeneezer had simply carried a measuring rope and a few tools for the executioner, but he watched very carefully all that was being done. He was deeply impressed with the hangman's attention to all the details: how well the scaffold was made; the testing of the trapdoor; and the measurement of the condemned man's height and weight.

Occasionally, the hangman joked with the boy, but while working, he was completely serious. "You got to be sure of the details, boy. You don't ever want to have a botched hanging. You do that, and you might not get another job."

Ebeneezer watched carefully. The hangman had the condemned man's information, so he knew his height and weight. "Got to know that. Got to measure how long the rope should be. Has to be long enough for the right drop, so's he breaks his neck when he falls through the trap."

He considered carefully, "Ain't like it used to be, boy. Was a time you could just let them drop, especially in England, and they took as long as they needed to die. If a condemned man wanted to be sure his neck broke when he got hung, he paid someone to just jump on his back for the added weight. Otherwise, they strangled slowly. Could take up to 15 minutes."

Ebeneezer was rapt with attention to the older man's lessons.

"Yep, them were the good old days. But now, boy, you got to be sure they snap their necks as soon as they reach the end of the line."

Ebeneezer wondered what that would have been like to see, but he tried to focus on what the hangman was teaching him. He could think about that later tonight, while in bed.

"Here, boy!" the hangman snapped. "Stop your daydreaming. You ain't no good to me if you don't pay attention."

"Sorry, I won't do it again." Ebeneezer feared he might lose his position, so he focused completely on the task.

"Now, boy, get over here and help me get this dummy ready."

"Yes, sir," Ebeneezer answered and hurried to the hangman.

The hangman had a dummy of a man made out of sheets tied together that the boy had pushed to the gallows in a wheelbarrow. "You get the information ahead of time if you can, and you learn to keep several of these dummies stored at each of the gallows you work. That way it's easy for you to measure what you need, boy. Now drag that up here."

Ebeneezer grabbed the dummy and pulled it to the steps and then stopped to gasp for air. He was a strong youngster, having done much farm work, but this was harder than he expected it to be. It was like trying to lift a human being.

Ebeneezer struggled. He locked his hands under the dummy as if he were lifting a real human being. It took a great deal of effort, but eventually he managed to pull it with him up the steps and then almost fell onto the floor of the gallows. He worked to catch his breath.

"Well now, boy," the hangman said and laughed. "Gotta say, there's an easier way to do it, but damned if you ain't determined. Now stop taking a rest and lug it over here." Ebeneezer, with sweat streaming down his chest and face, pulled the 150-pound dummy to the trap door.

Then he nearly collapsed.

The hangman laughed. "You'll figger it out, boy. But now, stop lollygagging, and hold it up, like it's a man."

Ebeneezer stood up. He went to the dummy and hoisted it as high as he could, grunting with the effort. Then he held it up with a wooden brace he had designed just for this purpose; when placed on it, the dummy seemed to be standing.

The hangman then placed the noose around its neck. "Now, you watch me, boy. Got to know this part down cold. Ain't never no room for mistakes."

He quickly tightened the noose and took all the slack from it. "You got to make sure the noose is tight and set. Don't want it sliding off his head. Or moving up and getting stuck around his ears. Got to get it right the first time."

When the hangman was satisfied, he stepped back and moved to a large lever that controlled the trapdoor. "You wondering what can happen if it ain't right? Well, boy. If it ain't tight enough, the neck won't snap."

The hangman smiled. "Like I said, that ain't good. Or it might slide up to his ears. The condemned won't like that. Nope. But it won't kill neither. And that is what we are here to do. Complete a good execution. That's our job."

The hangman waved Ebeneezer back. "Now, you be careful, boy and move back some. Away from the trap. But you keep watching to see how's it's done."

Ebeneezer stepped back and kept looking intently. The hangman gripped the handle. "Next, the preacher asks if there are any last words, and then the lawmen read the sentence . . . then," He suddenly yanked the handle. The trapdoor opened with a massive thunk, and the dummy fell through and stopped with a jerk about three feet from the ground.

The hangman released the handle and walked to the steps leading down. He briskly descended the stairs. "Follow me, boy, and learn."

He moved to where the dummy was hanging, and Ebeneezer followed. The hangman walked in a circle around the dummy. The noose had held as he wanted. "Do you see, boy?" he asked as he pointed at the noose.

Ebeneezer nodded.

Taking great pride in the efficiency of his craft, the hangman allowed himself a small and grim smile. "Done perfect. The condemned man's neck will snap, and he'll be dead immediately, just the way it's supposed to be done now."

He pointed at Ebeneezer, "Remember, in the future, when this is your work, if you mess up, and the man lives fall the fall and strangles to death, it can take up to 15 minutes. And that will probably be the last time you get called to do this job, unless, of course," he said and paused. "Unless they tell you they want him to really suffer. But be sure, boy. You don't want to make any mistakes."

After the hangman let the dummy down, he turned to Ebeneezer. "Always remember two things, boy. You got to take pride in your labor, and this is God's work we're doing."

The next day, at the appointed time of nine o'clock in the morning, the execution was carried out. It was the first Ebeneezer witnessed, and he would never forget the thrill of it, how much he enjoyed it. He had been worried he might get sick or be afraid. Nothing like that happened. He loved watching the trapdoors open, and the hooded man fall. He could hear the thud as the man's body was suddenly stopped on its rapid descent. He swore to himself he could even hear the sound of the man's neck snapping. He was exhilarated.

Later that day, as he lay in his bed, Ebeneezer was happy.

This began his long career as a hangman.

Chapter 3

June 26, The Present

Sam sat at the counter at Bethberg Diner. This longtime institution of food had been one of the original "rail car" structures that were used to make diners throughout Pennsylvania, New Jersey, and parts of New England. Many of these old buildings were long gone, razed, burnt down, or simply replaced by newer structures, but this monument to a different time still remained as a strong business in downtown Bethberg, PA.

This eatery had a faithful following, including families, teens who hung out there after school, and older men like Sam who would go there both alone and with friends, usually the other members of the Investigative Paranormal Society—Roosevelt, Jeremy, and Helen.

The structure itself was long and somewhat narrow with two sets of stools along the bar letting about 12 people eat there and booths that could fit four at a table lining the other wall. A very small room had been added two decades ago at the far end which allowed about six more tables.

Generally, the entire staff of the place at any one time consisted of two wait staff, one cleanup person, and one cook, which was the norm around the clock in this 24 hour joint.

This was the place where the Investigative Paranormal Society typically gathered twice a week for breakfast, but their primary purpose was split between socializing one day and Society business on the other.

Originally, their society consisted of Roosevelt, Jeremy, and Sam, along with occasional others who would help out. But now Helen Murray was a full member of the IPS.

After the battle with Maledicus, Helen had decided to become a full member of the Investigative Paranormal Society. She cared for these older men as close friends and respected their intelligence and abilities, as much as they respected and cared for her. Helen was guardian and mother figure to her 6 year old niece, Helena, who was now in her first year of Kindergarten. While a full-time history teacher at Bethberg High School and full-time mother, she, nevertheless, was committed to participating in the IPS' investigations into the supernatural.

Since her the addition, having proven to be one of the most important people in their battle against the demon Maledicus, they would meet with just the guys for a get together on Tuesdays and then have another diner meeting on Saturday mornings, which allowed Helen to bring her niece, Helena, with her.

They adored the little girl, and she now had three "uncles" who doted on her. She might not have grandparents who were alive, but the little girl did not lack for people who loved her and who had fought for her before and who would give their lives for her now if needed. They were now Uncle Rosy, Uncle Sammy, and Uncle Jerry.

As they usually did, the three men suggested an odd group—with Roosevelt, tall, slim, and dapper in a tailored British three-piece suit, Jeremy, slight and casual in slacks and a polo short, and Sam, overweight, balding, and wearing old jeans and a black tee shirt.

They seemed, on the surface, to be disparate, but they were deep and very old friends, connected by the loss of loved ones to death. Roosevelt lost his beloved wife Sarah to cancer, Jeremy lost his longtime partner David to a severe stroke, and Sam lost his son Josh, to suicide. This bond of deep grief, as well as old friendship and the combat they faced in defeating the demon Maledicus, forged their relationship into something like spiritual granite.

Even Roosevelt, who typically detested nicknames and who tried to get people to call him by his full first name, loved the way the little girl addressed him. It was both charming, and it reminded him of when his nephews, Patrick and Michael, had been little boys and had called him the same thing.

But this morning was different for Sam—this wasn't a meeting, and he had come in alone. He couldn't stop remembering.

It had been almost ten years since Josh's death and eight since Sam's divorce from Mary. Sam and Mary's marriage had seen the all-too-common deterioration brought on by the stress of his work in the police force. Except for their son, by the time Josh was a teenager, they barely spoke except when necessary.

While their marriage had not been good before the suicide, afterwards neither one of them seemed to care anymore.

Since the initial shock had worn off, they had placed guilt on each other in terrible fights, never with anything physical, but the horrible things they said to each other were perhaps worse.

Both blamed the other for Josh's death. One day after he returned from a very late day on the job, trying to track down a lead on a man suspected of killing his wife, Sam trudged in at 2 P.M. tired and frustrated. He figured Mary would be asleep, but she was up, sitting at the small kitchen table, drinking straight vodka. He knew the faraway lost and angry look in her eye, like a sailor who spotted a distant storm but knew it would slam into their small fishing vessel soon with enough force to sink them. Mary was holding a glass poised almost to her mouth when he came in.

She looked at him and said, "You stupid shit, always at work, never any time for your own son. Always worried about others, but you, the big homicide detective, couldn't see this coming."

She suddenly drank the entire double shot like she was punching someone. Then she placed the glass down and poured another.

Sam sat down across from her. All he saw was another drunk, like the ones he used to roust when he was a beat cop. He hated her now. "You miserable piece of shit drunk. Look at you. I can't believe you were my son's mother."

Mary laughed and shoved another glass across to him and poured them both some vodka.

"And I can't fucking believe you were his father! If it weren't for the fact that I never whored around, I would wonder," she said looking directly at him.

"I can't believe you said that, Mary."

"But Jesus H. Christ, why didn't you see it coming? Why?" This she said in the softest, almost inaudible voice.

Sam looked at her one more time, wanting to hit her, aching to scream, but hating himself the most. "I don't know why I didn't see it either."

Mary raised her glass. "To the worst fucking parents, a boy every had."

Sam just looked at her.

Mary downed hers in one swallow. "Not drinking that one?"

He shook his head.

"May as well take it then." She reached over and pulled the glass to her. "Waste not, want not as my miserable excuse for a mother used to say."

Sam could see she was drunk, but unless she passed out, she wasn't going to be able to forget. He had tried that too many times, and it never worked.

"Mary, you got to stop the booze. It ain't going to help."

"You think I don't know that? You fucking moron. I been trying this almost every day."

"Every day? Jesus Christ, Mary. I didn't know."

"Of course, you didn't know, Sam. Why would you notice this, O great detective?"

Sam just looked down at the table and felt tears of anger and sorrow building.

"All that happens now is it takes more booze to black out. At least then I can get some peace without the dreams."

"I can't ever sleep without the dreams," Sam said.

"At least I go that on you, you bastard."

"I can't fucking believe you, Mary. All you do all day is sit around and stare at the walls and get plastered. At least I am out there working, trying to do something."

"Well, Mr-trying-to-do-something, it don't mean a thing! If you had really done your job, maybe our boy would STILL BE ALIVE!! But no, you can help everyone else out there, but you can't help your own family. What the hell kind of cop are you anyway?"

"I'm fucking useless, and Mary, so the fuck are you!"

Sam pushed himself up from the table and went to their bedroom. He took out a single bag, packed some clothes, and the small locked bag with his second piece. Then he left the house and never returned.

That was the last real argument they had.

Sam sat alone and avoided talking with anyone. He opened the local newspaper and pretended to read it, but he could not comprehend a single word.

Chapter 4

June 29, The Present

In Atlantic City, the board of a very large casino—Utopia World—was frustrated with their attempts to move into Pennsylvania. Since the opening of gambling into many other states, most casinos had expanded their operations in order to survive the changes in the betting world. Several other casinos had made inroads into Pennsylvania, a state that the operating board believed would serve them well, but they had lost out at every turn in the Poconos, the Lehigh Valley, and in Philadelphia.

Despite their failures to set up shop in PA, the board understood that the circumstances of gambling in the United States were changing rapidly. The days were long gone when Atlantic City was the new player on the scene and when Las Vegas and A.C. ruled most of the American casino world. Now not only were casinos emerging on Native American reservations and in other states, but also internet gambling was cutting into their take in a very significant way.

The board understood that they either had to adapt to changing times or go extinct like the dinosaurs.

The board kept feelers inside the business world, the underworld, and in politics, although they were no longer sure where one ended and the other began.

Now, they had inside information from their connections from lobbyists in Harrisburg, PA, that a few more casino licenses would be issued. The state was desperate to raise more money, and this was an easy way to do so.

The board was determined not to lose out again.

Several men of different ages sat around a large table in a gleaming modern office that looked out of the 20th floor at this casino. The view was spectacular, giving the men inside the room a stunning vista of the beach and the Atlantic Ocean.

Michael Flannery stood before the others.

Much had changed since the days of Michael's father, Joseph Flannery, running the family business. In the old days, first in Las Vegas and then in their current home of Atlantic City, the establishment and running of the casinos was more direct and forceful. If someone cheated, they had their legs broken, or if it was too much money, then the offender might disappear.

Today, they used a hired security force which used sophisticated electronic surveillance and a number directly connected to the police department to deal with cheaters.

As Michael often pointed out to the men he considered to be dinosaurs, "P.R. matters more than a few dollars. In fact, we can't survive without it." Michael smiled as he spoke, the huge winning grin that made so many fall for whatever he said. In his Armani business suit and with his PowerPoint presentations, he looked more like the CEO of a mutual fund company than that of a casino. "We have the best opportunity right now that we are ever going to have to made inroads into Pennsylvania. I don't want to cast any blame," Michael said and smiled wider.

He knew the others had made a mistake when they voted not to try to get a casino license on Pennsylvania. They had thought their situation safe, that no one would be able to compete with them in Atlantic City, and they had been wrong. Then when they changed their minds and tried to put in an application after the deadline, they had already been beaten to the end of that particular race.

"It's time to move forward now, to see the future, the opportunities it presents, and to make our company, our brand, grow there."

The other men in the room, all significantly older than Michael, represented the old way of doing things. They had been his father's men, and when the corporation had been formed to run the casino, they had been appointed to the board.

In those days, when Michael was still a child, they had simply approved anything his father wanted, and they had enforced his will without hesitation or mercy. Men disappeared at his command. But things had changed. The old man was retiring, leaving his son in charge.

Now with the old man stepping aside, while still holding a function as senior advisor in name, they wanted to try to keep things in the spirit of the old ways of doing things.

Money, however, can be very convincing. Michael was also determined to show the older men that he was the one to lead them into a new age, that he was the one who understood the way the contemporary world functioned, and that he was the one who was now in control of the entire company. This was Michael's world now.

After the loss of the previous opportunity to gain a foothold in Pennsylvania, Michael had his accountants draw explicit reports and charts on monies lost as the casino industry faded in Atlantic City and monies missed out on from not expanding when the time was right.

The figure was staggering, in the tens of millions of dollars. It was such a huge amount that they could no longer ignore Michael's approach. They realized that they had to listen to the son.

They finally understood that something had to be done, and Michael explained that he had from "inside sources in Harrisburg, PA" learned that a few more casino licenses would soon be up for application, so the time to move was now.

That was a few months before. They had voted quickly to approve Michael's plan, and with the right "lubrication," they were awarded a license. Michael, in addition to applying new economic models from his MBA program to the business, also invested in numerous political campaigns in both Pennsylvania and New Jersey, and he distributed the money equally between Democrats and Republicans. He did not care at all about their politics, only the potential influence he could purchase. While no bribes passed anyone's hands, because Michael did not want to risk any kind of prosecution, enough money was donated so his company was well taken care of.

The company also found what they considered to be the perfect place for their operation: Bethberg, PA.

Before the official process had begun, Michael had scouted potential places that he thought would work well. Casinos had located in Bethlehem, PA and in the Poconos, which left, he reasoned, a wide swath of territory to claim right in-between the two places, and he found the perfect place to build—the old, long abandoned steel mill outside of the city limits of Bethberg. It was the kind of place that had been successfully used as the basis for casinos in other areas. And since it was outside of the city, there would be no issue with any land-use taxes for fees. To Michael, it was perfect.

Michael's father was superstitious, and he heard the stories about ghosts in the old steel mill. This was a problem, not because Michael believed in them. Michael was a modern man, and he had no time for such superstitions. His father, however, was a man of the old world. He had brought the Irish beliefs from the Northwest where he had been raised with him to the United States. Whatever the old man thought was still important. Not because he had power, but he had influence. Even though his father was no longer in control, if he wanted to, he could put serious problems into the project.

His father, Joseph, believed in the old ways. He had been born and raised in Ireland, and he knew the old beliefs, those that predated Christianity. "Never make fun of the evil eye," he had said to his son one day. "Most who do it are just assholes. They got no clues what they're doing, but some do, and you got to watch out for them."

When he began speaking of such things, his father could continue for a very long time. "And you can never build anything...nothing at all...on a fairy mound. The Sidhe will hate it, and they will get you." He had stopped previous deals if he thought any kind of evil influence could affect the building of a project.

Michael did not want to risk this project. It was too important, so he had a plan.

Michael humored his father, but for him, magic and the supernatural existed only in the way numbers could be used to build and hide fortunes. Computers were the real sorcerer's wands of today, not old superstitions.

There was just one problem now.

The old man.

But he knew that his father believed in witches and curses and ghosts. Somehow, in spite of that, he had still managed to be a powerful and successful owner of this casino. His influence, even though he was retired, was still powerful in the organization.

Michael had an idea of how to deal with this situation.

Michael loved shows and internet sites about the paranormal, even though he didn't buy into it himself, but he was always interested in the possibility. *Never hurts to be prepared for anything,* he thought. He had read about a small group of old guys who ran a paranormal investigation group right in Bethberg.

The Bethberg Investigative Paranormal Society. They sounded like something of the Victorian Era—Michael was proud of his literary and historical knowledge. His minor in literature, as well as his major in business, from University of Pennsylvania, an Ivy League School, served him well. This group of old guys said they never charged for their services, but he thought that if he offered a sizable donation to a charity of their choice, that they would agree to investigate and clear the place of any supernatural entities.

Then his father would be satisfied.

Then the construction could begin on their newest casino.

Chapter 5

June 29, The Present

Bethberg, PA had not been insulated from the opioid addiction epidemic that was sweeping across the country. No place was safe from it, not high-priced suburbs, not inner cities, not farm lands, not small cities, and not small towns—nowhere. With the incursion of meth dealers and opiate sellers, certain areas in Bethberg had become more decayed and destitute.

Bethberg had struggled to reinvent itself after losing many jobs with the closing of the steel factory and clothing mills. Through the use of various festivals and the encouragement of opening specialty stores and galleries, the small city had reinvented itself as a tourist shopping destination. It had taken its cues from Jim Thorpe to the north and Bethlehem to the south.

But the creeping effects of drug addiction and selling was starting to push into the main part of town, and that alarmed many people. If tourists did not think they were safe, then that business would quickly dry up.

The IPS knew people on the police force and fire departments, and the police had told Roosevelt and Sam that they had to respond to overdoses at least twice a week, and that was in a relatively small area compared to the larger cities to the south in the Lehigh Valley.

The Bethberg Police force did its best to try to handle the situation, but the opioid epidemic was far past their capacity. Too many people were addicted, and two few police and social workers were in the community.

The best they could hope to do was to respond well when needed and to try to shut down some of the drug pipelines. They hoped that the public and the government of the United States would recognize this problem and not simply ignore it while spouting platitudes. This was a true epidemic, and it showed no signs of tapering off.

The men and women of the police and fire departments, emergency responders, and social workers knew they were fighting, at best, a holding, if not a losing, battle. They would, however, not give up.

Nor would the sellers of the poison.

Roosevelt, Sam, and Jeremy walked down the street on a small excursion after their Thursday morning breakfast at the Bethberg Diner. They had decided it would be good to try to walk off some of the very large breakfast. They had consumed pancakes, bacon, home fried potatoes, toast, and a great deal of coffee, as well as tea for Jeremy.

"I don't know about you guys," Jeremy had said. "but if I keep eating like that and not do any kind of exercise, I'm going to turn into a fat slob." Jeremy had nothing to worry about, but he was ever conscious of his waist line. He still was the same weight he had been at 35 years old.

"Unlike me, my friend." Sam laughed his loud belly laugh. He gripped his large stomach in both hands. "Now this is the image of perfect fitness!"

Roosevelt simply looked at him and smirked. "You really do need to lose some weight and be in fighting trim."

"Yeah, like I'm planning on going a few rounds in the ring in the near future sometime. Don't think so, Rosy.

But I tell you what, if you decide to start running, let me know."

"Really, Samuel? Will you join me?"

"No, Rosy, but I will sit and watch you!"

They laughed and continued on their late morning constitutional. Roosevelt noticed the attempt at humor Sam was putting on. When Sam had first arrived at the diner that morning, he had been morose, and Roosevelt knew why—it was coming up soon on the tenth anniversary of Sam's son's death.

Roosevelt and Jeremy had arrived at the diner at 9 A.M. punctual as always, and they thought nothing at first of Sam being late. He typically was 10-15 minutes late for everything. "I plan on being late for my own funeral if I can do it," he liked to joke. But when he still wasn't there at 9:30, Roosevelt called him on his cell phone. "I hate these things—a curse on humanity and courtesy," he grumbled before calling. All he got when he called was a curt, "I'm on my way." Then Sam hung up.

Sam arrived at about 9:45 looking disheveled, even for him. Sam was not a man given to caring about his dress, but he looked like he hadn't showered or shaved. Neither Roosevelt nor Jeremy commented like they usually would have. They knew the pain Sam was experiencing.

Gradually, during the breakfast, Sam had become a little more talkative, but nothing like he usually was. Typically, when goaded, he could hold forth on almost any subject, and he loved to engage in good natured debate. But not this day.

They turned and continued down an old road, one of the original roads in the town—Williams Way—once a place of business and wealth, now a forgotten and decaying area, inhabited mainly by homeless and drug addicts. The men were not frightened of either, but they had turned this way quite without conscious plan—their feet simply seemed to take them there.

And they heard something unusual down that darkened road, with old buildings that seemed to overhang each other like those in the old London of Charles Dickens.

Sam held up a hand to silence his friends. He immediately took on the attitude of being the detective on a case. His joking demeanor changed to one of concentration.

The three men looked down an alley and immediately saw something deeply disturbing—three thugs terrorizing a boy. These men were all somewhere in their 30s and decrepit looking, but also mean. And they were holding a boy of about 12, who was skinny and terrified, up against a wall, while one waved a knife near his face.

The boy was crying, and the men were leaning near him, talking to him, but Roosevelt, Sam, and Jeremy could not hear what they were saying to the boy. They were sure though it was not to discuss anything pleasant like whether or not the Philadelphia Phillies would become a contender one day. No, they were intimidating this youngster.

Roosevelt, Sam, and Jeremy looked at each other and then moved down the alley towards the men.

"Well, well, well. Look at this…three assholes, and I recognize each of you, doing what you do best, being fucking morons. Picking on people smaller than you."

Jimmie, Clint, and Little Smitty looked up at Sam in surprise. It had been years since their last run-in with the detective, and that hadn't ended well—with them being convicted of running a small meth lab and serving several years in prison. Now they were out, and they couldn't believe that he was in front of them, like a gift at fucking Christmas time.

"What the fuck?" Marty said and laughed. "Can you fucking believe this?"

"Yeah, our old buddy Detective Sadlowski…Wait, it isn't that anymore is it?"

Clint laughed a braying sound, almost like a donkey.

Jimmie, the leader of this little crew, continued, "Yeah, we hear he's retired now. Sure looks like you got the geezer group along with you. What the fuck are you going to do now, old man? This ain't none of your business. Now, just turn around and get the fuck out of here. We'll all make like you ain't never seen none of this shit."

"Well, we seem to be at an impasse then if you believe that we will simply obey you," Roosevelt said in a very low and clipped tone. "Before anything else happens, you will release that boy."

Bill suddenly held a switchblade up to Sam's neck. "Get the fuck out of here, or I'll cut you up, old man."

The thugs did not expect any resistance from these three older men, especially the smallest of the group. They did not know, that after fighting the demon Maledicus, Jeremy was no longer the frightened man he had been before. Jeremy wasn't afraid of street hoods anymore And he never went anywhere without his preferred weapon—his precious cane. It connected him to his lost David.

As soon as the words were out of Bill's mouth, Jeremy crashed the heavy wolf's head of his walking stick, that had been his beloved David's, against the man's wrist. They all heard bones in Bill's wrist break like small, dried twigs that had been trampled underfoot. He screamed, dropped the knife, and fell to his knees.

"Nobody threatens my friends. Nobody."

Sam smiled and nodded at his friend. Then the other two thugs attacked.

These men were enraged and high on meth, so they ran forward, expecting simply to overcome the much older men by sheer force.

They were wrong.

Jimmie, the youngest of the crew at 25, was sure he would eventually become its leader. He was ambitious and mean but also not very smart. He thought he could just impose his will by force—always. He figured these old fucks would be no problem. They would simply crush them.

He ran straight at Roosevelt.

Little Smitty, named because of his size, 6'3 and 350 pounds aimed for Sam. He liked the idea of taking down the one who seemed to be the biggest of this stupid group of geezers.

Jimmie stopped no more than 10 inches from Roosevelt, stood there, and opened his arms wide in the too common street assertion of you-want-a-part-of-me?

Roosevelt shifted slightly, assuming the orthodox right-handed posture of a boxer and quickly pumped out two ramrod left jabs, both connecting solidly. The first caught Jimmie on the side of the jaw, the second directly into his nose, which immediately broke, squashing like an overripe melon and spraying blood.

Jimmie's head bounced back. He screamed from the excruciating pain.

Roosevelt shifted his weight slightly and continued with the basic "one-two" combination he had been taught many years ago: a left jab followed by a right cross. This was Roosevelt's favorite combination, and even though he was almost seventy years old, he delivered the punches well, with accuracy and with his weight behind them, especially the cross.

The right cross caught Jimmie on the point of his chin. His head snapped back—he slumped to the ground.

Roosevelt watched the man collapse with satisfaction. But he also thought *Damn. I think I broke my hand.*

Little Smitty roared and charged Sam.

But Sam was ready for him and much more agile than he looked.

He sidestepped the huge man as he lumbered by, and Sam pulled his homemade sapper, a weapon he always carried in his pants pocket, made of several roles of quarters inside a very strong wool sock, and gave a serious swat to the man's head. Little Smitty groaned and fell to his knees. He started to rise slowly when Sam kicked him hard in the groin. Little Smitty fell into a curled giant heap on the ground.

The IPS looked around. Jeremy stood ready to attack with his cane, Sam hovered over Little Smitty, and Roosevelt was cradling his right hand. "Rosy, you ok?"

"I will be Samuel, but I believe I have broken my hand with that right cross." Roosevelt's face was red with pain, but he refused to leave until they had tended to the boy and these thugs.

The boy was cowering against a wall in the alley, crouched down as small as he could get and hiding his face.

Jeremy went to him, crouched down and spoke softly, "It's okay now, son. They can't hurt you. And we won't let them."

Sam called the police and a social worker he trusted to come and tend to the boy. Once they had arrived, they gave statements to the police, who arrested the three dealers.

"You sure you want to testify against them? It could bring trouble," the young officer asked. He was afraid for the safety of the older men, although he wondered if he should be, considering how the fight ended.

"Yes, we are sure," Roosevelt answered, and Sam and Jeremy agreed.

Chapter 6

July 5, The Present

Bethberg, PA seemed to have more than its share of ghosts, or at least what the average observer might think. In most respects, however, it was an ordinary mall city in the northeastern U.S.A.

The center of Bethberg was a circle around which traffic traveled from two main streets and which housed the most important businesses and offices in the small city. City Hall, several businesses, and an old Victorian building converted to holding offices dominated most of the circle. On the northwest quadrant stood the Bethberg Public Library.

The library was housed in a grand old Victorian building that had once been the opulent home of the Petersons, one of the wealthiest families in the city. Eventually the children of the most recent generation wanted to live in even larger and more ostentatious suburban homes, so they a made the home a donation to the city to be used in perpetuity as a public library. This was in accordance with their father's wishes. They might have been able to challenge his will in court, but all of the children had inherited a substantial amount of money, so they saw no point in not simply carrying out his desires. Besides, they realized it would also make them look good in the eyes of the community.

Mr. Thomas Peterson, one of the investors in the Bethberg Iron Works, had wanted to be remembered as more than an industrialist; he also wanted to be known as a philanthropist, and he made several bequests and foundations for that purpose. As a bibliophile, the donation of the family home to serve as the town library seemed a proper remembrance. In fact, some of his books were the foundation for the collection in the library. Some of the more scholarly works were donated to the Bethberg University Library.

Over the several decades since the establishment of the library, reports were given of odd occurrences—file cabinets opened on their own, books moved seemingly by an unseen presence, and a "feeling" of someone being there. While no one had been threatened in any way, the present head librarian, Sharon Buchlieber, was concerned that some of the staff, especially the volunteers and the part-time workers were feeling uncomfortable.

Ms. Buchlieber was a friend of Helen Murray, so when they met for coffee one day, she expressed her concerns. They had met at the Bethberg Coffee House, a recently opened spot that was favored by the local artists—it was decorated with original paintings for sale and offered a wide variety of roasted beans from around the world. Additionally, they ran open-nights for local poets and musicians. It was a place Helen had come to love.

"Helen, I'm getting pretty desperate, and I'm not sure what to do."

This surprised Helen, because Sharon was the kind of person who was decisive and usually could figure out the solution to any problem she faced.

"I've already had two volunteers tell me they would not be coming back because they are too afraid. I don't really think there is any danger, but if word gets out, I will have a hard time finding enough volunteers to staff the library. And with cutbacks of government funding, I don't know what will happen. But I want to keep our library running. Do you think you and your organization can help?"

"I cannot speak for the others without first meeting with them, but I can promise you that I will bring it up, and I will let you know what we decide."

A few days later, Helen met with the others, and the Investigative Paranormal Society decided to take the case.

"Of course, we will investigate, Helen," Jeremy said after hearing her relate Ms. Buchlieber's fears. Do you agree, guys?"

"Absolutely," Sam said. He remembered how much Josh had loved the library as a little boy, so it was an easy vote to make.

"Libraries are the last bastion of civilization." Roosevelt was very serious and quiet as he spoke. "Even our modest collection in the Bethberg Library must be protected, so I vote yes also."

Their decision was unanimous.

Late, on the next Saturday night, after the Library closed, Sam, Jeremy, and Roosevelt conducted their investigation of the library. Helen, who had left her niece, Helena, with Dr. Wilson and his wife for babysitting. "We always love watching her. She is our little angel," they had said to her. After caring for the little girl during the climactic battle with Maledicus, they had grown to love Helena.

While the library building was a three-floor structure in addition to an attic and full basement, they decided to focus their inquiries at the main places where phenomena had occurred. That seemed the most fruitful way to proceed. If either nothing happened, or a great deal of activity occurred, they would return the following week to continue their investigation.

Approximately two hours into their initial exploration, around 11 P.M, Roosevelt and Sam went to the basement.

"Rosy, this must be one of your favorite places to investigate," Sam said. "I mean it has almost as many books as you have at your house."

"Well, perhaps I will have to make a donation to even out our holdings," Roosevelt answered and smiled. The two men were in the basement, in a storage area for files and the old card catalog. When the library had updated to a new computer system, the librarians couldn't bear to dispose of it.

"This is Sam and Rosy, beginning an EVP session—electronic voice phenomenon, believed to be recordings of voices that cannot be heard by human ears—in the basement of the library." Sam had turned to an official tone, as if he were conducting a police investigation. "Is anyone here with us?"

"Hello, my name is Roosevelt, and I love books. In fact, they are my passion, and I can see the care that is given to them here. Are you someone who also loves books?"

The men would pause after each question to give any spirit or ghost the opportunity to communicate, as if they were having a conversation with a living person.

"My name is Sam, and like my friend, I also love books. I may not look like it, but I am a lover of art books in particular, and I think this library has a fine collection. Have you looked at any of them?"

Roosevelt moved to another spot in the basement and looked around before he asked his next question. "May I ask what your name is?" Roosevelt was as polite as he always was, unless provoked by someone who was a bully.

Roosevelt moved to the old card catalogue. Several rows of long, dark wooden cabinets ran the length of one wall. They were oak and still in good condition. "This is a particularly beautiful item. The wood is, by itself, lovely, but I have always preferred using card catalogues to look for books over computers. Do you agree?"

A few seconds later, they heard a faint knock, as if someone had gently tapped on the side of the card catalogue.

"Did you hear that, Samuel?"

"I sure did. If that was you, can you please do that again?"

They waited for about 30 seconds and then heard another similar sound.

"Thank you so much," Sam said. "That was great."

"Yes, it certainly was. We appreciate your help. Some of the library staff have mentioned that the drawers of the catalogue open and close. Is that you? Do you think you could do that for us?" Roosevelt asked.

They waited, hoping for some kind of response. Then they heard a creak, and on the farthest end from them, one drawer opened very slowly.

"Wow, Rosy. That is amazing."

"Yes, it certainly is, Samuel. And I believe we captured it on the camera." Prior to beginning their active work, they had set up cameras and recorders throughout the library, including one focused on the card catalogue. "I hope we can continue to capture more activity. Thus far, this has been fruitful."

"Although, before we jump to any conclusions, Rosy, remember we have to carefully check all the recordings for other evidence."

"Of course, Samuel. That is, indeed, correct."

Later, while Sam and Roosevelt sat at the command post, Helen and Jeremy investigated the second floor, where other activity had been reported. They sat on two office chairs and began.

"Hello to whomever is here. My name is Helen Murray, and I want to tell you that I love this library. I spent many happy days here as a child and an adult, and my niece, Helena, also loves coming here and reading children's books. Are you someone who also loves this place?"

Jeremy paused for a few seconds, and then he asked, "My name is Jeremy, and I also love libraries and books. Were you a patron here?"

"Is there some reason, in particular, that you seem to be on this floor so much?" Helen continued.

After about 30 minutes with no apparent activity, Helen said, "I have an idea. Let's go down to the first floor to the children's section."

They ended the EVP session and went immediately to the Kids' area.

"EVP session begun with Jeremy and Helen, at the children's area." They settled in on very small benches and smiled at how silly they both looked.

"Hello. Is anyone here in the children's section?" Helen began the questioning.

"Do you like seeing the children read?" Jeremy asked.

"Did you read to the children?" Helen picked up one of the books, an old Dr. Seuss book and paged through it. "The Cat In The Hat. This was one of my favorites when I was a child. Have you read it to the little ones?"

"If you are here with us, can you show us that you are? Perhaps, by moving or opening one of the children's books on the tables," Jeremy suggested.

They sat very still and waited. Soon a book opened. It was Winnie The Pooh.

"I loved that book as a child," Jeremy said with a huge smile. "Please turn two pages if you can."

It took about one minute, but then one page and then another turned at the rate they would if an adult were reading the text on the pages to a child.

"Oh, that is so wonderful," Jeremy said.

"Thank you so much. You are very kind," Helen added.

Several hours later, at around 4 A.M., they all agreed that they had covered the entire library. Because the building would be closed on Sunday, they let a few cameras and voice recorders running to see if they could find more evidence, and they packed up the rest of the equipment. They would return in the afternoon to collect what they left behind, review the evidence during the week, and then come back to speak with Ms. Buchlieber.

Chapter 7

1967

"No son of mine is going to be a goddamned artist!" Paul, Sam's father, thundered from the head of the family kitchen table. He wasn't a very tall man, but he was broad and strong from his decades of working in the steel mill. "You think I've been working in this fucking mill this long, so you can waste my money by going to college—with the rest of the pinkos there?"

Paul was short and squat, with most of his hair gone, and the rest that remained was now completely white. Years of being a steelworker had made his hands rough with layers of callouses, and his arms were thick with muscle, not like a body builder's but powerful and corded.

Paul's wife, Violet, said meekly to her husband, "Please watch your language at the table, and let's talk about something pleasant." She always felt that dinner conversation should be easy and never about anything that could cause any kind of argument. No politics, no religion especially. It was the way she was raised.

Typically, Paul listened to Violet and respected her authority in the house, but this time he was too upset not to say anything.

Here was his son, going on 18 years old, almost a man, and wanting to throw away his life by going to college and studying art.

Paul fumed internally. *What the hell was that boy thinking? It would be one thing if he wanted to be a doctor or a lawyer—now he could make a really good living doing that. But an artist. No fucking way.*

Paul speared a piece of the pork roast and ate it, chewing like he was punching someone. Then he looked at Sam again, pointed the fork at him, and said, "You hear me, no son of mine is going to be an artist. You can't make any money doing that shit. It's fucking ridiculous."

"I'll find a way."

"Yeah, right. You mean you'll come crawling home and try to live off the money I make at that fucking place. Ain't gonna happen, boy."

Sam looked down at his plate and said nothing. He could feel anger growing, and that was the last thing he wanted now, to have a confrontation with his father.

"Besides, boy," Paul said while eating another mouthful. "Are you a fucking homo or something?"

"Paul!" Violet said in a shocked tone. "You don't say something like that to our boy." She was horrified, but she had also wondered a bit, since Sam didn't seem to say anything about dating girls. It wasn't that she would stop loving him, but she knew how hard the world treated men who preferred men.

"No, Dad, I am not homosexual, or a pansy, or whatever you want to call it. And I don't want to be an artist. I want to study about it."

Paul stopped eating and stared at Sam. He couldn't believe what he was hearing. "That's even worse. You mean you won't even be able to sell something you paint? Holy Jesus-H-Christ, boy, what are you thinking anyway?"

Well, that was just too much for Violet. She threw down her napkin and ran out of the room. She couldn't stand confrontations to begin with, and this, taking the Lord's name in vain, was just too much for her to handle.

Violet ran up the steps to the bathroom and stood shaking in front of the mirror. *Why did it have to be like this? Why couldn't everyone just learn to get along?*

Violet hated arguments and had ever since her father would bellow at her mother, who would yell back. In those days, Violet ran to her room and hid in a closet to get away from the strife. Now, she opened the medicine cabinet and took out the special pills her doctor had prescribed for her, "just to help her relax" as he had said as he wrote out the prescription. She popped one in her mouth and washed it down with a little water. Then she went to the bedroom, shut the door and lay in bed. Soon, she would relax and probably sleep until morning.

"Now, you see what you did, boy? I hate when she runs off like that." He shoveled in another mouthful. Paul couldn't stand this. Now his favorite meal, roast pork and mashed potatoes was ruined. Now it just tasted like cardboard, and he felt like an ass for getting angry at the table.

"Sorry, Dad." Sam lowered his head.

"I hope you get my meaning, boy. I ain't fooling around here. You think I'm going to fork out God knows how much money for you to go to college to study fucking art? Especially when you can't make any fucking money from it. Ain't happening boy—you got that?"

Sam shook his head yes but didn't say anything. He was getting angry and could feel it building up. After his mom leaving the table, he didn't want to do anything to upset her further.

Sam knew that she was popping some pill that quack of a doctor gave her, and he didn't want to do anything else to her, but he felt like he was going to explode.

"And don't think you're gonna do an end run around me like some fucking flashy running back, boy. Ain't gonna happen. You ain't going to college on my dime, not unless you study what I tell you, got it?"

Sam didn't say anything.

"I said, boy," he paused. "Do you get me?"

"Yes, I do." Sam kept control over his voice. He was afraid of shouting and a real argument breaking out. He knew his old man was strong, but he also knew how much stronger he had become. Plus, a fight would be something he could not fix. It would be the end to something, and he was terrified of what might happen.

"And you ain't gonna stay here and do nothing. You graduate. The next day, you do to the mill and put in an application or sign up for the army. You got me, boy?"

Sam would never forget that he was so scared of his father that he chose to go into the Marines rather than try to work in the same steel mill as his old man did. He wanted to be somewhere far away from his father, some place where he could completely separate himself from this man forever. The steel factory itself would be too close to home, and he could never keep away from his old man in there, but in the Marines, he knew he might go half a world away.

Chapter 8

July 8, The Present

The IPS was meeting at Helen Murray's house on Saturday morning. "After what we have experienced together," she had said one day to Sam, Roosevelt, and Jeremy. "I can't call myself an agnostic anymore. That always meant that I needed evidence to say that I believed in an existence past our earthly one."

The men nodded in agreement. They had similar thoughts and listened with complete attention.

"I now know," Helen continued. "Not believe, but know, that there is much more than is immediately apparent to us. Our battle with Maledicus proved that. And Roosevelt, what is that quotation from Hamlet that shows what I mean?"

"There are more things in heaven and earth, Horatio, than are dreamt of in your philosophy. And I think it certainly does apply. Would you not all agree, gentlemen?" Roosevelt smiled as he remembered the visitation of his beloved wife, Sarah's spirt. She had saved his life.

Sam and Jeremy also had similar experiences of intervention and aid by the ghosts of loved ones: Josh, Sam's son, and David, Jeremy's partner both returned and aided in the conflict against the demon. Helen's sister and brother-in-law had been there to aid her. All of them now had similar perspectives on religion and an afterlife. They were not sure of the details, but they knew something existed. Helen had prepared coffee and tea for this

Helen had prepared coffee and tea for this Saturday meeting. Typically, they had rotated residences of the 4 main members for their weekend meetings, but now they usually met at the Murray house. It was easier for them, especially Helen, to gather there. This way, she would not have to arrange a babysitter for Helena. This had the added benefit of the 3 men visiting with the little girl, whom they all loved. Helena had become their "niece." Helen saw not only did the little girl love their visits, but also she made them smile, and Helen knew Sam needed that bit of happiness, especially now.

Helena was almost empathetic in the way of some children, able to sense when someone was upset and sad. She said to Helen one day after a meeting, "Why is Uncle Sam so sad, Aunt Helena?" Helen was startled at the little girl's question. She knew Sam was suffering from this being close to the tenth year anniversary of his son's suicide, but he also tried very hard not to show it, especially around Helena. When he was with her, he laughed, smiled, and hugged her.

"Uncle Sam smiles, but there are tears no one can see." Helena became sad for him, then brightened and said, "I'll try to make him happy."

Helena decided to make Sam a "get happy card", and she designed, with Helen's help, of course, a card that said, "I love you Uncle Sam!" and that had a big red heart drawn on it with crayon. When she presented it to him, he started to say something, stopped, and scooped the little girl up in his arms and hugged her, closely but gently.

"Thank you so much, honey. I love you too!"

Roosevelt and Jeremy both saw the tears in their tough friend's eyes.

Since that day, Helena always spent some time chattering will all the men, but she paid special attention to Sam. "He needs me," she whispered to her Aunt Helena.

After they visited with Helena for a while, Helen took the child into the next room to play with her toys while they discussed Investigative Paranormal Society plans.

"Helen," Jeremy began. "We did a small preliminary investigation as agreed and some historical research, and it is now time to decide if we wish to continue this case or not."

"We have completed what we initially agreed to with the casino investors," Roosevelt said with a slight sneer on his lip. "And they have agreed to donate $1000.00 dollars to the Bethberg Children's Fund."

"That is a tidy sum, but. . ." Sam hesitated. "But, we had said we would never charge anyone for our services."

"True, Sam. But this isn't charging, and we won't make any money on this. We give them a set figure, and it goes to charity. We are aiding these kids, and they need our help." Jeremy's voice was clear in his statement. He believed in this cause.

"What do you think, Rosy?" Sam wasn't sure this was a good idea to continue.

"Ordinarily, I would have agreed with you, Samuel, but this situation is unusual. We have the opportunity to help a charity which we support normally, but with a much larger donation that we could do. And it is a very interesting case."

"I can't believe it, Rosy. You'd think I'd be the one to find the grey area, not you."

"We all have not spoken yet. What is your opinion, Helen?"

She was surprised by this discord, which was something she was not used to seeing with her friends. "When you set the rule about not charging anyone, did all of you agree on it?"

"Yeah, we did," Sam answered, and Roosevelt and Jeremy nodded.

"Was the point to keep being a non-profit group, which is what I believe you formed, correct?"

Again, they nodded.

"Did you discuss the issue of accepting money that would be delivered directly to charities, or not accepting any money, but having a group give money to charity?"

"No, it never occurred to us, did it, guys?"

"Then I suggest we decide now, as a group, what we should do. And we put it to a vote. Do you gentlemen find that acceptable?" Only Roosevelt noticed that Helen was using her teacher's voice and presence, and he appreciated it.

"Yes, of course, Helen," Jeremy said, and Sam and Roosevelt nodded.

"I think it is simple, really," she began. "If we want no one to pay us ever, then we make that rule never to be broken. That is fine, but it does not answer the question about donations to charity in return for our services. That is a clear, and sorry, Sam, not a blurred distinction."

Sam looked sheepish, like he had been a student who was corrected in a classroom.

"So, do we agree never to charge? All in favor, say 'aye'."

All responded, "Aye."

Helen shook her head and acknowledged their vote, then she continued.

"Now, to the question of allowing donations to be made to specified charities in return for our investigations, those in favor, say 'Aye.'"

"Aye." Jeremy was the first to answer.

"Aye." Then Roosevelt.

"Aye," said Helen.

Sam sighed, then said, "Aye."

"It is decided: we agree to accept donations to specified charities for certain cases."

"Well done, Helen. I think you kept this from becoming a potentially bad argument."

"It was nothing, compared to dealing with a class of rowdy teens!" She laughed, and they did also.

Jeremy asked, "Do we continue with the investigation of the old Steel Mill?"

They all agreed.

"Then we must contact the casino people and make it clear that we are undertaking the investigation, but not as paid employees or as contractors. And we will undertake this investigation as soon as we have completed our others. Do we agree?"

They all said yes.

Chapter 9

1870

"You are all sinners! We are all sinners, every one of us!" began the Sunday sermon at the Bethberg Reformed Calvinist Church. Schwarznacht stood straight and erect in the front of the simple, bare pulpit, which reflected the sparse nature of the church. The building itself was tiny, not much more than a single room, and it was only about one half filled with people in the pews, but it was his congregation, and he took his religious work seriously.

Dressed in black from neck to foot, he wore a long, plain, ebony gown over his pants and shirt. No color was allowed on his person while he preached. Like his posture, his face reflected the stern appearance of his clothes and the plain, unadorned atmosphere of the building. The walls were whitewashed, and no adornment was permitted.

"And all sinners must be punished!" He slammed his hand down on the pulpit, making a sound almost like a thunderclap or that of a musket being fired indoors.

"No one is exempt from the wrath of the Lord. No one can expect to commit sins, even in secret, and not be found out. God has eyes everywhere. He can see not only what you are doing, but why you are committing sin, and what is in your filthy heart when you do it!"

Schwarznacht spread his arms wide, but not in a welcoming manner; instead, his fingers pointed straight out at them. It was as if he were accusing each and every person there to be the worst sinner possible.

Schwarznacht surveyed his flock. While it was not large, perhaps only 30-40 people, it was one of the most loyal groups in Bethberg. These people attended regularly, frightened by the preacher's sermons that they might burn in hell forever if they missed a Sunday meeting.

He knew that he carried the joint authority of the pulpit and the power of being the hangman in the gallows. And he loved to use imagery of hanging in his sermons.

Schwartznacht moved from behind the pulpit and stood at the center of the stage. He was now only a few feet from those parishioners in the front row.

"Do you wonder what is going to happen to your souls after you leave this world of sin?" He looked directly into the eyes of a man he knew to be a fornicator.

"Will you be judged fitting, as one of the elect, and receive a reprieve from the Lord's vengeance? Will you then have the executioner's hood taken from your head, the noose removed from around your neck, and will you be led away to climb the stairs to Heaven, where you will find eternal bliss?" He smiled what was for him a wide grin, although it resembled more of grimace of severe pain than an expression of happiness.

Schwarznacht then paused and surveyed the entire congregation slowly, holding their attention with his fierce gaze. "Will, you be a good Christian and be one of the elect, or, will you be found guilty of being an unrepentant sinner, one who cannot be forgiven, and will you hear the sound of the trapdoor on the gallows, on which you are standing, open?

Schwarznacht felt the power of God flowing through him. "Will you feel your soul fall through to be snapped at the neck, as if you were alive, and then fall to the depths of hell, where Satan's devils await you?"

He stepped down from the stage, only two stairs above the floor of the small church. He walked to the very first row.

Schwarznacht then paused and pointed at someone in that first row. "The choice is yours!"

He walked slowly down the central aisle, moving his head so he could look at everyone who was in attendance. No one spoke or moved at all as he made his slow procession down the aisle and then back to his starting point.

"Remember, sinners. The noose of the Lord awaits all of you. The choice is yours."

He paused and then said solemnly, "Amen," and his flock responded in unison.

Others, not in his flock, found him to be a very odd figure in the community. "He'll take your life at the gallows, and then condemn your soul in the church," one wag said in a local taproom and laughed. The other fellows around him looked a bit uncomfortable. "C'mon," he said laughing. "He ain't my preacher, not that man."

Still, the others worried a bit about laughing at a preaching man, even one like Schwarznacht.

Chapter 10

July 13, The Present

"Natural Gas? You've got to be kidding, the young man said as he read the geologist's report. He looked at the report he had insisted be delivered by courier, on paper, because he did not trust the so-called security of the internet. He had seen too many go down by being tracked by the FBI online. If they needed records, he wanted to be able to control the physical copies of what existed.

The report was titled: The Feasibility and Risks Connected with the Site of the Former Bethberg Steel Works. Prepared by Dr. Nathan J. Kurtokov. It then listed the company information supplied to him—but what was, in reality, a dummy corporation, in order to keep everything secret.

Michael Flannery stood by the window in his office overlooking the boardwalk in Atlantic City. It was a large room with a beautiful dark wooden desk and a wide corner window that showed much of the Atlantic Ocean, a vista he believed he deserved. And he wanted to maintain his position and all the perks that came with it.

Michael needed this casino deal to go through, for the future of his business, and his personal plans. Now, it seemed that obstacles kept being thrown in his path.

But no matter how many hurdles he would have to leap over to complete his plan, Flannery would find a way to win. This would be the act that would culminate in his being in complete control over this business.

He continued to examine the report, with its formal tone and format. He read it through carefully and then turned to look out at the ocean. No matter how upset he might be, if he were to look at the movement of the water, to let himself be drawn into the rhythm of the waves coming in and then receding, it almost always calmed him.

So, he thought. *What are the obstacles my plan faces?* Michael believed in being organized about all business decisions, no matter the kind.

First, the ridiculous situation with his father's superstition about evil spirits had to be dealt with, but he was sure that was being handled by those equally absurd old guys in Bethberg, PA. Michael had found the IPS through their website and quickly realized they might be useful to him. He had contacted them before and made them a very compelling offer to investigate. *Hell,* he thought. *I'm sure the old man will believe them...they are all stupid believing in ghosts. Show me something with numbers, then I believe it, otherwise, it's worth shit.*

But now, Flannery had a potentially far more serious issue than nonexistent ghosts to handle. He had just received the official geologist's report for the land under the old steel Mill.

He had learned, in college in a required science course, Geology 1, affectionately called "rocks for jocks" that getting such a survey done was extremely important for all real estate building or buying.

He now was almost sorry he paid attention to the professor. The Geologist he had hired was a very good one, from a top firm specializing in researching land for real estate projects. This one had a Doctorate in Geologic Engineering from Penn State University.

He looked over the document again and scanned it quickly, moving to the most pertinent information that it contained. *Ah, there it is,* he thought. *Fuck. Fuck. Fuck. Now that is a serious problem.*

Actually, there were three problems.

The report contained the one word that he was hoping not to see at all: subsidence. The head geologist stated that conditions were developing under the old mill that might lead to an incident of subsidence. It was not a certainty that it would happen, the collapsing of ground that could lead to a swallowing of cars or even buildings and make development of property very dangerous, but it was listed as a reasonable possibility. Why this might occur was still speculation, ranging from lack of upkeep on the land to changes in the underground aquafers to increased fracking, which seemed to be causing earthquakes and other geologic disturbances across the country.

Son of a whore. That could ruin everything. If subsidence is a problem, we might have to dig a much larger foundation for the casino than I had originally expected. And that could cost way too much.

And there was a second issue with the land. There was a substantial pool of natural gas, deep under the layers of shale and slate that was the foundation of the former factory. Apparently, this pocket of gas, formerly stable, had become unstable, probably as a result of the nearby fracking.

The digging for oil was the reason, the geologist had speculated, that small faults nearby had expanded, and he was concerned about a particular fault, the third problem, that ran under the ruins. If it caused a large enough earthquake, it was possible it might produce enough friction and sparks to ignite the natural gas.

Such an explosion might not be noticed as more than an odd geologic event, if it were confined to underground, but if an earthquake opened a path to the surface, then the resulting blast might be devastating to the immediate area.

Michael paced around the room and thought about the risks. He had to have this new casino. He was placing his entire business reputation at stake on this project. If it didn't work, he had no idea about his future. It had to work.

The young man in the expensive Italian suit placed the report on his desk and turned to look out his window, where a beautiful seascape vista of the Atlantic City seashore and ocean presented itself.

Most others would be upset, frustrated, he thought. *But this can work to my advantage. Yes, there are problems here, and my ideas might need to change, but this is still an opportunity. I just have to be smart about it. I have to handle the situation and all of its complications correctly.*

These problems might eliminate the possibility of building a casino there, but they should still move forward with the purchase of the land—for commercial development, a suitably vague term.

Michael smiled. He was certain that he had the solution within his reach.

More money might be made from entering the natural gas market than from another casino, and besides, that was a more ethical way to take people's money.

Chapter 11

July 13, The Present

The members of the IPS were enjoying a breakfast on a Thursday morning after their last meeting at the Bethberg Diner. Helen's niece, Helena, was not there because she was enjoying an overnight visit with Dr. and Mrs. Wilson, who had come to think of the little girl as part of their family.

Helen was enjoying her small lecture to her friends. Jeremy had asked about earthquakes, since he was reading about California and wondered about where they lived in Pennsylvania. "Well, Jeremy," she said and smiled. "Earthquakes are not a real problem or danger around here, but they do occur, but almost never with any lasting damage. The last real one was the one in the early 2000s that centered in Reading, PA—it didn't cause much damage, but it was loud enough and produced large enough tremors that we felt the shaking, and many heard the noise here, over 40 miles away."

The men listened to her lesson with interest, as they always did. Both Roosevelt and Helen were given to going into long explanations about topics they were fascinated by.

"Yeah, I sure did," Sam said in reply to Helen's statement. "I was still on the force then, and we all felt it at the station."

"And some of our stuff in the antiques store almost fell off the shelves and displays," Jeremy said.

"That must have been terrifying," Helen added.

Jeremy remembered clearly the look of terror on David's face during the tremors, something Jeremy had rarely seen in his older partner.

"This is not something I experienced. I was on a trip to London at the time, and only heard about it when I got back." They knew it was one of Roosevelt's yearly visits to get a new suit measured and made, one of his few indulgences.

"Well, there is a much more common geologic event than earthquakes in our area," Helen continued. She was having fun now. The men listened, because they respected her, and she had their attention. "We are far more likely to experience subsidence—when a sink hole that is caused by weaknesses in the underground limestone formations throughout much of eastern Pennsylvania suddenly appears. Sometimes they can swallow cars, like the one last year near the downtown or whole houses like in Bethlehem and Easton."

Jeremy, Sam, and Roosevelt sat back in the diner booth and listened as Helen expounded on one of her favorite side interests.

"That is quite a lesson, Helen," Roosevelt said and smiled. "And I am serious. I am, like you Helen, fascinated with so many aspects of life and our world."

Helen laughed, and her face glowed. She loved learning about everything, and she adored talking about and sharing what she had learned. She loved sharing her knowledge and seeing the spark of learning come alive in others.

"Well damn, Helen. You even got me interested. The last time I really cared about weather or … geologic events was when I was in a storm, watching for a perp."

"Now, Sam, that sounds like fun!" Jeremy said and took a bite of rye toast. "Yeah, it was a fucking blast, especially when I had to chase some fucking asshole through the rain."

"Samuel, language, please!" Roosevelt scolded. "This is a family establishment."

Sam reddened and looked around. The only other patrons there were two retired farmers at the counter who were laughing. He looked back at Roosevelt, who laughed loudly.

Sam glowered, then he also laughed. "Damn, Rosy. You got me good."

"Yes, I did. And Samuel?"

"Yeah?"

"Don't call me Rosy."

They ate some more, and before they finished, Jeremy asked, "Do you think those casino guys checked the ground at the old steel factory for chances of subsidence?"

"That, Jeremy," Helen said. "is an excellent question. You would think, wouldn't you, that with all the money they have, they would check on such a possibility."

"Yeah, you'd think so," Sam growled. "But money-grabbing bastards, you can never tell."

"True, and even though earthquakes are rare here, you also never can tell if or when they will happen."

Chapter 12

1967

Sam had always considered himself to be brave in high school. He thought he faced challenges well, especially in athletics. He also wanted to hang out and be friends with many different kinds of kids. He refused to be a part of any clique. He was artistic and loved hanging out with painters and those who considered themselves to be hippies, but he was also an athlete playing backup catcher on the baseball team and fullback on the football squad.

He wasn't a huge kid, but he was, as his father liked to tell him, built like a peasant for working the fields. Sam was 5'10, 200 pounds, with huge, broad hands. While he was strong, he was also not particularly fast, and he knew he would probably not win an athletic scholarship to any college, especially considering Bethberg High School's teams couldn't compete with those from the powerhouse schools nearby of Easton High School and Phillipsburg High School just across the Delaware River.

But he loved the competition and the physical contact. He enjoyed the stupid horseplay in the locker room almost as much as he did the philosophic conversation he had with his artist friends.

He was also a decent, but not spectacular, student. He earned mainly "B" s with the occasional "A" and "C". Except for the ongoing tension between his father and himself, Sam was a happy kid.

For the most part, little of the troubles of the outside world seemed to make their way into the small city of Bethberg. The Vietnam War was in the background of life, and except for a few minor student protests at Bethberg University, little of the social conflict that was seemingly ripping the country apart had affected this community.

It was almost as if time there moved more slowly than in the rest of the country.

Sam also enjoyed a healthy dating life. He saw several girls, but he never had a regular girlfriend. *I'm way too young to settle down,* he thought. *I just want to have fun.* He loved the girls' company, and he was always as horny as a regular teenage boy, but he was also a gentleman. If there was one important thing he had learned from his old man, it was that you always treated girls with respect.

Sam hated one thing about the locker rooms—it was the bragging that many of the guys did about girls. He knew—he could tell that most of it was lying, that they were just trying to impress the other guys and build up their own reputations, but he never added to it, only laughing so he wouldn't be noticed. And he hated that he did that. *I shouldn't have to make myself fit in.*

Still, even though he didn't want to be tied down, Sam still wanted to find a girl, a special girl who he could connect with, someone who was different from the others.

Like most of the kids in Bethberg High School, Sam went to his Senior Prom. He asked Nancy Deangelo, a pretty dark-haired cheerleader, and he was surprised when she said yes. He really didn't think that he stood a chance, because he knew that the quarterback of the football team was interested in her, but he already had a different date.

Sam had planned ahead for this occasion for several months. He rented a tuxedo that he paid for from his part-time job at a local produce store on weekends. He put his money in a secret savings account in a bank on the other side of town so his father would never know about it. He didn't want to hear about any opposition from his old man.

When Sam arrived at her house to pick her up, he was struck by Nancy's beauty: she wore her long hair done up in a fashion that he had never see, showing her neck and a prom dress that an adult woman would have envied. He could not believe his luck in being able to escort her to this dance.

He also arrived with a corsage for his date and a bouquet of flowers for her mother. He knew that his mother would be proud of him.

At first, he had a good time at the prom, dancing with Nancy. He felt so happy, holding her, especially in the slow dances. But this happiness did not last long. After about an hour, she started spending more time flirting with other guys. "Sam, you don't mind if I dance with Donny, do you?" she smiled as she moved to the arms of one of his football teammates.

"Sure, no problem," he replied, but he felt his gut move like he had been punched hard.

Finally, after watching her spend the next hour dancing with other guys, he went to her and asked, "Are you here with me or not?"

"Sam, you're a nice guy, really, and I like you. But I thought you would be, you know, more fun. And I'll be going home with Donny. I hope you don't mind."

Donny stood there smiling at him like he had just won some kind of contest. In that moment, Sam hated like he never had before.

Fuck him and fuck her, he thought. *They deserve each other.* He wanted to yell at both of them, to tell her off and to threaten Donny. Sam's pulse was pounding, and his head felt like it might erupt.

Sam felt his hands tighten into fists.

Then he forced himself to unclench his hands. He glared at them for a few seconds.

"Sure, have fun," was all he said as he turned and left.

He left the prom and drove to a path on the outskirts of town. It was a place he often went to when he wanted to think.

Sam parked, locked the car and began walking. The night was clear and bright because of a full moon. He didn't need the flashlight he had brought with him from the car.

Then he heard the sound of soft crying.

He walked nearer and saw it was a pretty black girl in a prom dress, alone and sitting on a bench. He recognized her. It was Martha Nicholls, one of the brainy advanced science kids.

He walked a little louder, so she wouldn't be startled. When she looked up, he said, "Hi. Are you ok?"

"Hi," she answered. She looked away and blew her nose. Then, "No, not really."

"Can I sit with you?"

She looked directly at him for several seconds then nodded her approval. At that moment he thought, she has the most beautiful eyes I have ever seen.

Being careful to keep a respectful distance between them, Sam sat down on the bench. He took out his carefully pressed handkerchief and handed it to her.

She glanced at the handkerchief and smiled. This was such a gentlemanly gesture. "So why are you here, on this lonely bench? You're one of the cool kids, and that cheerleader was your date."

"Me? One of the cool kids? You're kidding me, right?"

"Yes, you, Mr. Football and Baseball player. Not to mention Mr. Artist." She smiled and playfully poked his arm.

"O, I'm not cool. I just like being with different people, not being in any clique. You know? Besides that isn't the real question."

"Oh, and just what is the real question?"

"Why are you here? Where's your date? Didn't you come to the prom with Jeff Stander, Mr. Popularity?"

Jeff Stander was one of the star basketball players at Bethberg High School—the point guard, and was tall, slender and handsome.

"Yes, I did go with him, but let's just say….he is not a gentleman. Not at all."

"Martha, I'm sorry to hear that."

"Yes, well he is one of those guys my Daddy warned me about—all smiles, charm, and then wandering hands."

Sam nodded. Stander had a reputation among the athletes as a ladies' man. Sam was sorry Martha had gone to the prom with him. Sam barely knew her, but he already felt protective towards her.

"Well, don't you worry," she said and smiled as she wiped away tears. "My Momma and Daddy didn't raise no fool. No sir. I was not going to be one of his conquests, let me tell you."

As she spoke, Martha's eyes flashed with anger. "That fool took me to his car, leaned me against it, and tried to put his hands inside my dress—right there, in the parking lot, in the open!"

"What an asshole!" Sam blurted out. His face reddened like a painted kickball. "I'm sorry, Martha. I didn't mean to swear in front of you."

She smiled, and her face transformed, turning from a threatening summer storm to a bright sunny autumn day.

Chapter 13

July 17, The Present

Helen, Roosevelt, Sam, and Jeremy were gathered at the Bethberg Public Library a week after their investigation. They congregated at 5 P.M., immediately after closing hours, to discuss the results of their investigation into the building's possible haunting.

They, along with Ms. Buchlieber, were assembled around a table in the office and were sipping coffee and tea. "Well, Ms. Buchlieber, we have quite a bit to tell you," Roosevelt said.

"I hope there is nothing bad," she replied. She looked uneasy and started tapping her fingers against the small teacup in front of her.

"No, not at all." Jeremy said in his best reassuring tone. He looked at her and smiled gently. "I'm certain you have nothing to worry about or be frightened of."

"That's good to hear." But Ms. Buchlieber did not seem to be completely reassured. She had been worried about the possible implications of this investigation even though she was the one who initiated it.

"So, Sharon," Helen began as she spoke to her friend. "We came last Saturday after closing and set up our equipment. We decided to focus on the areas you spoke of having the most activity, the second floor, the basement, and the children's section."

Helen took a drink of her coffee, giving Sharon a chance to take in what she was saying.

After Sharon nodded, Helen continued, "Since you know this building better than anyone else, we thought we would follow your lead. That is always the best course to take, especially with someone who knows a place very well, as you do."

"Then we went in groups of two and conducted EVP sessions, which we explained we would do and covered as much as we possibly could," Sam continued.

"We worked from about 10 P.M. until 4 A.M., then we gathered most of our stuff, but left some of it still working, in the hopes that we might find something after we were gone." Jeremy was very proud of their technological capacities.

"So, you can see that we covered all the areas you suggested and over a significant amount of time." Roosevelt also smiled.

"We then spent several days going over the recordings and doing more historical research, which you know I love to do." Helen was happy that she was able to bring her academic skills into their work, and Roosevelt was pleased to collaborate on this process. "And we have quite a lot to show you."

Jeremy opened up a large laptop and connected it to a bigger screen that he brought for demonstration purposes. The IPS wanted to be sure that anyone with whom they consulted could see and hear clearly any evidence they compiled.

"First, we would like to show you some visual evidence we were able to get. Here's the first." Jeremy keyed the laptop to play an image on the screen: it was of the old card catalogue in the basement. Roosevelt's voice was heard over the image saying, "Some of the library staff have mentioned that the drawers of the catalogue open and close. Is that you?"

Roosevelt paused, waited, and then continued, "Do you think you could do that for us?" Then one of the drawers of the catalogue opened and closed.

Ms. Buchlieber gasped and put her hand to her open mouth. "Did I really see that?"

"Yes, you did. Let me show it again," Jeremy answered in a gentle tone. He then played that small video recording for her again.

"That's just...I don't even know what to say."

Helen smiled at her. "Sharon, we have more to show you. Look at this piece. This happened when we went to the children's section, and I asked whomever was there to open a book or turn a page." They waited and saw the slow turning of pages from the children's classic book.

"Oh, how lovely!" Now Ms. Buchlieber was smiling. Her apprehension seemed to have vanished with this viewing.

"And you're not afraid?" Jeremy asked.

"No, not at all. May I see more?"

"Those are the main visuals that we captured, but we do have some voice recordings for you," Roosevelt added.

"Did you hear voices? I have, on occasion, but almost more like a whisper than anything else, so I simply dismissed them." Ms. Buchlieber was deep in thought over this possibility. "I didn't really make anything of them."

"Actually," Jeremy explained. "These are recordings, EVPs or Electronic Voice Phenomena, of voices that we cannot hear with the human ear, but that we pick up on our equipment. We are not sure why that happens, but it does."

Jeremy switched to the audio recordings. "This first one occurred while Roosevelt and Sam were conducting an EVP session."

They heard Roosevelt ask a question about liking books, and a faint response came, "I love books."

"Oh my god," Ms. Buchlieber said quietly and then looked at the IPs. "I could hear that clearly. But it sounded, I don't know, let me think about it."

"Certainly, Sharon," Helen said. "Jeremy, please play the next one."

Jeremy pressed the button. First was Roosevelt's question, then shortly after a response. "May I ask what your name is?" Then "Eleanor Smith."

"Do you know that name, Sharon?" Helen asked.

Sharon thought for a few minutes, then she smiled. "Yes, I do. She was one of the original librarians here in the 1940s through the 1960s."

"You're right, of course, Sharon. After we heard this evidence, I did some research on her. She was one of the original librarians here, and she worked here until she died."

"Did she die in the building?" Anxious to hear the answer, Sharon leaned forward.

"No. She lived in a small apartment nearby and apparently died of a heart attack. Her friends hadn't heard from her in a few days, and they were worried, so they went to her place. One had a key for emergencies, and they let themselves in. They found her in her favorite sitting chair, with a cup of tea on the side table, and an opened book on her lap. She was an avid reader. She loved books and children, and even though she was childless—I can't be sure why—she was devoted to the children's area, and she often held story days where she read to the little ones."

"And that would explain," Sharon said. "Why the turned pages happened at the Children's area."

As she spoke, a look of curiosity came over her face.

"One thing I hadn't told you, only because I just thought of it, is that somedays the books seemed to be in better order than when we left. I never really put much consideration into it, but now, I wonder."

"That is all of what we found, but I think it is safe to say that you have a pleasant situation here," Roosevelt said. "Your ghost seems to be a kindly old lady who likes to look after the books and the children. I certainly do not believe that you have anything at all to worry about." Roosevelt was very happy with this outcome. He had had enough of dangerous demonic creatures to last him a very long time.

"Sharon, you can assure your people that there is no threat in anyway, just a sweet old lady who helps to watch over everyone." Helen smiled and reached over to put her hand gently on Sharon's. "In fact, I think she is more of a watch angel, than anything else."

"And, Ma'am," Sam said. "If anything bad does happen, or you do think there is something to be frightened of, just call us, and we'll be right here to help. We never let anyone alone to deal with these situations. We are always available."

"Well, I am certainly relieved about the situation now," Sharon said. "I will have a meeting over tea with the staff and the volunteers to try to assuage any fears they might have."

"That is a very good idea." Jeremy was relieved it had gone so well. "And if you need us to come and talk to the staff, we can also do that. Just give Helen or me a call, and we can arrange it."

"Thank you so much. You are all very kind."

After leaving the library, the IPS was very happy with the result—of a friendly ghost.

Chapter 14

1967

Sam would soon be out of high school and away from his old man. He hated the way his father treated him. Nothing was ever good enough to please him, especially when the old asshole was drinking. *You'd think he'd be proud of me,* Sam thought. *At least with sports, but he hates everything about me, and I can't fucking stand it anymore.*

"Boy, you planning on getting a job when you finish high school? I ain't paying for you to go to college," his father said to him one evening. "I didn't go. You sure as hell don't need to. I made a good life for your mom and you. You got everything here you need, boy—a roof over your head, plenty of food, and clothes on your back. You trying to be better than me, boy?"

Sam knew better than to take his father's bait. It would only lead to an argument, and Sam was sick of arguing.

"Didn't think you got anything to say, boy," his father said when Sam refused to speak. "Now, you remember, boy. You ain't never going to be better than me."

Sam hated when his father talked to him like that. He hated that he wouldn't be able to go to college. He hated that he couldn't be with the girl he loved. He hated this damned little hicktown.

Sam had his own plans. He had just turned 18, so he didn't need his parents' permission to do anything.

He had already spoken with the Marine Corps recruiting officer about joining. Sam knew he was likely to be drafted anyway—he had no college or medical deferment and he sure as hell didn't have a rich daddy to get him a spot in the National Guard, which everyone knew was the wealthy way to dodge the draft. Since he was probably going to be called up, he wanted to at least control in what branch of the Armed Forces he would serve.

Sam liked the feel of the Marine Corps. He wasn't sure what it was about it, but he liked the sound of Semper Fidelis—that sense of honor spoke to him.

He had walked home from high school and went to the recruiting office on Harrison Street, next to a doctor's office. As soon as he entered, he felt at home. He liked the posters of Marines on the wall, and he liked the respect he was shown by Sergeant Miller. He didn't talk down to Sam the way his father did. He was direct and clear.

"I'm not going to lie and tell you it will be easy. It won't be," Sergeant Miller said. "The United States Marine Corps is the finest fighting force in the world, and it is certainly not for everyone. Do you understand?"

"Yes, sir, I do," Sam replied instinctively.

"If you enlist, the hardest part will be boot camp. We will put you through hell there, but you will emerge as a Marine. Do you want that?"

Two days later, he signed the papers. He would get on the bus for Parris Island the day after graduation. *Finally,* he thought. *I'll be away from that son-of-a-bitch. I'll show that miserable old fucker what tough really is.*

But he had one more thing to do before he left, one more loose end to tie up—Jonnie Esel. That asshole had made his life miserable as a kid. Esel was 3 years older than Sam, and he delighted in tormenting him, as he had so many other little kids. And now, the asshole wasn't simply bullying smaller kids—he was selling drugs to them and trying to recruit them to be his workers.

Sam was going to put a stop to that.

Sam had a buddy set up a meet that night in the woods to the west of the Bethberg Steel Mill.

Later that night, Sam pulled up to the pre-arranged spot. Esel and one of his lackeys was there as muscle—a huge guy over 6'2 and about 230 pounds.

"Well, well, look at this. If it ain't little Sammie Sadlowski. Used to kick the shit out of you just for the fun of it...Well, good times, right? Now, let's do some business, right?"

Sam smiled, and two figures stepped out from behind a wall—both wore ski masks and were holding shotguns.

"What the fuck is this? Cops?"

"Do we look like cops, asshole? You can't be that fucking stupid."

"What the fuck then? You trying to rob me, shithead?"

"No, Jonnie, I don't want your money. I don't want your fucking drugs. But you're finished here. No more peddling this shit to schoolkids. Man, I hate that."

"You sound like a fucking pig."

"Nope. You could say just a concerned citizen. Now drop that bag and your guns slowly."

Jonnie and his friend looked at each other and tried to decide what to do.

"Don't be dumber than you are, asshole. If my pals think you're trying for your guns, they shoot, .10 gauge shot, you know what that'll do to a man at 10 feet."

They nodded, dropped the satchel, and their guns.

"You." Sam pointed at the guy with Jonnie. "On your knees, hands behind your head."

"What the fuck! You going to shoot me?"

"No, asshole, though it is tempting. No, it's simple, simple enough even for you to understand. Jonnie and me are going to fight. That's all. But your stash...that's going to the cops, along with both of your names. If you're here in the morning, they'll find you. But stay the fuck out of this town. We know who you are, shitheads."

Sam looked at Jonnie. "Now we fight. I'm not little Sammie anymore. We're going right now."

Jonnie was angry. This sucked. He was building up a good business—saw a future in turning kids onto LSD and heroin. *Guaranteed customers. Now this fucking kid wants to ruin it all. Fuck that. I'll kick his fucking ass.*

Sam was waiting for him with hands raised and his right foot slightly back.

"What're you, Sammie, some kind of fucking idiot? You think I don't know you got people waiting to jump me? Maybe some fucking pigs around?"

"Now you sound like just what you are—a fucking coward. You think the cops would use me as bait? Really? C'mon, asshole. Fight or admit you're afraid of me."

"Ok, Sammie, since you put it that way." Jonnie signaled with a snap of his fingers, and two other men came out next to him, both holding pistols

Chapter 15

1967

Jonnie's two new men spread out and pointed their guns at Sam, who stood there smiling. Two more figures in ski masks moved out of the darkness, also holding shotguns and pointed them directly at the men with the pistols.

It was a growing circle of men with guns.

"Thought you might try that stunt, asshole," Sam said in a very steady voice. "They, like my other friends, have .10-gauge shotguns. They shoot from here—your heads'll be gone." These newest two were friends from school, who, like Sam, had just enlisted in the Marines. They didn't hesitate to back him up.

"Semper Fi," was all they said when he explained his plan. Sam now belonged to a force that would always protect its own.

"Now, Jonnie, you tell your two buddies to put their guns down and stand still...very still."

They did. They could see the men holding the shotguns knew what they were doing. Their men holding the shotguns were not shaking at all. They projected readiness.

Sam looked directly at Jonnie and waved him forward.

"Now, asshole...fight."

Jonnie seethed. He hated to fight when someone else started it. More, he hated fighting someone who was not frightened of him. And this fucker, Sammie, had grown from a scrawny kid to a big man with wide shoulders, and baseball size hands, with knuckles that looked like rocks.

But Jonnie knew he couldn't back down, not if he wanted to keep building up his drug empire. *Can't let anyone know I backed down from a fight. They got to be scared of me. Fuck it,* Jonnie thought.

Jonnie roared and charged.

But Sam easily sidestepped the clumsy attack with simply a pivot on his right foot. He stepped forward as Jonnie tried to regain his balance.

Jonnie's arms flailed as he tried to regain his footing.

Sam took one step forward and launched a vicious left hook to Jonnie's stomach.

Jonnie doubled over and gasped for air.

Sam brought his knee up, straight into the dealer's face. They could all hear the sound of his nose breaking.

Jonnie gave a high-pitched squeal of pain.

"Get up, you fucking bastard. Get up!" Sam wasn't finished with this asshole yet.

Jonnie arose slowly, with fear in his eyes. Blood poured from his nose, which would never be straight again.

As he stood, Sam landed a left jab, followed by a perfectly delivered right cross to the tip of Jonnie's chin.

Jonnie's head snapped suddenly, almost like it wanted to leave his body. His eyes rolled back, and he collapsed to the ground like a heap of trash.

"No need to count to ten." Sam looked at the others. "On your knees assholes. Shouldn't have come along. We were going to give them a chance to leave, but this prick Jonnie, ruined that."

They tied all of them securely and left the bag of drugs with them. Then they place an anonymous phone call to the Bethberg Police about "a rival drug gang." They knew that would get the interest of the police.

They made sure they had left no fingerprints anywhere, and they left. Sam was sure no one would mention his name, because that would have brought shame to Jonnie, being brought down by a local kid.

The next day, the friends were all on the bus to Parris Island, to be followed six weeks later by tours of duty in Vietnam.

Chapter 16

1870

Ebeneezer Schwarznacht conducted hundreds of executions over the years, some in his preferred area of Gallows Hill, and others in varying locals and judicial precincts. He had become known as the best, most efficient hangman in the eastern part of Pennsylvania. He was, however, always available to travel to another jurisdiction if needed, unless he were already committed to a hanging elsewhere.

His life, otherwise, was Spartan. He lived in a small rental on the outskirts of Bethberg and kept his money carefully hidden. He needed little — a few sets of clothes, food, which he ate at the local pub, and the occasional book. His supplies were furnished by the courts which he served, and he did little in the way of entertainment. His work and his preaching were the only points of his existence.

He did understand that he could not do his work forever, so he put half of his earnings aside, buried in a tin container, hidden near Gallows Hill in Bethberg, PA. When he finally retired, he wanted to depend on no one.

Schwarznacht's personal relationships were practically nonexistent. He had no real friends, with whom he spent his personal time and no recreational activities that could take his mind from his occupation. To Ebeneezer, besides preaching, hanging human beings was the sole purpose of his existence. He took no pleasure from seeing nature or beauty in any way.

He seemed to have no interest in women or in men sexually. His whole being was wrapped up in the act of killing people by hanging. When he saw their bodies drop and heard their necks crack, that was the closest moment to happiness he experienced.

At that moment, if the people watching the executions could see behind the executioner's mask, they would have observed a grim smile, but a smile nevertheless, form on Schwarznacht's grim features.

When he was preparing for an execution, Shwarznacht spent all his waking time thinking about the weight of the condemned and the drop needed to do the job correctly. Doing his work exactly and with no mistakes was the measure of his life. He felt this was his aim in life. *I have been put here to do God's work, to eliminate the corrupt from the land. He has placed great responsibility in my hands, and I must be certain to do it correctly and with great humility.*

He always prayed, in private, before and after the executions. Before the hanging, he prayed to God to be guided by His wishes and that he might carry out the work in the proper and sedate fashion. After the work was complete, he prayed again in private, in his rented bedroom. There he often asked for forgiveness, *because, I know, O Lord, that I have committed a grave sin. I have taken pleasure in carrying out the act that is an extension of Your justice. I have felt carnal pleasure, and that is a terrible sin.*

One day, only a few years after his first execution, while he was still a young man, Schwarznacht returned to his chambers, tired and worn out.

Even though he was exhausted, he was also exhilarated. Ebeneezer went straight to his chambers, stripped, and masturbated. Even as he did so, he despised himself, thinking that he was in the grip of Satan.

I must be punished for my sins.

But he continued to find erotic pleasure after the act of killing.

After finishing, he would clean himself, then take a scourge he had fashioned from rough rope and whip his back repeatedly. Then he would kneel and pray for forgiveness, for hours.

After several years of performing the executions, Scwarznacht noticed a change. Not only did he take masturbatory pleasure in his deeds, but also he grew to anticipate the victims. He hoped that they were younger, and if possible, that they protested their innocence until the very end. Ebeneezer had no doubt about their guilt— as far as he viewed the world, especially human beings, it was a place corrupted by the devil, and all humans were born with the stain of corruption on them, one that could never be removed. He had heard of the Papists, who said a person could be forgiven if they confessed their deeds to a priest and then followed his orders about penitence, but he did not believe this. All were guilty. All deserved to be put to death.

He wanted to cleanse the world of their filth.

Now, he certainly understood that he could not simply kill everyone to rid the world of its stinking infestation, nor could he act on his own, as much as he ached to do so.

He often lay awake at night, thinking of ways he could devise to capture people, to bind them, and take them to the gallows alone. There, unobserved by anyone, he could carry out the executions in the most painful way possible. He would not use the correct drop so that the neck snapped. No, he would let them hang and very slowly suffocate. He so wished he could do this. But he knew the risk involved.

For many years, he shoved the urges aside, satisfying his desires by the official hangings. But then came the lessening. Fewer and fewer people were being executed, and his need grew stronger, almost making him burst with anticipation and desire.

As the use of the gallows slowed to almost nothing, Scharznacht took to staying there at night, reminiscing about the glories of the past. He also chased away children who had begun to come around as a place to play and scare each other. He also cleared the area of drunks who found it a good place to imbibe privately and fall asleep. He realized that he could have simply killed those rummies who polluted his sacred ground, but they were already well on their ways to death, and it would have brought him almost no satisfaction.

There were also rumors spreading in the town that investors, some of the local robber barons, were eyeing the location as a potential place for a new economic endeavor—an iron mill, similar to what Asa Packer had built in Bethlehem, just to the south of Bethberg.

Schwarznacht was appalled by the idea. *They can't do that, not here, not on this place, where I have carried out God's will—it would be an abomination!*

Shwarznacht soon had a plan in mind. And he came prepared.

He would stop the desecration of this site by removing the main player among the businessmen. Jacob Miller was a man who had come from a well to do family that made its money in lumber, and he had been educated at

Harvard. He believed the way to maintain his family's wealth and prestige was to understand the direction of the future. While lumber was certainly a strong enterprise, he could see that the vast forests of the land were already diminishing. There might come a time when they would no longer be able to sustain the economic machine his parents had created, and he did not wish to see any lessening of his family's wealth.

He had spent most of the evening with his two business partners, Mr. William Stevens and Mr. John Doyle. Both, like he, had a large fortune and wished to keep expanding it. They hoped one day to be able to rival the other emerging men of wealth in the United States. They had dined on the finest steak and potatoes at the dining room in the Bethberg Hotel, and then moved to a private sitting room for drinks and cigars.

It was a wood paneled room, with deep leather chairs, tables with large enameled ash trays, and a serving man who came around to keep refilling their glasses with whiskey. This was what they saw as their reward for their hard work and enterprise, the ability to indulge in the finer things in life and not have to worry about the cost. And soon, their bank accounts would rival even those of the largest capitalists. They were, indeed, very satisfied with themselves.

Miller was a jovial man, slim and tall, always ready with a laugh and a handshake for anyone. He wanted to be known as a tough but kind man, because he had ideas for running for public office in the not too distant future.

He opened a box of top-level cigars and shared them with his business partners. They snipped the long cigars and lit them with special matches.

Stevens, a man of very large tastes, was the opposite of Miller. Standing just over 5'9 inches, he weighed about 350 pounds. He consumed as much good food at every meal as he could, drank copious amounts of beer and whiskey, and smoked long imported cigars. He also kept several pretty young mistresses, with whom he enjoyed the sexual pleasures he would never ask of his very conservative wife. She, of course, knew about them, but as long as he was discrete around her, she didn't mind. She loved the large house and estate he had built for her and their six children, and she loved her position in high society not only in Bethberg but also in Bethlehem. She felt certain that her husband's influence would continue to grow and move her into an even more rarified and sophisticated social atmosphere. If that came at the cost of her husband having a few "doxies" as she called them, then so be it. She was perfectly happy with the arrangement, providing, of course, that no scandals ever arose to disturb her life.

Doyle was neither jovial nor large. Rather, he was a dark, little man, who often fidgeted and wore ill-fitting suits. Stevens had tried to get him to change his appearance, but nothing seemed to work. Neither Stevens nor Miller actually liked him, but they understand his astounding talent with mathematics and his understanding of strategy. Had he been in the military, he would certainly have been a general in charge of planning battles. For these two men, he was in charge of charting their business war.

For this night, they ate and drank and laughed.

Then they departed and went their separate ways.

Miller, you are the heart of this abomination. I am waiting for you. If that doesn't halt the progress of your damned ironworks, then I will execute Stevens and Doyle next. Schwarznacht was prepared, and he intended to do everything he could to stop their plans.

Miller emerged from the hotel and tried to steady himself in the night air. It was a chilly October night, not yet cold, but the brisk air helped to sober him a bit. He didn't usually drink as much as he did this night, but he prided himself on being able to hold his drink, and he never asked for assistance. He would have taken a room in the hotel if he really thought he could not walk the four blocks to his home.

Schwarznacht waited until he saw Miller emerge and thought, *This, is the night. I will never have this opportunity again. I will have my vengeance tonight.*

He hurried down the other side of the street and was certain that Miller did not see him in the murky darkness. It certainly helped that a misty rain was falling, like a curtain to obscure the vision on the street.

He waited until the block just before Miller's home. There was a patch of trees that would completely hide him. That was where he had put his needed supplies and a horse and wagon, waiting on the street.

Soon he heard Miller slowly walking along, often stumbling. Schwarznacht held a large wooden club in his right hand. As Miller stepped by him, Ebeneezer stepped behind him, looked to be certain no one was watching and swung the club hard.

Miller moaned and sunk down. Schwarznacht grabbed him and dragged him to the waiting wagon. With Miller still dazed, he hefted him into the back, gagged him and tied him securely with his hands behind his back.

Then Schwarznacht covered him with old blankets and secured them with a variety of old farming tools. He would look like just another farmer on his way home.

Of course, he wasn't headed home.

He drove the old wagon out of the town limits and to the dirt road that made its way up Gallows Hill. As

Schwarznacht approached the gallows, the sky lightened. Almost as if he had commanded them, the clouds opened up and revealed a brilliant Autumn evening with an almost full moon and a wide array of stars casting light down below. He smiled. This would give him light he needed to carry out his task without worrying about igniting any torches that might be seen in the distance.

Chapter 17

July 21, The Present

Sam's most secret room in his house was on the second floor. It faced the east, away from the street, in the working-class section of Bethberg. No one, not even Roosevelt, had been allowed in there, and it was where he kept his most hidden self.

The house itself was a modest brick single on a small plot of land. He had purchased the home after selling and splitting the profits from the other house, the one were Josh died. It wasn't very large, only about 1200 square feet, but it served his purposes.

He slept in the front bedroom, which was small and intended to be a guest room. But he didn't care—he only needed it for storing clothes and sleeping. The best room was the larger bedroom in the back of the second floor.

That was the room he focused on.

This room, with the best light in his small house, was his painting studio. It was here that he allowed himself to be what he had wished he had been since he was a child: a painter. Or at least, it was what he tried to do.

He did not have many regrets over the course of his life. His time in the Marines had prepared him to become a police officer, go to college part-time, and move up the ranks to become the main homicide detective in Bethberg.

His major goal to be a painter was a failure, but that was nothing compared to the loss of his son.

That would haunt him more than any ghost the IPS might have found. He still believed he should have seen some signs, so he could have found help for his boy.

Through all of his life, and now 69 years old and retired, he had maintained his love for art. Both Roosevelt and Jeremy knew this about him, and they often visited galleries and museums together, but he never told them that he still tried to paint. Never told anyone. And he never planned to. He had no desire to show anyone his paintings. As far as he was concerned, this was completely for his own satisfaction, and he had no desire to hear what anyone else might think of his art. Especially because he had been unable, in the last few years, to complete any piece.

Sam had tried numerous times, but without success.

Sam would go to the studio, set up a canvas, and stare at it. He sometimes arranged his paints and even placed a photograph or two nearby of local scenery so he could work from them on a landscape.

Sometimes Sam would stare for hours at the canvas, but he would produce nothing.

Sometimes Sam would throw his brushes down in disgust and leave the room.

Sometimes Sam would sink to the floor and cry.

Chapter 18

1870

Schwarznacht had arrived at the gallows. He stopped the horse and wagon and climbed down from the seat. He secured the wagon to a hitching post and then went to the back, where he heard moaning from under the blankets.

It was nighttime, but the full moon gave a fair amount of light, and Schwarznacht knew the trail leading to the gallows as if he could see it with his eyes closed.

He stood for a moment and savored the sounds of fright coming from under the tarps. He pulled the coverings off the prone Miller, who was awake but in serious pain from the clubbing on his head.

"Now don't you worry about that ache in your head, Miller. That pain will soon enough be gone. That's right. It'll soon fade away, and you won't feel a thing." Schwarznacht gave him a hideous smile, like something from a demon from the pits of the netherworld.

Miller tried to say something but was unable to produce only inarticulate groans because of the gag in his mouth. He struggled against his bonds, but the rope was tied too well, and he had no chance of escape. And every time he tried to move, a shock of pain coursed through his head, making him nauseated. He was afraid he might vomit into the gag and choke to death.

Schwarznacht grabbed him and pulled him roughly out of the wagon and held him standing on very unsteady feet. Miller looked at the man holding him and felt fear cascade over him as if he had been immersed in a sudden ice bath. He looked into Schwarznacht's dark eyes and saw death there.

Schwarznacht didn't untie Miller, but pulled him, holding him from behind, with his arms locked around Miller's chest. When they reached the edge of the gallows, Shwarznacht propped him against it and climbed up the steps. On the main floor of the gallows, he lowered a rope with a loop in it, then he scampered back down to Miller.

He fastened the rope tautly around Miller's chest and went back to the top. There, with a winch he had installed, he cranked and pulled the trembling man up to the gallows platform. Miller's body banged against the wooden frame as he was raised up. Finally, Schwarznacht grabbed him and heaved him all the way onto the platform.

With tears running down his face, Miller groveled on the platform, curled up in a fetal position.

Schwarznacht reached down and pulled him up to a standing position and held him upright.

"It is time, Miller for you to pay for your sins," Schwarznacht said to him and marched him to the trapdoor. Miller was crying and shaking, his whole body wanting to collapse in fear. As the executioner stood over the sobbing man, the light from the moon broke through a temporary cloud cover and showed him in complete power over his chosen victim.

Miller looked up at the man towering over him. The moon was directly behind his head and backlighted Schwarznacht, casting an almost demonic glow that seemed to emanate from the smiling hangman.

"I sentence you, Miller, for the crime of sullying the sacred nature of this ground with your evil plan to make money from this soil, which has seen the sanctifying of justice delivered to the guilty and their souls delivered to their maker. Soon, you will accompany them."

Schwarznacht pulled Miller to his feet and put the noose around his neck and tightened it so that the man was now forced to remain standing or strangle if he slumped down. Then the hangman secured a weighted sack around the terrified man's feet. This would cause him to break his neck when the trap door opened and die quickly as the executions were designed to be. "While I despise you, Miller, I'm going to send you on your way, the proper way, the way I always have. It'll be quick. One snap of your neck, and you'll be finished."

Miller whimpered and tried to beg, but his mouth was still stopped with the rag from the wagon. Tears streamed down his face.

With Miller secured on the trapdoor, Schwarznacht stepped to the control lever. "Jacob Miller, for your crimes of desecration of sacred land, for choosing greed, one of the seven deadly sins, and for your unholy life, I find you to be guilty, and I sentence you to hang by the neck until dead. May God have mercy on your soul!"

Miller closed his eyes and tried to pray. Then Schwarznacht held the lever in both hands and pulled. The trapdoor opened, and Miller fell through. A crunch, like the sound of a semi-rotted tree branch cracking in half, barked in the air. Then silence.

Schwarznacht laughed and shook his fists in the air. "You have paid for your sins!" he shouted with great glee.

He ran to the stairs and nearly jumped down them. Hitting the ground on both feet like a boy playing a game, he whirled and ran to the hanging Miller. The hanging man's neck was clearly broken, and a spread of urine covered his pants.

"I have done your most holy work, O Lord. I have cleansed the earth of another sinner! I thank you for allowing me to be the instrument of Your justice."

Just two more to do, and this foolishness of building here will be over, he thought. *Now to remove him and bury his damned corpse.*

Schwarznacht had planned the evening carefully. He had already dug and covered a grave in the local field that had been used as a dumping ground. No one would think of looking there for a burial site. Soon he would have this part over with, and he could continue with his plans of holy justice.

As he was cutting the noose, he heard footsteps and shouting.

"There he is!" someone shouted. "Get the bastard!"

Chapter 19

1965

"I hope this is all right, Martha," Sam said as he opened the door for her. He looked just like what he was, a frightened and uncertain boy on the verge of becoming a young adult. Sam had saved up a bit of money, and he had rented a room in a small motel on the outskirts of town. It wasn't an upscale place, more one likely to be used by truckers stopping for the night or for trysts conducted outside of general public view. It certainly was not the kind of place where Sam would like to have taken his beloved Martha, but it was the best that he could do.

"Please wait in the car while I sign in, Martha," Sam said to his girlfriend.

"Are you ashamed of me?" she asked.

"No! I'm proud of you. I'm ashamed that I have to bring you to this place. I would rather take you to a five-star hotel in London or Paris. That is what you deserve, not this place."

"Sam, I am happy to be with you, anywhere, anytime. I love you."

When Martha told him that, his heart soared like he had been aboard one of the space rockets. He looked into her beautiful eyes. "And I love you."

They kissed, and Sam went into the motel office.

Sam was extremely nervous and felt his hands shaking He paused at the entrance to try to steady himself.

Then, he went in. Sam had signed in, with Martha waiting in his old Buick sedan.

The old man at the desk seemed to be so ancient that Sam thought he had died but never noticed and just kept tending to his motel. He also never asked embarrassing questions as long as the room was paid for. Because Sam was paying in cash, even fewer were asked.

"Just sign here."

Sam wrote Stan Renoir in the register. He thought using the artist's last name added a touch of class to a dismal place, but the old fellow didn't notice, nor would he have cared if he had paid attention to the signature.

"How many nights?"

"Just tonight," Sam answered.

"Yep." The fellow turned and found a key from the rack behind him. "That'll be 15 dollars, up front."

Sam gave him the money, and the man quickly wrote out a receipt, then handed Sam the key. "Checkout's 10 A.M. Sharp. You're still there after 10, you owe another day."

"Yes, sir," Sam replied.

"Ok. Room 25. Around to the right. Can't miss it."

Sam left and went to his car.

Sam went to passenger's side door, and he held it open for her.

"Why, thank you, kind sir." Her eyes smiled as she looked at him.

I've never seen anyone so beautiful, he thought. *I don't think I ever will again.*

Sam held out his arm, and Martha slid hers easily around it. As they walked to the room, they looked like a couple that was completely comfortable together and had been with each for many years.

Sam unlocked the door to room 25 and held it open. He turned on the light and followed her inside.

The room, while clean, was beige and drab, with a double bed, a chair and table with a phone on it, and a small black and white television set, complete with rabbit ears. These were rooms that were utilitarian and certainly not decorated for romance. Just the opposite.

Sam and Martha didn't care. They might have been in the grandest honeymoon suite in the Waldorf Astoria, with a large king-sized bed, and a view overlooking much of Manhattan. Because they were together, they were happy.

Sam went over to the chair and held it for her to sit on.

"You are a gentleman, Sam." Martha smiled. It was an honest smile, with absolutely no mocking or sarcasm in it. They had dated twice since they met at the disastrous Senior Prom, and the most they had done was kissed.

But they had felt an immediate connection, and both knew it wasn't the stuff of teenaged infatuation. This was different. This wasn't the here today and vanished tomorrow desire for someone, simply driven by hormones. Both felt that the happiness of the other mattered more than their own. Sam had never felt this way towards anyone else before.

And they were also frightened, because they knew that Sam would soon be going into the Marines, and Martha would be going to college in California in the fall. Both paths had already been chosen by the two young adults. When she found out that he had enlisted, she had asked him why.

"I have to get away from this place and my old man."

"From me, too?" She had asked, her eyes, clear but also worried and determined.

"No, no! Not from you. I can't get out of my commitment to the Corps—I'm signed up now, but I probably would've been drafted anyway. This war is getting worse, and it looks like they are going to increase the number being called up. I know I am not the type to protest, and I'm not going to Canada, so I wanted to choose what branch I would serve in. And I'm not going to college."

"Like I am?" Martha was scared he was jealous of her opportunity. "Do you blame me too?"

Her words were sharp.

"No, Martha." Sam spoke in a quiet voice. "You have no idea how happy I am that you are going to college. It's your ticket out of here. Besides, you're the smartest person I've ever known. You shouldn't waste your mind at all, and you also need to get out of this one-horse town. It would be a tragedy if you didn't make the most out of yourself that you can be. I want you to have all the success in life you possibly can have."

Martha smiled and kissed him. "Well then, my Sam. Let's not waste the remaining time we have together." They planned to meet at the motel later that day.

Martha stood and looked at Sam. He was wearing jeans and a blue chambray shirt. "You are the handsomest and best man I know, Sam."

He blushed a deep red. She stroked his face.

Martha wore a light blue blouse and a modest skirt. She had a simple necklace of turquoise and matching earrings.

"And you, my sweet, lovely, Martha. You are beautiful."

The kissed then, slowly, at first, hesitantly. They then pulled each other into a tight embrace.

After they kissed, Martha looked at Sam. "Sam, I have to tell you something."

"What is it?" He was worried. Was something wrong? Did he do something wrong?

"No, nothing is wrong. It's just. . . I've never done this before. I don't want you to think I'm a slut."

"Martha, I would never think that about you." Sam became very serious and held her face gently between his large hands. "You are the best person and a lady. Plus, I have something to tell you also."

Martha looked at him.

"I've never done this before either."

Sam awoke the next morning, holding Martha, and he knew that would be the best night of his life, the night by which all other loves would be measured.

Chapter 20

July 22, The Present

"I don't fucking believe it," Sam said and looked across the table at his former partner from when he was a homicide detective and one of his closest friends. They were sitting at a table in a small diner, The Get-A-Way, an old and regular hangout for cops, both working and retired.

For the last ten years of his job as a homicide detective, Sam's partner, Steven Goodman, had been not only Sam's investigative partner but also one of his closest friends, with bonds formed from connections he had with no one else: work and children. Sam had been godfather to Steven's daughter Maria, and Steven had been the same to Josh.

Maria had been born with cerebral palsy, and she had not been expected to live long. Steven and his wife, Monica, had two other children, but they loved them all, and the thought of losing Maria tore at them. But they persevered with their love and attention to all their children. Maria, also, proved to have the strength and fortitude of her parents. She was an extremely determined child with a very strong will.

The disease slowly decimated her frail body, but her mind was strong, and her intellect grew daily. She excelled at school, and though it was difficult, she became valedictorian of her class.

Maria won scholarships to several colleges, and after graduating from high school, she elected to attend Muhlenberg College in Allentown, PA, which offered very strong support for those in need and was also a nationally ranked liberal arts college.

Because Maria and Josh were the same age and the connection of their families, the two children grew up with an unusually close bond. Monica once said that Maria was more of a sister to Josh than she seemed to be to her siblings. Maria's older brother and sister didn't mind though; they were happy to see the strong friendship she had with Josh.

Unfortunately, too many children judged Maria immediately on her physical appearance and her difficulty in moving. Josh, however, did not care at all— to him she was beautiful, and he soon became her protector. If any other kid, no matter how big they might be, teased her or mocked her, Josh always came to her aid.

He did develop a reputation as a tough kid, but he was never seen as a bully. While his defending Maria sometimes landed him in detention in school, he never stopped being her protector or her best friend.

With his friendship and her fortitude, she blazed her way through her high school classes, at least until Josh's death.

Even her extraordinary determination came into question when Josh committed suicide. Steven and Monica thought she might succumb to the grief at having lost her life-long friend and simply give up. But Maria seemed to find a fathomless well of strength from somewhere and kept going, as she said, "to show what Josh and I can do and could have done together."

She never explained what she meant by that, except to say that, "I'm sure that Josh understands."

Maria did survive and emerge from her grief, and she enrolled at Muhlenberg College. This was an accomplishment of which her parents and her unlikely godfather were deeply proud.

More than two decades earlier before sitting at the same bar and talking together, Sam was astonished by what Steven and Monica had asked him. They were sitting at a picnic table in the Goodman's back yard. "Me? Really? I haven't been to mass for over 10 years." Sam, since his tours of duty in Vietnam, had not considered himself to be much of a religious man.

"Do you think that matters at all to us, you dumb shit?" Steven was amused by his friend's perplexity. Monica, however, was offended by her husband's language and swatted his arm.

"Now, mister, you do not talk like that around me!"

Steven was very quickly chagrined. He knew that parameters of what was considered acceptable language at home. "I'm sorry, honey. I just was so amused by the look on Sam's face."

Monica smiled. She loved her husband completely, but she also set very high standards of behavior at home, and she expected them to be followed by her family. She could forgive friends, but her looks of disapproval could make hardened men like Sam feel like they were children being punished. But she also adored Sam, and she and her husband has agreed completely on this request.

"Sam," Steven continued, watching his words carefully. "You don't really think I was much of a church-going man before getting married and having kids, do you?"

"I have to admit, Steven, I never really thought about it."

"Well, I didn't. But now I do, and the boys are better for it, and so am I. It really isn't about me though. I want to give them everything I can, the same way I know you feel about Josh. I've watched your face when you talk about him and show me pictures of him. I have to say, I've never seen you as happy as when you talk about your baby boy."

"Well, you're right."

"Of course, I am, Sam! When am I ever wrong when we talk about something anyway?" Steven laughed hard, and Monica swatted him again.

"Only, mister, when you try to argue with me!"

"We both know that our little girl faces the hardest of fights. We don't know how long she has." Steven paused and wiped his eyes, while Monica hugged him. "But, we'll do anything and everything we can for her. She is such a sweet and well-behaved child, and she was given such a raw deal, but we can do the best we can, and that includes having you in the family as her godfather, to help watch over her. I want you to have my back with her."

"Ah, man." It was all Sam could get out before he started blubbering also.

"Look at you two tough guys. Well, I'll be right back with some coffee for you." Monica gave them a little time to recover.

Josh had been born about four months before Maria, so he knew exactly what Steven was talking about. Josh had become Sam's world, and Sam had also tried to be a better man than he had been before.

Since Josh's birth, he had begun exercising daily, and he was making a serious attempt to give up smoking. But he had to admit, he wasn't doing so well on that particular front.

"But, Steven, man," Sam said while thinking. "There's another problem."

"Yeah, what is it? Don't tell me you don't want to do this." Steven looked at Sam with an odd sideways glance. "Don't tell me it's because I'm black."

"Fuck, no, man! What're you even thinking? You know me better than that." Sam then looked around in a panic to see if Monica had heard him swear. "You're my brother, and I love Maria like she was my own daughter."

Steven glared at Sam with the same stern look he used on perps when questioning them in the interrogation room. He held Sam's eyes for a few seconds. Then a wide smile slowly creased his handsome face. And he laughed, with a deep booming sound that came from the center of his being. He kept laughing and finally pounded his palm on the table to be able to stop.

Sam had seen this laughing fit before and waited for it to end, though he drummed the table with his fingers and snarled a little.

Steven saw Sam's face turning red, a sure sign his partner was getting angry. "Sammy, I'm sorry for laughing like that at you, but you can be a total idiot some times. I know you don't care about color—I was just busting on you, and man, you always bite."

"Well, that really helps, jerk." Sam felt like a kid trying to get the last word in.

"So, tell me, Sammy, what is the other problem anyway?"

"I'm sort of embarrassed by it."

"C'mon, Sammy."

"This is going to sound stupid, but, man, I'm Catholic, and you're Protestant."

"So, tell me something I don't know. Sam, don't you get it? I don't care what religion you are or are not, and my minister doesn't either. I already talked to him about it."

"Really?" Sam felt foolish now, like a child caught stealing a cookie.

By this point Monica had returned and placed cups of coffee in front of them. She looked at Sam and smiled. "You are one of the best people we know. We both think that, Sam."

Sam could only smile and nod. He felt too choked up to say anything.

"Yeah, besides I pointed out to the good Brother Micah, if there was a problem with you being my daughter's godfather that I would take myself, my family, and we're a damned big extended family, and my friends, and go to a different church. He knows I am serious, and he knows that I know he's having a hard timed filling the pews on Sunday, so he can't risk losing even more."

"You'd do that?"

"Yes, we would," Monica answered. "God isn't the property of any one Church, and you are family. We would do that for our family."

"Ah, now. . ." Sam couldn't continue. He was wiping his eyes.

"And, Sammy," Steven said and grinned. "I would never tell anyone what a softie you are."

"Better not! And now I feel like a moron for what I said before."

"Sam, my man, sometimes you are a moron. But that is besides the point. So, what do you say? Will you be Maria's godfather?"

This time Sam answered with no hesitation. "Yes, I will."

Sam dealt with the Catholic issue by simply not mentioning it. He figured that he doesn't tell the Pope what to do, and the Pope doesn't tell him what to do.

And Sam was true to his word. He learned about the Methodist religion and attended services with Steven and Monica every two Sundays; the other two he went to Mass.

That was about 23 years earlier. Maria had since grown, attended, and graduated from Muhlenberg College with a degree in history. Sam was as proud that day as he had ever felt in his entire life. He cheered loudly as the now fragile and frail Maria was pushed across the stage in her wheelchair by her parents to accept her diploma. Though her body was clearly weakening, her smile was wide and healthy.

Still, it was a bittersweet moment for Sam. He had hoped to see Josh graduate also, not be a memory etched into his mind, a terrible moment of hell—of cradling his dead son's body in his arms and wailing

Chapter 21

1870

Schwarznacht turned and saw a group of men running towards him. *Noooooooo,* he thought. *This will ruin everything. They can't despoil my plans. I have to save this sacred place, and I cannot let anyone stop me.*

"Get him! Get the son-of-a-bitch!" one yelled as they advanced from the bottom of the hill. They moved forward like as mass of undulating jelly, with their drunkenness making them lurch in various directions.

"Look! Look at what that bastard has done!" one of them shouted, and they surged forward, with the moonlight occasionally illuminating the path as clouds passed over it quickly and then revealed it.

"What is that?" one called out.

"I can't see…it's too dark." For a few seconds, the moon was obscured.

As they looked, the clouds parted just enough for part of the moon to emerge and through a misted light onto a tableau of death. Schwarznacht was on the ground below the gallows, and he had cut the hanging rope, but the noose was still around the dead man's broken neck.

Eight men were standing there, not believing what they saw. The fog of too much beer clouded their minds at first. Then they saw the preacher/hangman holding the body of one of the investors, the very dead body.

First, there was only a murmur, as the men were shocked by what they saw.

Their movement forward came to a halt.

The moon shown fully on the unholy scene. Schwarznacht looked like some kind of demon out of hell. He stood before them, holding the body of the dead man and grinned at them.

Then understanding set in to the drunk men, and one of them pointed.

"Look! He killed Miller!"

Understanding slowly spread throughout the mob of men.

Then a roar slowly went up, beginning as a soft murmur and building to a loud and violent thunder, but absent any lightning strike in the sky.

Then the posse of men charged him. They lumbered up the hill, some falling, and getting back up. Others charged forward.

Schwarznacht was still holding Miller's body as they swarmed around him. He gripped the corpse hard, his fingers digging in like talons, as he tried to keep them from taking the corpse away from him.

The struggle was hard. Schwarznacht's fingers clutched Miller's body like a man trying to hold onto a life raft in the ocean in a terrible storm.

Eventually they wrenched the dead man free. As they pulled the body away, the executioner still held material torn from Miller's clothing.

They shoved Schwarznacht to the ground and held him there.

The night changed again. A sudden surge of clouds swept over the moonlight, and lightning began to flash.

"You cannot keep me from doing the Lord's work! I will have justice on all of you! I will bring the wrath of God down onto you and this place forever!"

"He's evil! He's a demon!" one called out.

"He's summoning the devil. Look at the sky!"

A bolt of lightning flashed across the sky, and for a brief moment, the dark had turned to daylight.

Then just as suddenly, darkness returned.

"NOOOOO! Release me, you fools! I must complete my task!" Schwarznacht struggled against the men pinning him to the ground, but he was not strong enough, even enraged, to break free of their grasp.

"Let's take him to the police. They'll know what to do," one man offered.

"No, we can't do that. He's in with them, and he'll get off. Look at what he's done. He's killed one of the men who would bring prosperity to our town, and he would probably try to kill the others."

"I will! I'll kill them and then all of you, you unrepentant sinners! Fornicators! Agents of the devil!"

"Listen to him—he's crazy. We have to do this now. And we have to swear to each other not to reveal what happened here this night."

Before they did anything else, they took rope from cart and bound Schwarznacht with his hands behind him.

The men who were there stood around the now bound and still struggling hangman and looked down at him solemnly.

"Now, we have to swear not to reveal this to anyone."

"I swear," the leader said.

"I swear," came the next and so on until they had all made their vows.

"Remember, no one can ever speak of this. We were not here. We will simply let Miller's body where it is and then hang Schwarznacht. Everyone will think he killed Miller and then committed suicide. It has begun to rain, so our tracks will be obscured in the mud. Besides, no one will have any reason to think otherwise."

They forced the hangman onto his stomach and bound his hands together tightly.

Then they pulled him to his feet and shoved him to the stairs.

He tried to resist, but they dragged him along. They had tied a rope around his neck, so they could lead him like a roped cow. As they pulled him up the stairs, the rain began.

"Remember to untie his hands when done!" the leader of the men called out.

Schwarznacht refused to walk, so they pulled him up the stairs banging his shins against the wood. Then they went to the trapdoor. Two men pushed it shut, and they forced him to stand there while they formed another noose.

Three held him in place, while another put the noose around his neck and tightened it.

"Any last words, you murdering scum?"

"I curse you all. I curse you and this land you are standing on. This is sacred ground, for purifying the guilty, not for profit. I tell you now—I will never leave this place. Never! As long as this gallows is here, I will be here!"

"You got that right—you ain't ever walking away from here!" one of the men holding him said and laughed. "Now you gonna die, you murdering asshole."

They stood back from the man who looked at them and laughed. "You are fools and sinners, all of you!"

The man at the lever yanked it, and the trap door fell open.

Schwarznacht fell through, but the drop wasn't long enough to break his neck, so it took 15 long minutes of his kicking and moaning to die of strangulation.

His eyes bulged, and blood vessels broke as his orbs seemed to try to escape from his face. Then his mouth opened, and his tongue hung out like a strange animal caught in a trap.

The men, who had climbed down to the ground moved back. They didn't understand why he hadn't simply died. But they were amateurs, and they had seriously misunderstood the needed knowledge to execute another human being properly.

Finally, they were certain he was dead, and they left in the pouring rain.

Schwarznacht's body moved in the wind from the storm.

His spirit rose to the platform.

"I will never leave."

Chapter 22

July 22, The Present

Every day, that image of Josh's death came to him, and every day that pain was as fresh as that terrible day when it happened. The only thing that helped was that Josh's spirit has appeared to him and aided in the climactic battle against the demon Maledicus, and Josh said, "I love you, Pop." Sam held onto that moment deep in his heart, and he always carried Josh's beloved baseball card that had served as a talisman in the battle with him.

Sam and Steven were sitting at the diner where they had shared many meals while on the job as detectives. It was a place they had some privacy from the all too prying eyes of the people of the town.

Sam couldn't believe what he was hearing. "You got something to tell me about Josh? Now, after all this time? Are you sitting me, man?" Sam was completely astonished. He wasn't angry, not yet, but he just couldn't believe his friend would have held something back from him, not after all they had been through together.

"Samuel, listen to me."

Sam sat stunned. Steven never used Sam's formal name unless something was very wrong.

Steven looked directly at Sam, hesitated, then continued, "I just found this out. I never held anything back from you, and I never would. Shit, I can't believe it myself."

Sam nodded. "Go on."

The big man who sat across the table from Sam, the one whose sheer physical presence usually intimidated criminals, who despite his recent retirement still looked like he could play linebacker on a college team, seemed to shrink in front of Sam.

First, he looked down and gripped the table with both large hands, then he slowly moved up to face Sam again, but with large tears welling in his eyes and then running down his cheeks like a dam that had burst open. "Maria's dying."

"Oh, shit. No, Steven." Sam couldn't say anything else.

Steven nodded and wiped his tears with the sleeve of his sports coat, suddenly looking like a very large child in deep pain. "Yeah, a week ago, she had some kind of seizure, different from anything before, so we took her right to the hospital."

"Man, why didn't you call me? I would have been there. You know that."

"I'm sorry, Sam. We thought it was just another progression of her condition. She seemed to get better in a couple of hours. But. . ." Steven held his head in his hands and cried again.

Sam waited. He understood his friend's grief and immediately went back to the pain he felt at being there when Josh died. He felt his heart breaking. . . again.

"Cancer." Steven spoke again after regaining his self-composure. "Brain cancer, the worst kind of the connective tissue, the stuff that runs through the entire brain, and it's advanced and it is now in its final stages."

"Ah, man. Steven." Now Sam was also crying. "Can't they do anything?"

"Nothing. And they said we might have been able to try chemo or radiation if it was caught earlier, but they also said it would not have done anything, only made her sicker."

"Fuck, man. This is awful."

"Sam, my baby girl's going to die." He started to cry, louder this time, with his shoulders shaking, looking a bit like a volcano on the verge of erupting.

Some of the other customers were staring at the two crying men. Sam slowly turned to a couple and glared at them. "You got a fucking problem, pal?" he said to the biggest man there.

The man, a guy used to fights, wanted to say something back, but the look in the older man's eyes told him it was better just to turn away. He was accustomed to fighting people afraid of him, and this guy showed no fear. "Sorry. Sorry," he muttered and turned back to his food. When he did, all the others looking also looked away.

Sam stood and went around the table and wrapped Steven in an enormous bear hug and let Steven cry on him. After about a minute, Steven moved back and sat back down.

Sam returned to his seat.

"Sammy, that ain't all. It gets worse."

"What? Fuck, man. How can it be worse than that?"

"It can, Sammy. It can." Steven paused.

Chapter 23

July 22, The Present

"It gets much worse, Sammy," Steven said. Usually, when they talked, Steven would look directly at Sam; in fact, Steven had one of the most piercing stares he had ever witnessed. Many being interrogated often collapsed under his gaze, and in friendly conversation, he always kept his eyes on the person he was speaking with. But as he was talking with Sam, Steven's eyes first clouded a bit, and then he looked away from Sam.

Sam sat back and waited. He had never before seen the odd look that went over Steven's face. "Just, tell me, Steven."

Steven looked up. "I told you that Maria is dying and doesn't have long now."

Sam nodded.

"Maria is in hospice now."

Sam looked hard at Steven.

"I was going to tell you, but now, I have something else you need to know." Steven's voice caught for a moment as he continued to talk. "She told me something, and I got to tell you what she said." Steven's eyes almost glazed as he spoke.

"We were alone in Maria's room at the hospice. Monica had gone home to take a shower and rest. We were doing on and off shifts staying with Maria." Steven had to stop and compose himself, so Sam simply waited. Steven continued, "Maria was sitting up in her bed, and she looked at me with the most frightened eyes I had ever seen on her.

"'Daddy,'" she said. "'I have to tell you something, and I want you to promise me that you won't hate me after I tell you.'"

"I had never heard that kind of fear in her voice before."

"Babygirl, you can tell me anything, anything." I reached out and took her hands in mine, and they felt so small and so fragile. What could my little girl say to me that would make me think any less of her? She was my angel, and I loved her so much that my heart was breaking watching her die slowly."

"'Daddy, it's about Josh.'"

"Well that had thrown me off. I never expected to hear anything like that. Had something happened with them? Had they become boyfriend and girlfriend? I tell you, that is something I often wished had happened. I couldn't think of a single boy who would be better for her. If they had gone too far and done something, well, that's just human nature. How could I have felt bad about her?"

"'Daddy, I know what happened to Josh. Why he, why he . . . did what he did.'"

"Now, that really floored me. All these years had passed and she was telling me now, on her deathbed. This really didn't sound good at all."

"'Daddy, I couldn't tell you before, because I promised I wouldn't. And you taught me never to break a promise.'"

"Now that was a bind I really didn't expect. I had taught her that."

"'Daddy, Josh and I were really close.'"

"She laughed when she saw the look in my eyes. Even though I had hoped they would be a couple, I was still her Dad."

"No, not like what you're thinking, at least not for a long time,'" she said with a smile. "'He always acted like an older brother to me, always. I liked him, but he was always there to protect me, against anything. Daddy, it was back when we were both 16. He was driving around in the car Uncle Sam had got for him. I remember how proud of it he was, how he took care of it, always washing it and shining it. He had told me one day he would drive to college in it, and he would drive me to wherever I went to college also.'"

"That sounded exactly like Josh. I just couldn't understand where this was going."

"'Daddy, one of my friends, Jennifer, got in trouble by hanging with the wrong crowd. I know I should have come to you and said something, but I didn't want to tell on her. Well, she started, what do you call it? Delivering drugs for one of the local dealers. But I didn't know that. And she asked for a ride one day, and Josh said sure, so the three of us were together.'"

"Now, Sam. I knew this would be bad."

"'Well, it turned out that Jennifer was supposed to deliver a bag of money, a lot of money, but she had spent it already, and she hadn't told anyone. Well, it got really awful when we got there. There were several guys there, and Josh was mad and wanted to fight, but there was nothing he could do against them. The gangsters were really mad, and they wanted their money. Josh couldn't keep his tongue and told them they would be sorry when his dad found out. I knew it wasn't good to say, but he wanted to fight them so much, and that was all he could do.'"

"Maria started to cry then. I just waited for her to continue. When she was ready, I asked if she heard any of their names."

"Sam, the leader's name was Max."

"Fuck, I should have known," Sam said. "It was that asshole, Max."

"We both should have known."

"Well, I know what I'm going to do to him."

Steven shook his head slightly in agreement, then he continued. This is what Maria told me then, "The leader of the gangsters looked at all of us, but he especially looked hard at Josh. One of them got quiet and serious. He said he had a phone call to make, about detective Sadlowski. When he came back, he was smiling and said there's been a change of plans. Got direct orders to carryout. Daddy, he pulled out some handcuffs and put them on me. He then turned to Josh and said, 'You want to be a hero boy? Here is your chance. And you only get one shot, boy. You got to go home, lock yourself in the garage, keep the car running and stay there. You got it, boy. You do anything else, anything, like calling your old man, saying something to anyone else, anything and we kill your little nigger girlfriend. You got me boy? You don't do this, and you go free, but she dies. Then daddy, they put a gun to my head and pulled the hammer back. I thought I was going to die that day."

"Maria got really quiet then."

"'Daddy, Josh made me promise not to tell anyone. He said they would know and come for me. Daddy,'" she said and started to cry again. "'I promised him. And...and...and...he died to save me.'"

"Sammy, he died to save Maria, and I just found out. She gave me a letter Josh wrote to her.

Chapter 24

July 22, The Present

Steven looked across at Sam. Then he reached into his coat pocket and pulled out an envelope and handed it to Sam. "I haven't read it."

On the front in Josh's clear handwriting was one word—Maria.

It had been opened before. "Maria read it. She said it arrived in the mail a day after Josh's death."

Sam nodded very slightly. He took the letter out and read it.

My dearest Maria,

I have been waiting to call you that for many years. I know that sounds silly because we are so young, but I need to tell you this now. I can't wait any longer.

Since we have been little kids, I have loved you, but in the past, it was like an older brother. I hope it doesn't sound weird or anything, but my feelings for you have changed.

There is no way to say this without simply jumping in and doing it. So, Maria, I have grown to realize that I love you—and I want to be with you the rest of our lives. This is not the fantasy of some kid. Both of us know your situation, and how precious every day is. I know if everything were normal, we would take our time and wait until we are much older.

But everything is not normal, and we have always been completely honest with each other. I have always been able to tell you anything, so I need to tell you this. And I can't wait any longer.

And from the way you have looked at me recently, I am sure, or at least I hope, you feel the same way.

So, we need to meet after you get this letter—alone, my beloved Maria. I have a ring and a very important question to ask you. I am sure you know what it is.

Until we see each other,
Your loving Josh

Sam felt tears running down his face. He handed the letter to Steven. "You should read it also. They were in love with each other.

Chapter 25

1880

Several years after the destruction of the gallows, and after a period in which the land lay vacant and avoided, a new group of investors decided to buy the field and move forward with the abandoned original plans—to build an iron works there. The original cadre of capitalists had been so shocked by Miller's killing that they decided to pull out of the plans, but others soon came forward with greed driving them. One of the circumstances that could usually be counted on to happen in the USA was that there was always someone ready to make money, often from the remnants of the misfortune of others.

The economy of the United States was moving forward, and investments were spurring the development of industry throughout the east and middle parts of the nation. While the United States of America was not yet a military power in the world, its economic might was beginning to be recognized, especially as industry continued to spring up throughout the growing young nation.

The people of the Bethberg area did now want to be left out of the expansion.

With funding arranged from the new consortium of capitalists, the building began and moved forward quickly.

It was, however, not without danger. Several men died in the construction process from accidents, as was often the case with large construction projects during this era. Working on building these structures paid well, but it too often came at the risk of not only bodily harm but potentially death.

At the construction of the Bethberg Iron Works, what would eventually become the Bethberg Steel Works, some were crushed by falling material. One fell over debris and broke his leg; gangrene set in, and despite amputation, he died soon from an infection.

Still another died back in the westernmost part of the construction.

"Desecration, vengeance, destruction, execution." The voice was angry and sounded like a curse shouted on the wind by an Old Testament Prophet. No one was sure where the voice came from, but they could hear it shouting curses at different times, and they always heard it at the far western part of the construction, nowhere else. "You will all pay for your sins!"

The company was pushing its men to work harder and faster. They were losing money whenever the construction fell behind in its schedule, and they would not tolerate that happening.

So the work went well into the night, even with insufficient lighting, and that helped to contribute to many more accidents occurring.

Eamonn McConnor, 20 years old, was born in Easton, PA, the son of immigrants who had escaped the Great Irish Potato Famine and somehow survived the voyage on one of the crammed former slave ships out of Cork to Liverpool to Canada.

They made their way down from Canada, like so many others who had escaped the starvation, to settle in the small city of Easton, where his father, Michael, worked as a day laborer and his mother Mary as a maid to one of the very wealthy families in the city. They raised him to be a good Catholic boy and a hard worker. "In the United States of America," his father often told him, "even though you're Irish, if you work hard, you can make something of yourself. You can be somebody."

Eamonn didn't know if his father was right or not, but he was strong and willing to work hard, so once he heard there was a call out for laborers on the Iron Works that was being built, he decided he try to get work there. If he did well, maybe he could stay on at the factory itself. He had spent most of his years from 13-20 doing odd jobs and helping out on farms as he could. He never made much money that way, but he was diligent and always wanted to work.

When he heard of this opportunity, he took it immediately. This might be the way to a better future.

Eamonn was terrified of water, which kept him from taking any kind of job in shipping, including trying to work in the navy or on merchant ships. Several of his friends had gone that route, but he couldn't. He did not know how to swim and dreaded the idea of being on water.

But, unlike so many people he knew, Eamonn loved heights, so he became one of the men who would work on the highest parts of the construction.

There were beams on the outside of the building going up like a strange black skeleton. Eamonn worked on them, easily walking along the crossbeams and never losing his balance or footing.

Up there on those beams, as close as he could get to the sky, he felt completely comfortable. The troubles of the world were left forgotten below him.

Eamonn not only landed the job, but he also became noted quickly as one of the best workers on the beams.

One day, Eamonn was taking his lunch break, eating on a suspended beam that was about 50 feet above the ground. He didn't mind though. Sitting there with the air and the sky feeling like he could reach up and touch it, he loved the feeling of freedom and never worried about falling.

This day he was alone during lunch. The man he usually sat with, Mikey Turner, didn't come in because he had come down with some terrible stomach illness. It had to be very bad, because Mikey never missed work. "You don't work, you don't get paid," was the rule.

Well, Eamonn was reasonably sure Mikey would be back at work as soon as he could be, but that wouldn't keep Eamonn from working right where he was. When he was finished, he closed up his lunch pail, and drank the rest of his coffee. He had grown up drinking tea, but he hated it, and now that he was a grown man, he preferred what he considered to be a more American beverage.

Then he stood on the beam to get back to work.

"Time to pay, sinner."

The voice startled Eamonn. He looked around at its sound, but no one was there.

Eamonn was not a man easily frightened, and he thought it was someone playing a joke on him. Many of the workers liked to play pranks on the others, but there were unwritten rules about such things. It was never supposed to be done if someone was doing something dangerous. That was off limits.

While he enjoyed horseplay after work and banter at the pubs, this was different. It should not happen while he was up here—that was wrong, and he would give whoever was doing it a sound beating when work was over. That was certain.

The weather was clear and warm, with few clouds in the sky, and even though he was far above the ground, no real wind was blowing. He had excellent vision, and he scanned the area carefully. There was no one up there with him at the moment. Of that Eamonn was certain. Whoever said it must have scurried away quickly or simply hidden behind something. Oh well, it certainly wasn't worth getting too excited about now.

He stood to begin working again.

"You cannot escape the wrath of the Lord! You are a sinner, building a den of iniquity, and you are doomed to hell!"

The voice was louder this time—it was distinct, and now Eamonn was frightened. He looked around, turning his head from one side to the other.

No one was there.

Suddenly he became aware of how high he was. It had never bothered him before, but now he felt like he might lose his balance at any moment.

Eamonn did something he had never done before. He looked down, and he hated being this high above the ground.

He started to sweat—a great deal. He felt his palms get wet, and sweat, cold and slimy, ran down his face. His heart began to thud in his chest.

"Hey, asshole, whoever you are. Show yourself. Let's go down below and settle this like men. I'll beat you to a fucking pulp, you fucking bastard!" His words sounded brave, but he felt the worst fear he had ever known.

"Prepare yourself, sinner." This time the voice was almost gentle.

Eamonn had enough. It was time to get off this scaffolding. He might be going crazy or something, and he wanted to be down on the ground. He wasn't sure if he would ever be able to go back up high again.

He turned to go to the ladder, when he felt hands grab him.

"What? Let me go!" he said to no one he could see.

His hands were held behind him, as if they were tied together. He struggled, but he could not move.

He wanted to scream for help, but it was as if his mouth were stopped with a gag.

Then he felt something—it was impossible!

A noose was tightening around his neck.

No, no, no, no, he thought. Please no.

A sudden shove from unseen hands sent him plummeting off. But there was no scream as he fell.

One man, the only one who looked up and saw Eamonn plummet to the ground, later said, after he regained his composure, after several shots of whiskey, "You just don't get it, he told the police. "He jerked in the air once as he fell, like, I don't know, like something grabbed his neck, then he just fell to the ground. Just fell."

The police just thought this worker must have been drinking. There was nothing that would have made the man jerk in the air. But it didn't matter to them. Either way, this poor fellow had fallen off the construction beam and was dead. Broke his neck in the fall.

Chapter 26

July 23, The Present

As a retired police officer, Sam had reduced rates at the local YMCA. It was a place he hadn't gone to in years, but now he found himself in the boxing room, a small part of the gym, that was now almost unused. It was rare these days, with the advent of popularity for MMA, that young people took up boxing. *That,* Sam thought, *was another testament to the growing lack of focus and attention span that was pervading society. But sometimes I am just an old guy who can't change with the times. Fuck it. I'll take boxing over that MMA crap anytime.*

The room, like the building itself was old, and few people came to use it anymore. The newer gyms catered to the young with bright colors, a myriad of exercise equipment, including every kind of aerobic machine possible, and too many television screens.

This room, like most of this old place, was painted a drab beige, and in many places, the paint seemed to have worn off, leaving just the plasterboard showing underneath. It was as close to an old-fashioned boxing gym as might have been seen in the 40s or 50s, even with some posters of local fighters on the wall who had trained there in the past, before going on to larger and more professional training spots.

Here those who did show up to use this gym didn't dress in modern and expensive workout gear.

They were not there to see and be seen. This place was not part of a ritualized mating dance.

There was no longer a ring set up. The time of letting youngsters work out their differences in a ring supervised by adults had long passed, but they still have various training equipment. The ropes and turnbuckles sat in a chaotic pile in one corner of the room. But Sam didn't care. He didn't need the ring.

Sam hadn't seriously worked out in years, so he knew he should take it easy, but he needed to hit something, really pound something, so it might as well be the heavy bag.

He had dug out old handwraps and striking gloves from one of his closets. He was dressed in sweats and sat on a bench in that room and wrapped his hands with care. He knew he would be sore the next day, but he had no wish to break a hand or damage a muscle. He knew how to use the wrap to protect his hands, so he could hit the heavy bag as hard as he wanted.

After wrapping both hands, he pulled on the striking gloves then stood up.

He stood in front of the big, brown, heavybag that looked like it had been hanging in that spot for decades…*an old fucker just like me,* he thought.

Then he threw one, then two punches, hard.

That felt good.

He caught the slowly swaying bag, then hit it again, two, three, four hard punches.

I can't fucking believe it, he thought.

More punches. He was breathing hard now.

Josh, oh Josh.

He kept seeing the image of his dead son, slumped over the steering wheel of his car.

But Sam kept slamming into the bag.

Why didn't you come to me? I could've helped you. Oh fuck!

Sam's arms were aching, and his hands hurt regardless of the handwrap and gloves, but he kept on slamming his large fists into the unyielding bag that swung from the punches but always came back to him like bad memories returning.

They did this to you...those motherfuckers, It was Max and his crew. I will make them pay. I want to fucking kill them.

Sam hit the bag again, harder.

Oh, Josh.

More punches, but his energy was running out, and his heart was pounding.

Soon, he was exhausted. *Shit, I feel like I might have a fucking heart attack. I don't fucking care. Josh.*

But he didn't have a heart attack. Instead, exhausted, he slumped to the ground and covered his face and cried.

He couldn't get the image of Josh dead out of his mind.

Josh.

Chapter 27

July 23, The Present

Even though, despite the grumbling of some, many people were enjoying the balmy temperatures of this late summer, a few old-timers were warning whomever would listen of a coming storm.

Ed Whittaker, a friend of Sam's and a retired construction worker, who had coffee and an éclair every morning at the Bethberg Diner, was telling everyone he could about what he was feeling. He dipped his éclair into his black coffee, shook off the drips of java, and wolfed a large bite of the creamy treat. After wiping some of the cream from his lips, he turned to the fellow sitting next to him. "You don't have to listen to me, but I'm telling you – we're getting a storm soon – and I don't mean just rain, but a real storm, a Nor' Easter."

"Ah Eddie," answered his friend Tony, also a retired construction worker, who was sitting at the diner's counter next to him and having a breakfast of eggs, homefries, and scrapple with syrup. "You always think you can tell the weather from your bones. You know you sound like a kooky old guy now, one of the guys we used to laugh at. Besides I'd rather listen to Ralph talk about his fun with the ghost chasers."

"That may be, but Ralph is in the back now, and he gave up doing anything with our ghostguys, so instead of goblins, you got me, and I ain't so old."

Tony looked at him, smiled, and shook his head. Then Ed relented, "Well, maybe I am old now, but that doesn't mean that I don't know what I am talking about." He shook the remainder of his éclair at Tony for emphasis.

"Well, maybe you do, and maybe you don't. Me, I like to count on something a little more solid than some old fart's bones – the Weather Channel, our own Channel 96, and I even check the weather on the Internet on my computer."

"You – on a computer?" Eddie shook his head in disbelief. "You gotta be kidding me."

"Nope, my son set it up for me and showed me how to use it. After all, he is a big shot now – a what do you call it? Systems guy for his company. And let me tell you, the kid makes a helluva lot more money than I ever did. Uses his brains like our buddy Roosevelt, not his brawn."

"Ok, now tell me Tony. What does your Internet tell you?" Ed finished his last bite of his éclair and sipped his coffee.

Tony dipped his white toast into his over easy egg yolk and held it dripping the yellow yolk while he answered. "It told me that no storm is coming Eddie. The next five days are going to be clear and warm." He bit into the yolk-covered toast.

Eddie signaled to the waitress for more coffee. As she poured it for him, he simply smiled at his friend. "You always did love new gadgets and shit. Man, do you still have your eight tracks? I mean that must keep you right up to date with all the kids and their gadgets."

"Yes, I do, and you know what? It still works. I can still listen to Dean and Frankie on it."

Eddie laughed. "You probably even got the latest cell phone, don't you? Man, do you think having that crap makes you young again? Let the kids use that stuff."

"I like having the new stuff, and I'll buy it. You, my friend, need to get with the times and stop being such an old fogie. I mean, we aren't ready to die yet, are we?"

"I don't think so. Let me tell you something Tony – I really don't like the times we're living in, so I will happily avoid them if I can. I think, if I could, I would rather live a hundred years ago than today. Times were simpler and better then."

Tony shook his head and stabbed a piece of scrapple that he had drenched in maple syrup. "That's your problem, Eddie. You want to live in the past. What good is that? You got to change with the times, to see the world as it is, not as you want it to be."

"Really?" Eddie looked sad for a moment. "At least then people believed in right and wrong, good and bad....not like today, not at all."

"Ah, Eddie, it's not all that bad." Tony was putting the finishing touches on his breakfast. Soon he pushed his plate aside and pulled his coffee cup in front of him.

"Well, Tony, you go ahead and trust your weather on that damned intranet thing and listen to your oldies on your Eight Track, but make sure you have enough gas for your generator, and food and supplies because I'm telling you – a storm is coming, and it is going to be a son-of-a-bitch, something to remember."

"It's July, so sure, we might get something in the next couple of weeks Eddie. But wait a minute. I got a sure fire way to know." Tony picked up a section of the newspaper that was on the counter next to him and folded it and held it up to his forehead in an imitation of Johnny Carson's old "Karnak the Magnificent" bit. "When oh great prophet of the weather, do you see this storm coming? You think I got enough psychic power to get our buddies to use me on an investigation?"

Eddie started to say something, but Tony held up his hand to silence him. "I can feel an answer coming. Uh huh, uh-huh...yep, that's it...the answer is sometime, definitely not this week."

Eddie laughed. He loved Tony's goofy sense of humor. "Ok funny guy, don't believe me. But let me see the Sports section of the paper. I want to see what it has to say on the Eagles."

"Oh no, you don't get off that easy. If you really believe you can tell the weather by your bones, then let's make this interesting."

Eddie smiled. This was an old routine of theirs that went back decades. Whenever they debated anything, be it sports, politics, or even the weather, they would eventually reach a point where they made a wager. The bet was never anything substantial, never a large amount of money or stuff, often just a few bucks, a bottle of beer, or cup of coffee, or a meal, but it made life interesting for them.

"So, let's say," Tony smiled. "Since we're in here now, let's make a full breakfast ride on it. If you can predict a summer storm coming to within, oh, a day or two, then I will buy you breakfast, anything you want. But if you're wrong, then you buy it for me."

Eddie pretended to consider for a while as if he were not sure of himself, then he broke into a wide grin.

"Done." Eddie reached over and shook Tony's hand. "I'm calling the storm to be here in just 2-3 days. Any longer than that, and I'm wrong. And I ain't saying just a bit or rain. I'm telling you—it's going to be something unusual."

"Mmmmm. I can taste ham, eggs, homefries and pancakes."

"We'll see Tony. We'll see. I think I can see a plate of steak and eggs in my not-too-distant-future."

Chapter 28

July 23, The Present

His friends knew this was a day to let Sam alone. While Roosevelt and Jeremy were tempted to stay with Sam on this day, they knew better. Sam needed his privacy. It was nearing the time of the anniversary of Sam's son's suicide.

Reluctantly, they respected his wishes.

Sam called it the J.S. day, short for Joshua Sadlowski, and on that day, he retreated from the world, only speaking, if needed, with strangers. Even though almost ten years had gone by since Josh had killed himself, Sam's pain never lessened, not at all.

Many people believed that old adage that time heals all wounds, but it wasn't true, at least not for Sam.

Each morning, Sam woke with Josh in the forefront of his mind. His first image was that of holding his dead son in his arms that day, and he knew this memory would never fade. A parent should never have to bury their child, and he had lost his beloved son.

The memory of what had happened never faded. . . One day, when Sam was at the station, he received an urgent phone call from his wife. He could barely understand her—only that he should come right home. When he got there, other police officers and an ambulance were there, something he was used to seeing at other people's homes, not his.

His home was a place where normalcy and happiness. It was a guarantee he believed in and where safety and protection from the world's problems were givens. He panicked. He turned off his car. He jumped out. He ran into his house.

"Mary? Mary? Are you OK?"

Two young cops tried to stop him, but he pushed through them. His wife, curled up on the floor, was crying. He looked at her and then at the other police officers, who avoided his eyes.

"Mary?" he asked softly as he knelt down and tried to take her in his arms, but she wrapped herself into a tighter ball. "What is it? What happened? Did someone hurt you?" If someone had hurt her, he would find them and kill them. She only shook her head. Then she let out a low moaning keen. That sound suddenly amplified into a full wail. Then it hit him—Josh.

He stood abruptly, fear pumping through him like a balloon overfilled with helium, about to burst. "Oh god, oh god, not Josh, not my boy, not Josh."

He knew from Mary's reaction that this was bad, very bad. He had seen similar reactions too many times before from survivors in murder cases. He turned to one of the cops. He grabbed him by the uniform and pulled him aside. He looked into the young man's eyes. "Tell me, now!"

The young cop stammered. "He, he's in the garage." Sam released him and ran through the house and into the garage. The EMTs had turned off the car, an old Chevy Caprice that Josh loved, and they had opened the outside garage door. Even with fresh air moving in, the fumes were still thick in the small room. As Sam moved to the car, he saw Josh slumped over the steering wheel—dead.

Sam collapsed to the floor. He would later learn that Josh had left a note saying only "I'm sorry. I have to do this." Regardless of the following investigation, they never found any reason for his death. No one, including his closest friends, who were just as shaken by his suicide as Josh's parents, had any idea why the teenager had killed himself.

When he was a homicide detective, Sam had seen the grief and shock of the families and loved ones of the victims. He had witnessed the slow collapse of marriages, of families, and of individuals. Few people could withstand the pain and torment from this grief.

Sam, however, managed to survive, just barely. But little of the rest of his life did.

He was in his bathroom, steamy from his morning shower. He wiped the mirror of the small sink and looked at himself. "Not much to look at anymore. Fat and going bald. Yeah, I'm a regular fucking Tom Cruise. But then, I never was much to look at. Surprise I even managed to get married."

But his marriage, shaky as it was, did not survive their mutual grief. *Fuck,* he thought. *Our marriage went to shit, not that it was good to begin with. Like we had become different people than before. I couldn't even recognize her anymore, and I am sure the asshole I became wasn't like I was before. We didn't hate each other—just didn't know each other anymore.*

Still, Sam thought, *We just fucking gave up. Neither of us gave a shit after Josh was gone. It was like our marriage died along with our boy.*

Sam survived by immersing himself into his official work as well as conducting and unofficial investigation into Josh's death—to try to find out why he had done it.

Sam needed an answer, even though he knew he was unlikely to find one. The only clue he ever had was the maddening note Josh left behind that said, "I'm sorry. I had to do this."

An autopsy had been performed, and nothing was found to help—no trace of drugs, no secret illness, nothing at all. And none of the lowlife scum Sam, had leaned on had revealed anything.

Chapter 29

2005

Max, short for Maximillian Herbert Esel, a name he hated almost as much as he did the parents who gave it to him, knew they would be watching him, always inside the prison. The guards knew he was part of one of the fastest growing gangs in the state, and they wouldn't lose any opportunity to nail him for something if they could. Max's best approach, while in jail, was to seem to be a model inmate, except, of course, when it was necessary to kick the shit out of some asshole. Then he did whatever he needed to do to fuck the guy up bad. Or he had some of his guys do it for him. But he always made sure that this action could not be seen and that he had a complete alibi for that time.

Max was serving a 10-20 sentence on possession with the intent to distribute methamphetamines, but the fucking cops thought he was just a runner, a low level guy, and he didn't want to do anything to change their impression of him.

If it hadn't been that he had fought and seriously fucked up a rival gang member, his sentence would have been a lot less.

They didn't know that he was one of the up and comers in the outfit The PA RiotRiders that was becoming a major mover in the drug business in Eastern Pennsylvania. And the guys above him knew he had taken the fall for others, so they owed him, and if there was one thing that was certain about the PA RiotRiders, it was loyalty.

Those who weren't loyal to the gang were quickly eliminated; they had no desire for any loose ends. They might look like simply a motorcycle gang, but they were much more.

And Max had plans to use it as the base for his own operation. But for now, he would remain a loyal, if ambitious, member.

Their influence had spread into the prison he was sitting in located in northcentral Pennsylvania. He was quickly accepted as the senior figure in the prison gang, and he used that position to move meth inside the prison and to help distribute it into local small towns with almost no police presence. "Like a fucking fast food franchise," he had said to one of his soldiers one day. "Get the high school kids into it, let them make some money, get hooked, and you got a ready-made distribution setup. Anything happens, make sure they never see anyone above the guy handling them, and they go down. Remember, burner phones only, and never contact them on their home cells. Mommy and Daddy might find out otherwise. That would suck."

Max had to deal with situations like that before, and he hated it. Not because he was bothered by the ethics of destroying kids or families, but because of the potential fuckup it could bring to his organization. He always wanted everything to run as smoothly as possible. That way he could make as much money as possible and gather as much power as he could. In his fantasies, he hoped one day to be as powerful in this region as Al Capone had been in Chicago during Prohibition.

One of the first things Max did when he was incarcerated was to find the members of the gang. Then he made it clear he was the new head, which didn't go over very well with the reigning guy.

Ogre, a huge hulk of a man, in for life with no chance of parole for killing 3 people during a robbery, ran the unit, and he hadn't been told there would be a change. Well, this was something Max had told the guy who ran the RiotRiders on the outside, Willy T, "fuck it," he had said. "I ain't going to be nobody's fucking legman in there. I'm gonna find him and make it clear I'm the new guy. He don't like it, well then we just settle it."

Max delivered his ultimatum, and the gang met in a back room behind the prison laundry. Two guards, well-paid for their silence ensured there would be no interruptions.

Ogre stood 6'7 and weighed 330 pounds. He seemed to be as wide as he was tall. He was big, mean, and scared the crap out of almost anyone who opposed him. His reputation for cruelty was well known. The last guy who had made him fight, he not only beat, but broke both arms, stomped his fingers, and broke his jaw. That guy was lucky to still be alive. Others who had gone against Ogre did not survive.

Max saw his opponent and knew he had to make this fight fast. He didn't want to give the big fucker any chance of grabbing ahold of him. That would be very dangerous.

What Ogre didn't know was Max, while significantly smaller, at 6'1 and 185, was a former Special Forces Army vet who had received serious martial arts training. He was taught how to fight to kill, and he intended to do that very quickly.

Ten other men stood in a wide circle around them, all from the RiotRiders. They knew what was at stake here, and they fully expected Ogre to win easily. It was the way things always had gone in the past, and they all knew that challengers would come up every so often.

Max had arrived first, dressed, as always, in his prison outfit. He stood on the far end of the room and waited for his opponent to arrive.

"You a dumb fucker," one of the men near him said. "But got to give it to you for balls."

Max just nodded and looked at the door when Ogre came in. But as he always did, Ogre was accompanied by his guys. One entered first to check the place out, then Ogre entered, then the other bodyguard. It wasn't as if Ogre needed protection, but he liked the attention, and he considered the bodyguards as perks of the position.

"I'm gonna fuck you up, little man, and I'm gonna enjoy it." Ogre smiled and spread his arms wide, in the classic street fighting stance of – you want a part of me?

Ogre kept smiling and looked around at the men in the room. Then he turned back to Max, "Just gonna give you a chance to back down. Talked to Willy T, and he likes you, man. I don't want to fuck up a guy who is useful, so you want to just give up now? Only chance, bro."

Max simply shook his head "no" and stood there waiting. "Let's do this."

Ogre roared and charged forward. He expected Max to back up in a panic and be stopped from trying to run away by the men. They he would have the little fucker in his grip, and it would be over. At least the fighting, but not the fun. He would be sure to enjoy himself first messing with him and then destroying him.

Instead, Max waited until the last moment. Then he launched himself straight at Ogre.

It was a sudden straight right punch, with the combined force of the huge man's weight and mass and his own thrust. The fist landed just where he had aimed.

He drove it straight into Ogre's neck, through the windpipe, almost out through the back. He could feel the cartilage and bone breaking. He whipped aside and stood with hands up, waiting to see if more was needed.

It wasn't.

The huge man staggered. He grabbed at his throat trying to force air through. His face turned blue as his eyes bulged. He collapsed on the ground.

Others wanted to go to him.

"Stay back, fuckers. This is him and me. If he can get up, I'll fucking finish him. But I don't think that is happening."

It didn't. Ogre died on the floor of that back room. The guards made sure no one ever found out what happened, and from that moment on, it was obvious that Max was the new leader of the RiotRiders inside this prison.

That wasn't the only battle he had to fight to prove himself.

Over the next several years, just as he had challenged Ogre for supremacy of the gang, others came at him. Most of them challenged him in his first year at the top, but as he reputation for fighting grew, the opponents lessened. After a few years, his rule was complete inside, and it would be until he got out.

Plus, Max never forgot those who helped him or those who fucked him over. If some guy helped him, then they could always call on him if needed. But if some asshole tried to screw him, then it was just a matter of time before he dropped a proverbial sledge hammer on them and splattered their brains.

One guy in particular, stuck with him, one guy who had put him away when he was younger and busted up the ring he was setting up then. A fucking smartass detective. Fucking Sam Sadlowski.

Max had already fucked the guy up a bit—yeah, the asshole's boy offing himself brought him some satisfaction, but it wasn't enough. The fucker had not only destroyed his potential ring when he was younger, but he had shot his brother during the arrest. He couldn't forget that. Jonny was the only family he had, a not very bright younger brother, but he had promised his ma he would look out for him, and he knew that she must have cried so hard at the funeral he couldn't attend, because he was sitting in prison. Then the old lady drank herself to death a few months later.

He knew the detective had retired, but he didn't care. The old fucker wasn't going to be able to just sit back and relax the rest of his life. No fucking way.

Yeah, he still had plans for Sadlowski. And he would be getting out of this shithole soon—on good behavior.

Chapter 30

July 24, The Present

Sam woke up groggy. It was 10 A.M. and he could barely move as he rolled to the side of the bed and slowly sat up.

As always, the first thing into his mind was Josh.

Josh…why didn't you come to me first?

Sam closed his eyes as tight as he could. The image of his dead son stayed with him, as it always did. He waited for it to fade very slowly, then he tried to get up out of bed.

His whole body ached from the boxing workout the previous day. *What the hell was I thinking?*

He slowly stood, and everything, even his head hurt.

He shuffled into the bathroom, then slowly made his way to the kitchen.

I need coffee, he thought and went to his old-fashioned percolator. He took down a canister with coffee beans, put them in an old grinder, and made the correct grind. Then he put the coffee in the holder, filled it with water, and plugged it in.

Then he sat at his kitchen table.

Damn. It'll take about 12 minutes for the coffee to brew. I need something now. My head is fucking killing me.

Sam rose from the chair. Even standing made him hurt more.

Can't wait for the coffee.

Sam turned and went for a shelf in the other direction in the kitchen. He opened the cabinet and looked at the assortment of alcohol he had in there. He pulled down a bottle of vodka.

This should do the trick.

He got a glass and poured several inches into it. Then he sat down again at the chair.

He first took only a small swallow. He let it go down, then he quickly drank the rest.

It took some of the edge off his pain.

Sam reached for the bottle again.

Chapter 31

July 24, The Present

Sam stood in his studio. He had put up another blank canvas, recently prepared for painting, and he would try to create an image again. He had not been able to make any paintings for the last year, and he felt like he might burst in frustration. It was like a lava flow of pain was trapped inside him, but there was no geyser to let it out safely.

He was dressed in old jeans, barefoot, and an old torn tee shirt. He had placed a bottle of Irish Whisky on a table and took a swig from it. Then he put it back down and looked at the photo he had pinned to the top left corner of the canvas. It was the Junior grade High School picture of Josh, the last school photograph he had of his son.

Josh, Sam thought. *Maybe if I try to paint your portrait, I can do this again.*

Sam picked up a charcoal pencil to sketch in the outline of his son's face. As he held the light implement, his hand began to shake. The shaking increased as he moved closer to the canvas.

I can't do it. I can't fucking do it. I can't even paint my son's picture, and I want to do that more than anything. I'm a fucking failure.

Sam sat on the floor and reached for the whisky.

Chapter 32

July 24, The Present

The Investigative Paranormal Society's phone rang in their office at Jeremy's house. As the equipment manager for their group, they agreed it made sense to locate the office in a small room in his house.

Jeremy, as was his custom, listened to the message before answering. It was an old, but very efficient, way to screen calls. Too often, in the past, crank and prank calls were made to the IPS, and they wanted to be able to eliminate this problem. And this very simple solution worked extremely well.

He had just made himself a cup of his favorite tea, Earl Grey, when he heard the answering machine pick up.

"This is Michael Flannery. I am calling to find out your progress on the investigation of the Bethberg Steel Works ruins. This is very important, and I hope you are making it your main priority. Remember, gentlemen, I have hired you to do this, and I expect your complete cooperation." Then he left a call-back number.

Jeremy played the message again, and he fumed with anger.

He sat with his tea, waited a moment and then made a call to Roosevelt. He had wanted to call Flannery back himself, but he knew that doing so when angry was probably not a very good idea, and he could not simply speak for the group himself, so the best thing to do was to call his friend. Jeremy made a brief call to Roosevelt, hung up, and smiled.

Then he made another call.

"Hello, is this Michael Flannery? This is Jeremy of the Investigative Paranormal Society returning your call."

"Ah, I am so glad you could call back so quickly," the silky-smooth voice on the other end of the line replied.

"Yes, we got your message, Mr. Flannery, and there is something you absolutely have to understand before we proceed any further." Jeremy's voice had gone very even.

"And what is that?"

"We do not work for you. We are not your employees. We are not subcontractors for you. Do you understand that? We have signed no contracts, and we agreed to help you, but only in our capacity as nonpaid volunteers."

"You agreed to do this investigation in return for our donation to the charity of your choice!"

Flannery's voice was starting to rise in pitch as he became frustrated.

"No, we agreed to help you with this investigation. If you check carefully, you offered to make the donation. We still will do the investigation, but it will be as we prioritize it, not as you wish it. Furthermore, whether or not you choose to donate to the charity of our choice is entirely your decision. It is not founded on what we do."

"You agreed to these terms!"

"And Mr. Flannery," Jeremy said in a calm but serious tone. "If you should continue to make aggressive and threatening phone calls to us, then we will consider our relationship ended, and the matter will be turned over to the police. Is that clear?"

"So, are you backing out now? Really? Do you think I don't have any resources?"

"Of course you do. We certainly understand that, and we would prefer to have a cordial relationship with you. But WE WILL NOT BE BULLIED!"

Flannery went silent for a short period.

"Do you understand our position, Mr. Flannery?"

Flannery considered his position, and all he wanted was for these old guys to do their ridiculous investigation, so he could report to his old man that the place held no ghosts. He didn't need to rile them up and cause problems. He got control of himself. He had to be a businessman, a contemporary businessman. "I apologize for being rude. I am coming under intense pressure, so anything you can do to help would be greatly appreciated."

Jeremy smiled. "Of course, we will help. And when we have something to tell you, we will. Rest assured of that."

Chapter 33

July 24, The Present

Roosevelt kept ringing Sam's front door bell. He and Jeremy had been at Sam's house for ten minutes trying to wake him up. It was one o'clock in the afternoon, and they were concerned about their friend.

"I know that we have to give him time and space, but I am worried about him, Jeremy," Roosevelt said.

"I know." Jeremy was taking this situation very seriously.

"It is not like Samuel to disappear for a couple of days, even with what he is facing. I would expect to at least get a phone call or for him to answer his phone." Roosevelt banged harder on the door.

"Roosevelt, this isn't working." Jeremy stood immediately at the door and began rapping hard on the wood with the handle of his wolf's-head cane. The sound was loud but still not enough to raise Sam from the land of the sleeping. "Ok, enough is enough."

Jeremy opened the gate at the side of Sam's yard, one that featured a large BEWARE OF DOG sign, one that featured a large snarling face of an enraged German Shephard, but both men knew their friend didn't own a dog.

Jeremy went to the back of the house where Sam's bedroom was and began rapping on the window, creating a loud staccato sound. Jeremy didn't know if Sam had an alarm connected to his house of not, but he didn't care.

Jeremy made a brief call to Roosevelt, hung up, and smiled.

He was seriously pissed off at Sam for going down the route he was taking. There was no way he would let Sam do what he had done and become an alcoholic. There were only a few possible explanations for this vanishing act, and Jeremy was all too familiar with the most likely one. He was damned if he was going to let Sam make the same mistake he had. One miserable old alcoholic in their group was plenty, thank you very much!

Finally, he heard groaning from inside the house. Movement. Then the unmistakable sound of a very pissed off voice. "Get the fuck out of here. What the hell is the matter with you?"

"Samuel," Roosevelt said with as stern a voice as he could muster. "We are NOT going anywhere, and you ARE opening the damned door and letting us in. NOW!" He was now standing erect, reminiscent of the Marine Corps Officer he had been. *If this did not get Samuel's attention,* he thought. *Then nothing would.*

Ten minutes later, Jeremy and Roosevelt were sitting at Sam's breakfast table in his small kitchen. This was not a regular breakfast meeting of The Investigative Paranormal Society; Sam was sitting on one side of the little rectangular table, holding his head in his hands, with his friends on two other sides.

The kitchen was a complete mess, with an empty bottle of vodka on its side on the floor, and dishes unwashed. This was not at all like Sam, who was usually careful about cleaning up in most of his home.

"Samuel, we simply cannot allow you to go on like this." Roosevelt was drinking a cup of black coffee and pushed one across the small table to his friend. "Drink it. You need it."

Jeremy went to the counter to prepare a small meal for his friend. "You'll need more than that, and I know just the thing for a hangover like yours. Trust me. I know this." He poured a bowl of corn cereal with milk and sugar. "You need the carbs and liquid, because you are dehydrated, Sam. This comes from too much experience."

Sam just groaned. He held his head that was pounding from too much booze the entire day before. "Just leave me the fuck alone."

"Yeah, right, Sammy. Like that's going to happen." Jeremy placed the bowl in front of Sam. "Now eat this."

"Nooo. I don't want it."

"Well, Sammy, that really doesn't matter. We're here, and we're going to take care of you, whether you want it or not, big guy."

Roosevelt raised an eyebrow. He had noticed recently a change in the formerly timid friend. Since the battle with Maledicus, Jeremy had grown more confident. He no longer seemed to be hesitant about taking command or asserting himself when needed.

"Look, Sammy. I know how you feel. Believe me, and I have too much experience finding ways to be able to face the day after a particularly good night."

Sam looked at him to say something, but Jeremy cut him off. "Don't say anything. Just start eating this. Look, I'll even join you, not that I had anything to drink, because you know I left that behind me."

Jeremy prepared himself a bowl of cereal and sat down across from the scowling Sam. "And don't even think we're going to leave you alone. We gave you space already, my friend, and what you don't need now is to be alone. So get used to it. We are going to be a serious pain in your ass, and we are going to be here for you."

"Yes, we certainly are," Roosevelt added.

"So, Sam, after you finish this, you are going to get cleaned up. You will go take a shower and put on some clean clothes. I assume you have some in your place."

Sam groaned and nodded yes.

A few minutes later, Sam rose on very unsteady legs and made his way into his bathroom. When they were satisfied that Sam was showering, Roosevelt and Jeremy got to work cleaning up the kitchen.

When Sam was cleaned and dressed, they told him they were taking him out with them.

Chapter 34

August 1981

Hard days had hit the Bethberg Steel Works. Not only had the recessions of the 1970s and early 1980s seriously limited the firm's business forcing cutbacks and layoffs, but also it was becoming increasingly more difficult to compete with the steel giant in Bethlehem as well as the many other smaller mills scattered throughout the Lehigh Valley.

This part of eastern Pennsylvania was a heavy industry hub, filled with a variety of factories, and that meant that the smaller ones had the hardest time absorbing the economic downturns. The people running the office were becoming increasingly concerned about the viability of the plant, and the steelworkers understood their economic peril.

Additionally, the skeleton crew that worked the nearly eliminated third shift 11:00 P.M. to 7:30 A.M. was reporting "odd" and "creepy" incidents to the foreman of the shift. What bothered the plant manager, Henry Stanly, about these reports was they were coming from longtime steelworkers, tough men not given to over-indulgences of their imaginations. Had it been some of the younger guys who had spoken of such ghostly apparitions, he would have smiled and explained that such things do not exist. But these were tough, hardened men, typically concerned mainly about wages, work hours, beer and football and not always in that order.

"Mr. Stanly," Rinehardt, the longtime foreman of the third shift, said to him one night.

"I got to talk to you about something."

Stanly respected this man. He had started in the mill as a young man of 16, after dropping out of high school. After 20 years, he had done most of the jobs on the factory floor. Then he had become a line supervisor and finally, at the age of 50, he achieved the status of foreman of the third shift. Rinehardt hoped to stay in this job until his retirement, and he knew every square foot and every operation of the whole mill. If he had been formally educated, he might easily have become assistant plant manager, which Stanly would have liked, because Rinehardt was far better than the fool who held that job now. But Stanly knew that the corporation that owned this mill would never have approved such a promotion.

"Mr. Stanly," Rinehardt said to the plant manager, one late August afternoon in 1981. "The men are reporting seeing, um..., I don't know how to say this, but things late at night."

"What kind of things, Rinehardt? Kids breaking in and drinking, partying? We've had to deal with that kind of thing in the past. It's easily taken care of."

"No, sir. That'd be easy to spot, yes it would be. Our guards might not be as good as the regular police, but they can find the kids who want to get in. Nope, not kids."

Stanly waited with patience as Rinehardt gathered his thoughts. Stanly sipped his coffee and watched the older man struggle with what he wanted to say. The plant manager had learned long ago to let discussions with Rinehardt proceed at this pace.

"Well...I can't believe I'm even saying this, but, um...they, well, they said they seen a ghost."

"What? Are they drinking on the job, Rinehardt?" Stanly's eyes were wide. He could deal with much, but never drinking when working—that was too dangerous in a steel plant. Too many terrible things could happen, and this sounded like something that could come from too much booze. "C'mon, Rinehardt. You know we can't have this going on in the plant. I'm a fair man, but if the guys have been drinking, then we have a real problem."

"No, no, Sir. Ain't no drinking going on. I'm sure of that. I'd never let anything like that happen. You remember last year, when that new guy started bringing booze inside his soda bottle to work? The other guys were calling him six-pack, and it took a little while for me to figure it out, but I did. And he's gone from the plant now. No, I don't put up with any drinking on the job."

"No, of course you don't, Rinehardt. Please go on."

Rinehardt looked at the floor then up to the ceiling as if he were trying to find the correct words. "I don't know what to say, but even Dietz and Kaufmann are spooked. They both claimed they saw something that looked like a man, and just...poof!... he vanished into the air."

That worried Stanly. Kaufmann and Dietz were widely regarded in the factory as the meanest and toughest men there. *Hell,* he thought. *They might be batshit crazy, but I can't think of anything that ever scared those two.*

Both men had been known into brawls in some of the nastier bars in town, and they usually came out victorious, often against four-five other men. Stanly narrowed his eyes. This was indeed worrisome. And he didn't know what to do about it.

That, in itself, made Stanly nervous. He was used to being a man who made decisions quickly. Still, he didn't want anything upsetting an already fragile work environment any further.

"Okay, Rinehardt. I'll have security make more rounds on the cemetery shift. And, Rinehardt, let me know if there are anymore…sightings."

Stanly hoped this would be the end of this problem. So he left Rinehardt and went back to his office.

At two o' clock the next morning, Joe Pastelli, a college student at Bethberg University, who worked part-time as a security guard at the factory made his rounds. This was his job all year, but he was able to get more hours during the summer. The schedule worked for him, even with taking a couple of summer courses.

Security at the mill had not been a serious issue for many years, so the guards, especially the part-timers, carried only a flashlight, walkie-talkie, and wore a hard hat when in the plant itself. Pastelli, a slight young man still fighting acne, had hopes of becoming a corporate lawyer and had no intentions of ever intervening if he saw anything wrong. The most likely incident he might see would be a fight between two workers or perhaps a theft, and all he would ever do, if he saw something, would be to retreat to a safe distance and call it in.

Pastelli was in the outer perimeter of the facility, up on a catwalk that covered much of the west end of the factory, the original section that had been first constructed and was now called "the old mill." The catwalk was three feet wide and went in a semi-circle of about 100 feet. He hated this part of the job. Mostly his work was slow and gave him time in his outside cubicle to do schoolwork, but this place was just creepy.

As he made his way to almost the most western point of the walk, he stopped and stared ahead. He thought he had seen someone. *But who would be up there now? Was this someone playing a joke on me?* he thought.

The guys in the plant had done that a few times when he first started, but he had been working here over a year now, and he didn't think they would still try to haze him. Most of them ignored him, and he was fine with that.

Pastelli saw something again. He stopped walking and shone his flashlight in that direction.

It looked like a man standing in a shadow, but slowly moving away, like he was trying to hide or something.

I should just call this in, he thought. But he was curious. *I don't want them to think I'm some kind of idiot or coward. I'd never live that down.*

Pastelli, against his better judgement, moved forward about two feet and shined his flashlight in that direction.

Nothing. No one was there.

When he clicked the flash off, he could see the man again. He was odd and was wearing clothing that looked like it came from a much older time. Pastelli wanted to see more.

When he moved a bit closer, almost to the figure, it solidified, and the student could see a man who was definitely in the wrong time period. And he was holding something in one hand.

It was a noose.

Pastelli felt frozen in place, then he turned to run.

He felt strong hands grip in and hold him in place.

And his blood felt like it was now as cold as the air in a meat freezer. He wanted to run, but he was completely still, as if he were encased in ice himself.

Pastelli felt a noose go around his neck and tighten, and there was nothing he could do.

"You are guilty of desecration." The voice was like the sound of a knife scraping a piece of metal. It sent fear deep into the young man like an arrow penetrating to the heart of a hunted deer.

"You are hereby sentenced to death for your crimes!"

A sudden shove pushed Pastelli from the catwalk. He wanted to scream, but no sound emerged from his tightly constricted throat.

His fall jerked to a sudden stop. His neck snapped, killing him immediately.

In the morning Pastelli's corpse was found hanging with the rope attached to a guide bar on the catwalk.

The death was ruled a suicide.

Chapter 35

July 25, The Present

Sam stood at the booth in the firing range. This was a public shooting range, not the official one for the police department that he had used when he was still serving actively in the Bethberg Police Department. As a retired detective, he could still have used it, but he did not want to draw attention to himself. He almost certainly would have run into officers he knew who were still on the force, and they would inevitably have gotten around to asking him how he was doing. That was not a conversation he wished to have.

Sam drove an hour northwest to a gun-lover's range in a very small town. He wore jeans, boots, and a red flannel shirt and came in with both his .38 Smith & Wesson revolver and his 9MM. Beretta semi-automatic.

He gave a brief hello when he entered, then signed in and paid for his time. He was a semi-regular there, so the staff acknowledged him, then they essentially ignored him.

He went to the open lane at the far right of the building. No one else would be near him because it was a late morning on a weekday, and that was exactly the way he wanted it.

At the far end of his shooting lane was a standard target of a man on a paper with concentric circles. Sam donned the standard ear muffs and held the revolver first.

He took the classic shooting stance and rapidly emptied the gun. Then he pressed the button to pull the target forward. "Not bad," he thought as he looked at the placement of the bullets. Four in the inner circle, two outside. "But not excellent. I need to practice more."

He reloaded and fired, over and over, until he was able to place all six shots into the inner circle.

Then he paused, and replaced the gun into its holster.

Next he picked up the Beretta, checked its clip, chambered and a round into the gun and prepared to shoot.

He emptied the entire clip.

Then he checked the target.

He continued this process until he was completely satisfied with his results.

Then he packed his stuff and left.

Chapter 36

July 26, The Present

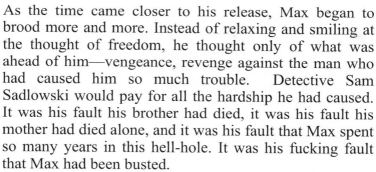

As the time came closer to his release, Max began to brood more and more. Instead of relaxing and smiling at the thought of freedom, he thought only of what was ahead of him—vengeance, revenge against the man who had caused him so much trouble. Detective Sam Sadlowski would pay for all the hardship he had caused. It was his fault his brother had died, it was his fault his mother had died alone, and it was his fault that Max spent so many years in this hell-hole. It was his fucking fault that Max had been busted.

Max wasn't afraid that something might happen to keep him from being released. He had a clean record that did not reflect the reality of his situation as the head of the prison unit of the Pennsylvania RiotRiders. He had simply grown impatient. He wanted to get to that fucker who had ruined his life.

Everything had been going so fucking well before Sadlowski's interference. He had his gang organized and ran the piece of property north of the Lehigh Valley from Bethberg to just south of East Stroudsburg. While to some it might have seemed smalltime, Max had his eyes set on taking over the drug distribution in the entire Lehigh Valley, from Easton to Allentown.

That would have meant a lot of fucking money and the respect of the gangs in Philly and Newark.

He even dreamed of replacing them, but he wasn't stupid or suicidal. That might have been too much to try.

Max wasn't the top guy in the RiotRiders, but he was fast moving up the ladder. He saw a time when he would be running the entire Northeastern region.

And then it all went to hell, in one fucking night.

It was in the early 90s, and he had overseen the receipt of a major delivery of heroin, aimed at being distributed throughout the area. With this stuff, he could make many new customers and have them coming back for more and more. Fucking pathetic losers was what he thought of drug addicts, but he loved their money and the power it gave him.

He knew that he couldn't let too many in on this deal, because it would be too many moving parts to have to control. And he always insisted on being in control. So, he only had two of his guys with him, his brother Jonny, —named for his father—for muscle, because, he had to admit, Jonny was pretty fucking stupid, and Mitch, a guy who had proven himself several times recently and was the opposite of Jonny, smart and resourceful. Jonny was big, 6'3, with huge shoulders...the kid had played football in high school, linebacker, and might have been able to play in college, but his grades were just too low, and his temper didn't help. He had been busted on several assault charges, usually from beating some equally stupid drunk in a bar fight, and after those on his record, no college wanted him anywhere around. Not a problem. His big brother was there to take care of him.

As Max built up his empire, he always kept Jonny near, both as protection for himself, but also to try to keep his little brother out of trouble.

Jonny soon developed a reputation in the area as a guy not to be fucked with. He was good with his fists, but preferred to use baseball bats in fights. Sometimes, he used guns.

Max didn't care, as long as the evidence could always be hidden. And some of the old abandoned coal mines in Schuylkill County, PA served as perfect hiding places for corpses. They were forgotten and had very long and deep tunnels. Max knew they were useful.

When one guy, Jay, thought he could be a snitch and get away with it, found out he was wrong, he ended up being punished by Jonny. Normally, Max watched everything Jonny did, but this time, it was too much even for him to see. So he waited until after his brother had killed the little asshole, after torturing him in an old warehouse.

Then they put the body in an oversized, industrial garbage bag, put it in the trunk of an old car—didn't want to be seen in anything too flashy—and drove to an old country road, pulled the car off to the side. It was far enough along that dirt road that it wouldn't be seen from the main road.

They got the body out of the trunk and lugged it about one quarter of a mile through the brush to a barely visible tunnel entrance.

Then with Max holding a large flashlight, they went into the tunnel. It was narrow and marked "DO NOT ENTER" and "DANGER—CAVE INS". They ignored the warnings and pulled the body along.

Then they came to the end of the path. Old wooden barriers had been erected to keep anyone foolish enough from exploring from falling, but they had been ripped down long ago.

They heaved the body over the edge and listened as it fell into the darkness far below. No one would ever find it.

Still, Max knew that he had to keep an eye on what Jonny did, because on his own, the fellow was likely to erupt and do something incredibly stupid. That would not only get him, at the least, put in jail, but it might also implicate Max. He would not have that.

Mitch was different.

Mitch, short, slim and dark, was not much of a physical threat. Although he didn't seem to be tough by his slight appearance, he was also not scared of anyone, even Jonny. There were very few reports of his having fought, but Mitch was very good with both knives and guns, and he let that be known.

Mitch, however, was someone who was excellent at planning. He was able to look at a strategy of action and see where something might need to be changed and where a weakness might be. Max had doubts about him until he insisted during a drop several months before that they change the arranged place. "It don't feel right," he had said. "It's too open, and I don't like us being exposed like that. Could be cops anywhere."

Turned out Mitch was right. Max had agreed to change the plans at the last minute, but he had a guy watch the original place, and fuck, if cops didn't show up. Proved to Max that Mitch knew what the hell he was doing.

Mitch became his right hand man, the guy he turned to. And they worked together successfully for several years. With Mitch's mind, Max was able to accelerate the growth of his power.

When it came to the largest deal he had made, Max wanted Mitch to be the one who did the planning. Mitch figured out the strategy.

"The best place is the old steel mill," Mitch pointed out. "Only people who go there are teens looking to party or get a piece. Lots of old shit laying around. It'll be easy to see whose coming and going. And I like knowing that. Got to look out for your enemy." Max was impressed. Mitch sounded like a fucking general in charge of his troops.

He had stayed with Max, in case he was needed, and Mitch would observe from a tower that was still standing, although it was severely rusted.

The lone car they expected, a black Lincoln, pulled up. Two men got out, leaving the driver inside. Both were dressed in long black overcoats and had hair slicked back. *Jesus Fucking Christ,* Max thought. *Could they look any more like they had just stepped out of a fucking gangster movie?*

They went to the back of their limo and opened the trunk. They had two briefcases there which they opened. Max liked what he saw, many clear bags filled with heroin. Still, he had to be careful. He opened his pocketknife, cut a small slit into one bag, and touched it to his tongue. He was satisfied. This was the real thing. They may look like assholes, Max thought. But they came through with the goods.

He waved Jonny over with his satchel of money. He took it from Jonny and handed it over. He liked being the one making the final exchange. By doing it this way, he could not only oversee the operation, but ultimately he was in charge of it.

As soon as he handed the case of money over, the two men pulled guns and badges. *Fuck!* Max thought.

The driver also got out, someone he should have known…fucking detective Sam Sadlowski.

Then everything went completely wrong.

Jonny panicked and drew his gun to shoot at one of the cops in the coats.

Sadlowski fired three shots and hit Jonny directly in the chest. He fell to the ground immediately.

Max froze.

"Get on your face on the ground, asshole! Put your hands on the back of your head."

Max kept waiting for Mitch to help out. He was packing two guns, one an Uzi, and he could easily have taken these assholes out. Finally he heard someone walk up. "Looking for me, Max?"

Max was now handcuffed and pulled to his feet. Mitch stood in front of him and showed a badge. "You fucked up good, Max. Now, we got enough on you to put you away for a long time."

Max was furious, but not as much at Mitch as he was at Sadlowski. "You killed my brother, you fucking bastard."

As he was being taken away, Max thought, *You cost me my family you son-of-a-bitch cocksucker, and now, I'm gonna complete taking everything from you, asshole. I'm going to destroy you* He yelled at Sam, "I'm going to kill you, motherfucker."

"Have fun with that in jail, asshole." Sadlowski turned and walked away from him.

I'll be out of here soon, Sadlowski, Max thought. *And then I'll be coming for you. First I took your son. Now I'll fucking destroy you.*

Chapter 37

July 26, The Present

Jeremy shook his head in disbelief and smiled at his friend. "Sam, don't you understand anything? You, the great detective—how can you be so oblivious?" Jeremy was enjoying Sam's complete oblivion, and he smiled at Roosevelt as if sharing a secret.

Sam looked at his friend sitting across from him and scowled, "I guess pretty easy, because I got no clue what the hell you are talking about."

It was a few days after Roosevelt and Jeremy had intervened at Sam's house, and they were doing a very good job of keeping track of him. They couldn't be with him constantly, but they were now reasonably sure that Sam was close to being back to normal.

Jeremy looked at Roosevelt, who was sitting next to him in the diner booth, as they were finishing up their breakfasts at the Bethberg Diner. Roosevelt simply looked at Samuel with apparent amusement dancing at the somewhat suppressed smile dancing at the corners of his mouth.

"Okay, okay. What is it with you two anyway? Will one of you geniuses tell me what the hell you are going on about?"

Roosevelt held his palms up. "I will defer to Jeremy on this issue."

"Thanks, Rosy. I can see your courage overflowing there," Jeremy said. "Sammy, I can't believe you couldn't tell. That lovely lady you were just speaking to…"

Jeremy was enjoying teasing Sam about the woman, Jenny, who had clearly been flirting with Sam. She worked at the bank down the street, and she had made it a point to come over to talk with Sam. She had practically sat down on his lap while stopping to talk with him. When she left, she had smiled and said, "See you later, Sam."

"Yeah, Jenny," Sam said.

"Well, Jenny is, how shall I put this, interested in you." Jeremy looked at Sam with an even and serious gaze.

"Go on, Jery. Nah, no way, you gotta be busting on me," Sam said and laughed, but redness coming into his cheeks.

"You can be such a dolt sometimes, Sam. That lady, and she clearly is a lady, couldn't have tried to make herself clearer to you unless she had climbed in your lap and kissed you. Which, of course, she wouldn't do because she is a lady."

Sam rolled up a napkin into a ball and threw it at Jeremy, who snatched it out of the air and smiled.

"Well, son-of-a-bitch, that was one hell of a catch Jerry." Sam's eyes were wide with surprise.

"What? You think just because I'm gay, that I can't catch a ball?"

"No, no, I would never think that. You know I don't give a shit about who anyone is attracted to, except, of course, if it is kids, then they have to be busted. You know that, man."

Jeremy laughed, a big hearty laugh. "Of course I know that, you idiot. You think I would be friends with you if you were a homophobe. But, I love busting on you."

Sam blushed deep red. One of his worst fears was if he lost his friends. He had lost his son and wife—he didn't want to lose anyone else.

"But," Jeremy continued. "I bet you didn't know that I played shortstop on my high school baseball team. I lettered for it."

"Jeremy, I am very impressed. I had no idea that you had been athletic." Roosevelt smiled and nodded at his friend.

"Yeah, well. In those days, I even dated a cheerleader. Had to fit in, you know. Not that anything happened, but we were close friends."

"Wow, Jery. A shortstop. Will wonders ever cease?" Sam was smiling now. "So, how did your team do? Did you have a winning record? What kind of batting average did you have?"

Jeremy was surprised that Sam cared. "Well," he answered. "I hit about .285 and not just singles. I had 10 home runs my senior year."

"Jeremy, you are a wonder and a nonstop series of surprises. I believe you will continue to amaze us with what you can do."

At first, Jeremy wondered if Roosevelt was being sarcastic, but the look of admiration on his friend's face convinced him otherwise. "But, Sam, you are diverting us from the subject at hand. MaryAnn is interested in you. If this still were high school, she probably would have given you a written note, but she probably assumed, and that is a mistake, that as a big boy, you would understand her meaning."

"And just what meaning is that anyway?"

"Well, Samuel. I think Jeremy is being very clear, but I suppose we will have to spell it out for you. She wants to go on a date with you. Why else would she have given you her number? She went out of her way to stop by and chat with you, put her number on a napkin, and handed it to you, so, be an adult and call the lady later."

Roosevelt wondered if Sam was simply avoiding the situation. Jeremy was correct...the lady could not have been any more clear.

"But please, Sam, please find a nice, appropriate place to take her, not some dump of a bar. If you need any help with suggestions, I can certainly put myself at your service." Jeremy looked smug.

"You two are idiots!" Samuel tried to sound angry, but he couldn't help smiling. He knew his two friends were looking out for him, and besides, they were correct. He had missed the signs completely. Plus, he had to admit. He liked the lady, and he also liked the idea of going on a date. It had been far too many years.

"Alright, will it satisfy the two of you if I agree to think about it?"

"Certainly," Roosevelt answered.

"Sure thing, Sammy." Jeremy was now happy.

Sam, hoping to get a crack in, was about to say something else, when he stopped even before a word could come out of his mouth. The door to the diner opened, and a graceful, older African-American woman walked in.

It was Martha.

Chapter 38

July 27, The Present

Sam, Roosevelt, Jeremy, and Helen visited the ruins of the Bethberg Steel Works during the day the week after their decision to begin a preliminary investigation in order to evaluate the situation. They wanted to see what kind of physical problems they might be facing if they agreed to take the full investigation of this facility. Helen had arranged a babysitter for Helena, so she was able to attend this first examination of the site. It was still about two weeks before the new school year began.

They pulled up to the old mill only after about a ten minute ride. Nothing in Bethberg was ever very far from any other part of the small city.

The drove the "official I.P.S." van, although they agreed not to have anything on it to indicate what they did. It was not out of any sense of shame of what they did, but they felt it was always better to be discreet, especially because they sometimes went to someone's private residence, and they never wanted anyone's privacy to be put at risk.

They pulled up to a spot that used to be the factory's main parking lot but now was overgrown by bush and grass. It looked more like something out of a post-apocalyptic movie set than an abandoned old industrial plant. "It does not take long for nature to reclaim its own from the human race, does it?"

"Now, Roosevelt. That was very philosophical," Jeremy said and smiled.

"I have my moments."

Sam just grunted. He had been unusually quiet during this ride. It was usually Sam who would tease Roosevelt or make some kind of crack, but nothing today.

"I can probably include this place in a lesson on the problems of pollution and industrialization in one of my classes," Helen said. She was always looking for anything new and interesting that she could incorporate into her teaching. She never wanted to be one of those teachers who never changed and who read from the same lecture notes year after year. One education professor at a local college illustrated exactly what not to do when teaching. While teaching education classes to undergraduates, all she ever did was read the same worn out lecture notes, year after year. *I promised myself I would never do that,* Helen thought.

They walked slowly around the entire perimeter of the old ruins, which was large, more than the size of several football fields.

"It is like something out of a science-fiction novel, guys. And it is really creepy. I never really looked at this place before. Always drove past it."

"Nor I, Jeremy. Have you Samuel?"

Sam kept walking slowly. Then, "Yeah, I have. Busted a few assholes here a while ago. Not since then."

They walked in silence for a bit further.

The sheer enormity of the size of the place impressed them. This would be the largest investigation that had ever attempted, in terms of square footage, even if they only did the western end of the ruins.

"This is going to be impossible to do if we try to cover the entire area," Jeremy noted.

"That is why we will only do the western end, the area where the incidents have been reported, or at least supposedly reported." Helen was certain that would be their best approach, and the only reasonable way to conduct this investigation.

Roosevelt looked at his right hand, wrapped in a cast as a result of the punch he had used to subdue the thug several days earlier, and noted, "We will have to be very careful with the debris that is scattered around here. It would be too easy for any of us to be injured, and I do not mean by anything supernatural. Only old metal."

"That is an excellent point, Roosevelt." Jeremy was in complete agreement about the potential hazards.

"We'll definitely have to get here early, so we have plenty of sun to set up," Helen said.

"Yeah," Sam said. "Let's get the fuck out of this place."

Chapter 39

July 27, The Present

The prison gate closed behind Max. This was the day he had been waiting for a very long time. He had collected his belongings and the meager savings he had made from working in the industrial laundry in the prison. It wasn't much, but that didn't matter. He had much more waiting for him on the outside.

But he had no intention of advertising that he did.

When he left, one guard said to him and laughed, "See you soon, Max."

He didn't reply. He didn't want to give them any opportunity to keep him there even a day longer.

And he had plans.

He walked to the taxi that was waiting and got in. Once he was far removed from this place, his ride would be better.

Chapter 40

July 27, The Present

"Gentlemen, I found some interesting history of the land on which the old steel mill lies." Roosevelt Theodore Franklin was in his element; he had done research both at Bethberg University Library and the Bethberg Historical Society, located in what had been an old tailor shop in the downtown area. Now he had naturally fallen back into the story-telling cadence he had enjoyed using so much as a history professor.

Sam and Jeremy listened to what Roosevelt had to say, but Helen could not attend because she had a mandatory pre-school year high school meeting to attend.

"Rosy," Sam said and smiled at his friend. The Investigative Paranormal Society was holding a discussion meeting after their brief and preliminary investigation of the old steel mill, making plans on what their next step should be. "Please, oh educated one. Tell us."

Roosevelt smiled back. He was grateful to see Samuel acting more like he usually did—a smartass.

"Well, Samuel, since your requested it. This, however, is not something the town fathers like to speak about. No community prefers to emphasize its sordid history. But it seems that the area of the western section of the old steel plant was the locale, from the early 1800s to about the mid-1870s of a place of execution."

"No shit." Sam was impressed.

"Wow, that is really amazing. Please go on, Roosevelt." Jeremy stopped his cup of Earl Grey Tea midway to his lips.

Roosevelt smiled. He had their attention, and he felt like he was, once again, back in the classroom. He had not mentioned it to his friends, but he missed teaching a great deal. He thought he could simply give it up with retirement, but it had been a central part of his life, and he needed it. Perhaps he would inquire about teaching a history course as an adjunct at one of the fine adult programs in some of the colleges in the Lehigh Valley like Bethberg's Rising Vision or Muhlenberg College's Wescoe School in Allentown. This was something he would consider very carefully. "Yes, gentlemen, executions. Public executions were held there for several decades. Please remember that the administration of justice was swifter in the past and often harsher than it is today."

"Yeah, and I bet they killed a lot of innocent people," Sam said.

Jeremy was surprised. "Sam, I wouldn't have expected that perspective from you, a former cop. Why you almost sound like a liberal."

"Now, Jery. Just because I was a cop doesn't make me some kind of uneducated hillbilly. I want justice for the assholes of the world, but real justice with actual police work and solid evidence. And I always hated any kind of corruption, especially among police!" He pointed right at Jeremy. "Don't you forget it!"

"Whoa, big guy. I didn't mean to get you riled up. I agree with you, and I know how much you like to have a...let's say...spirited discussion." Jeremy looked at his friend and smiled. He then said, "I was wrong for suggesting anything. I'm sorry."

Sam's face was red, and he sat looking down, like he was trying to control an oncoming eruption of anger. Then he let out a sigh, shook himself, looked up, and shrugged his shoulders.

"Are we good, Sam?" Jeremy looked directly into Sam's eyes. He was truly worried. Typically, when having an argument over some political issue, no one really took it too seriously. He knew how much Sam enjoyed the give and take, but knew when to end it before saying too much and causing any kind of rift. Especially after the recent incident of Sam's drinking and his moods. And losing Sam's friendship would be one of the worst things he could ever imagine.

"Yeah, we are." Sam's voice was low and soft. The redness drained from his face. "We're good, Jerry. It's just, you know. . ."

"Yeah, we know, big guy. We do, don't we, Roosevelt?"

"Samuel, we do understand. If you do not want to talk about it, we certainly understand and we respect your wishes. But, always remember, we are your friends, more than that, we are your brothers in arms, and we stand with you always."

"Against anything," Jeremy added. And he offered his hand to Sam.

Sam reached out and shook Jeremy's hand. He looked embarrassed, then shook his hand in the air like he was waving aside some bad thought or a pesky fly. "Alright, alright. Let's get on with what we are supposed to be talking about. You were saying, Rosy?"

"To continue, there were more executions carried out in that time than I would have expected, especially in an area that was not at that time very populated.

Roosevelt paused as he looked at his audience. "I suspect though, and I will follow up on this, that judges in Philadelphia and other county seats sent many of their condemned to Gallows Hill in Bethberg."

"Gallows Hill? You're shitting me?" Sam was genuinely surprised. "Are you making that up? It sounds like something out of a kid's campfire scary story."

"Samuel, I assure you that I am giving you the correct name."

"Wow, that's pretty amazing, guys." Jeremy added.

"So, Rosy, how many did they hang?"

"Samuel, the records, taking with some, ... ah.... consideration of the record-keeping of the time, there were well over a hundred at this one location."

Jeremy whistled a long, slow note. "And you think, Roosevelt, that there may have been more?"

Roosevelt nodded. "That is an excellent question, Jeremy. Gentlemen, given the lack of accuracy of some of the historical records, I believe that the number of executions was almost certainly underreported."

"And this spot, Gallows Hill?" Jeremy made the connection.

"It is at the western end of the old Iron Works, at the original location, before the expansion when it became the Bethberg Steel Mill. That is where the gallows stood for years, until they destroyed it to begin construction on the Iron Works."

Sam slapped his big hands together, making a sound almost like gunfire.

"Son of a bitch!" Jeremy yelled as both he and Roosevelt were startled.

"Sorry. Sorry." Sam held up both hands, palms out and smiled in a crooked grin.

Jeremy grumbled, then smiled.

Sam continued, "I just felt again, after a long time, when I was a detective and made a connection on a case. And, I got to say, it felt great."

"It is okay, Samuel. We are glad you felt better. But please, warn us next time. So, what did you connect?"

"That spot is where the casino 'investors' want us to pay attention to the most. I bet that is where the most activity, including what is seen as normal, happened most. If we checked the factory records, I bet we find that is where most accidents occurred. But only, if there is something there causing them. No real occurrence of accidents, then it would be my guess, that nothing is there."

"Yes, that's where most would be. But still, even if we don't find many accidents there, we should still do an investigation, right, guys?"

"You make an excellent point again, Jeremy, but let us not get ahead of ourselves, shall we. It happens that in my investigations of history of the place, I considered just this possibility, and I checked into them."

"And?" Jeremy asked as Roosevelt paused to drink some coffee.

"C'mon, Rosy. I know you like to build up suspense, but give already." Sam was smiling now, enjoying his friend's performance.

"It is the case that many executions, specifically hangings, were conducted at that very spot. Later, during both the building of the original Iron Works and then later, during the course of the entire existence of the Steel Mill, most accidents happened in that very spot. And. . ."

Roosevelt paused again. He took another sip of coffee, then continued, "And that is also the precise location where all of the plant fatalities occurred."

"All of them? Wow," was all Jeremy could say.

"Wow, indeed, Jeremy."

"Then, guys. We know where we have to focus our investigation. Right there. Roosevelt, this information certainly helps us, because the whole range of the factory is enormous. Way too big for us to cover well." Jeremy was already considering what equipment to use and where.

"Yeah, Rosy," Sam said. Now we have a spot to focus on, almost like a stakeout."

"But guys, before we can get started, we need to meet on Saturday with Helen, because she is a full part of the IPS now."

"Ah, Jeremy, you are correct. We should contact her and set up the meeting."

Chapter 41

1965

In the 1960s, American Steel was king of the manufacturing world. The two behemoths, U.S. Steel and Bethlehem Steel ruled most of this realm, but there was still room for plenty of other little dukedoms such as the thriving small factory known as the Bethberg Steel Mill.

With the surplus of money coming into the business, Mr. Henry Taylor, the CEO, had decided to cement his legacy at the factory and his place as one of the most important businesspeople in Bethberg, PA by expanding the mill considerably. He would purchase the land just to the west of the factory. This was scrubland, long unused and sitting collecting random garbage deposited there. He would clean it up and put a large expansion on the mill.

Taylor was realistic. He knew his name would never be compared to that of Asa Packer, the industrialist who was the founder of Bethlehem Iron Works, later Bethlehem Steel and Lehigh University, now considered one of the finest universities in the United States. Taylor would certainly not be able to achieve that level of notoriety, but he could still be seen as important and powerful locally, especially at the Bethberg Club, the last bastion of wealthy power in the small city.

This club was a holdover from the Victorian Era. Only men were allowed, and membership was exclusive and only by invitation. Taylor liked it just fine that way.

He was married with three children, and he considered this bastion of quiet masculinity a place where he could relax and mingle with important men in the community.

And with the work he was doing to expand the facility, he believed they would be impressed with him.

Taylor had grand plans, and he had no intention of letting anything stop him from gaining the fame and fortune that would satisfy him. He was not able to find any real happiness at home. He admitted privately to himself that he was not happy at home, and he was far too aware of his public image to do as other men in his position had and take a mistress. Building this extension and expanding his financial empire would bring him happiness—that is what he believed.

The construction crew had been working for over two months. Taylor had ordered an expansion of the factory, and they were working to finish it—this was a large extension on the western end of the plant. They were digging a hole that would serve as the foundation for a large crane that would be set in it, and when finished would be able to rotate in several directions to unload trucks coming in from the new docks.

The construction crew worked very hard, happy that there was a seeming explosion of work occurring on the edges of Bethberg. Not only was there this expansion in the steel factory, but there was also talk of a mall being built, and that would bring much work to those in the construction field.

The shop owners of the downtown of Bethberg were not happy with the idea of a suburban shopping mall, because they feared it might kill their downtown, which hadn't changed much in the last 30 years.

Regardless of their fears, changes were coming, and the city would either adapt or die a very slow death.

The construction workers had dug a pit about ten feet deep into the ground and about 15 feet in diameter. This was intended to serve as the foundation for the huge crane they were to install.

As they were moving towards their desired goal, one of them called out, "Hey guys, hold up a moment. You got to see this!"

Three men were in the pit, and they were gesturing wildly to their boss to come over. He scowled and approached. This was a man who hated any kind of delays, especially on this job because they were making good money, and there was a promise of further work to come. Jimmie Stiles had promised Mr. Taylor he would get the work done in as short a time as he could while still maintaining a high quality of construction.

"Yeah, what is it now?" He started to say something else, but he stopped before he could.

The men had uncovered some kind of wooden beam, and it was looking decayed. That, in itself, was not a big concern, but what was attached to it was. They had come across material from old construction before, but nothing like this had ever been seen.

An old noose connected to the beam was around the neck of a partial skeleton.

"Holy fucking shit," one of the men said.

"Mother of God," answered another and crossed himself.

"Fuck me," was all Stiles said at first. Then he said, "Cover it up with dirt. It's old. Don't mean nothing. We can't let it interfere with our building. Too much is riding on this, and I don't intend to let anything delay us."

"But boss," the man who had crossed himself said, "Don't we have to notify someone? I don't know. Maybe the cops."

"O'Malley. You really think we should do that? What, you think we got some kind of murder or something? I mean, for Christ's sake, look how old this shit is."

"Hey Anthony, he's right. Besides, what's it to us anyway?"

"Besides," Gilmanton, another of the diggers said. "It's just a piece of old junk. Don't mean nothing."

Stiles climbed the ladder down into the pit. He gathered the three men around him. "Look, we tell about this—you know what'll happen. The cops'll come around. Who knows who else? What I do know is it'll fuck up our schedule from here to kingdom come. All those nice checks you're getting from this job. You'll kiss them goodbye."

The men started to look worried.

"But, if we just act like nothing happened, then we're good." This meant everything to Stiles. He was falling behind on his mortgage, and he owed a bundle to a local bookie. *It's one thing to lose my house,* he thought. *But that fucker'll send some goon to break my legs.* He spoke in his strongest tones, "We got the hole deep enough. What's two more feet gonna mean anyway. We cover it, pour the cement, finish the walls, and we're out of here. No muss, no fuss. You guys go with me on this, and I'll add a bonus to your pay, but in cash. You got me?"

They all nodded. These were hard working men who were supporting families, and they could use the extra money. So, they agreed and recovered the beam and bones. They made sure the beam could not be seen, then they poured the cement floor and set about making the walls.

190

They let the cement cure, and all looked well with the floor. Then they started working on the cement for the walls.

"Got to let it sit a few days, then we get back to it," Stiles said.

A few days later, they met up in the pit again. The floor looked fine, but there was a potential problem.

As they worked on the cement that would finish the walls, the three men and Stiles were examining the walls of the pit. They were concerned about a crack on the western side of the wall that had appeared.

"I don't know, Mr. Stiles. That looks shaky. Looks like it could break apart under too much stress."

Stiles ran his hand over the six foot long crack that had seemed to have developed over night. "I think it can be fixed easily. I want this job done, and we can get the fuck out of here."

"Sinners," a faint voice said from seemingly the wall itself. "You must all be punished."

"What the fuck was that?" Stiles looked around. "Are you shitting me? Who the hell said that anyway?"

O' Malley crossed himself again.

"I said—who the fuck said that? Someone messing around here?"

All the men shook their heads no. They were frightened.

Stiles went up the ladder on the side of the wall to see if someone was pranking them from above, but no one was around. He then descended back to the floor of the pit. "Alright. It's nothing. Must have been the wind. Let's get back to work."

"Prepare for your fate."

The crack began to widen. The men looked around as other cracks formed in the newly made cement walls.

"Let's get the fuck out of here!" Stiles grabbed the ladder to climb out, but it toppled over as if it had been pushed. He crashed to the ground onto his back.

As they looked down to their boss on his back, more sounds of cracking split the air, almost as if a bomb had exploded.

The men looked in horror as the walls broke around them and fell like a mudslide onto them, crushing them to death nearly instantly.

This disaster, which resulted in the death of four men, ended Taylor's plans for expansion of the mill. After the corpses of the men were removed from the pit, the hole was filled in loosely, and marked "off limits". That wasn't truly necessary, because no one who worked in the plant wanted to go to that end anymore. Many believed it to be cursed.

While that pit was still off limits, later construction extended the western walls of the plant around it, but nothing was ever built on that spot, and few people, except the toughest, even wanted to work anywhere near it.

The western part of the factory was the first to go into serious decline, but that was a forerunner for the rest of the plant. Its finances were no better than the slowly rotting condition of the western section.

From that day forward, the factory started its decline, like so many others in the eastern and Midwestern parts of the United States of America that would later be known as the rust belt.

By the mid-1980s, the Bethberg Steel Works closed its doors forever.

Chapter 42

July 28, The Present

Sam led the way. Jeremy, Roosevelt, and Helen followed close behind. It was late in the day, and darkness would soon be falling.

Earlier that day the IPS had gone to the western end of the old Bethberg Steel Factory and set up their recording devices. Given the dangerous conditions of the place, with a multitude of fallen debris and failing structures, the place looked more like a place of recent warfare than the remains of an industrial building. It seemed like it could have been straight out of one of the documentaries of Europe in World War II.

They all carried flashlights and various recording devices: DVRs, EMF detectors, digital voice recorders, and various kinds of cameras, including infrared and full-spectrum. They looked like an odd group of tourists instead of serious paranormal investigators, which is what they were.

"Be careful where you step, everyone." Jeremy was worried about their safety in this urban ruin.

"You make an excellent point, Jeremy. These facilities are . . .ah . . .less than safe."

"Rosy, you got a serious way with understatement," Sam said. "Everyone, be sure to walk real careful. Every step here could be dangerous. Could easily fall or step on something that could break and you go through. So be careful!"

"We will, Sam," Helen answered." And I don't know what to expect here, but let's all be very alert."

"This feels almost like we were back in Nam, Rosy, going on search and destroy missions and looking out for mines on the ground." Sam didn't like this feeling. He had tried to put the war behind him a long time ago, but now, it seemed he just couldn't escape the past, no matter how hard he tried. These days it felt like almost everything about the past was intruding on the present, and it was building up.

"Ok, guys," Jeremy said. "This is where we set up for our main post. This is pretty high up, so be careful. And going in pairs has to be observed. Watch out for each other, okay, guys?"

"We will, Jeremy." Helen patted his arm and smiled, but she took his advice very seriously.

They gathered around the tables they had placed earlier upon which they had positioned their monitors. They also had four folding chairs and walkie-talkies for everyone.

"Rosy and I will take the first shift, while you guys stay here and keep in contact with us. Is that good?" Sam was now clearly in investigation mode.

Roosevelt was pleased to see that focusing on this task seemed to be helping his friend, at least for now.

"That's good, Sam. We have the walkie-talkies set, and so do you, so be careful." Helen's tone had changed to her very serious I-am-in-charge-and-serious-about-this voice.

"Yes, ma'am. Will do." He and Roosevelt then set off moving to the southwest corner, about 75 feet from the command post.

They stopped and stood about ten feet from each other.

It was now dark, but there was enough light from the clear night sky, with a three-quarter full moon and start to see by. If needed, they would use flashlights.

"This is an EVP session with Sam and Roosevelt, beginning at 11:00 P.M. Is anyone here?" Roosevelt spoke first.

"Is there anyone here who would like to communicate with us?"

"We are not here to bother you, but to try to find some answers. I hope you do not mind." Roosevelt said. As he did, he felt something like a feather or a soft whisper by his left ear. "Sam, did you hear that?"

"No, Rosy. I didn't hear anything."

"There was something. I am not sure what though. Maybe it will be on the recording."

"Did you work here? Did this place mean something to you?" Sam asked.

Sam and Roosevelt continued their questioning for a while, in the hope of recording an EVP.

After about 30 minutes, when nothing seemed to be happening, they moved further to the westernmost point in the ruins, where the original old iron mill had first been built.

"We are at the spot of the original mill, the iron works. This seems to be where many things have happened. Are you a part of that?" Sam's tone had become hardened, almost as if he were conducting an interrogation. Sometimes a change in approach worked if nothing seemed to be happening.

"Where you here before the mill was built?"

This time they both heard something. Roosevelt looked at Sam who put his finger to his lips. He wanted to listen further.

It was there. They both could hear something, but they could not make out what it was. It sounded almost like something falling, but very faintly.

They ended their session after about another 20 minutes and returned slowly and carefully back to the command post.

"Did you get anything?" Helen asked.

"Perhaps, we will have to see during our playback. I think it would be a good idea, if you and Jeremy started a new session there. Perhaps you will have better luck."

"But be careful, got it?" Sam added.

"Sam, we will." Helen nodded to him, and she and Jeremy headed to the suggested area.

They walked slowly and cautiously, keeping aware of any potentially dangerous footing. Soon they reached their goal and began. "Jeremy and Helen beginning an EVP session at the western point. Time, 1:00 A.M. Our friends were here before. Did you try to make contact with them? You can with us if you wish." Jeremy used a conversational, friendly tone.

"That's right. Do you have anything you wish to say to us?" Helen asked.

"Are you here for a reason?" Jeremy added.

"I'm going to move a little further over," he said to Helen.

They moved with great care because the walkway was narrow and about 30 feet about the ground. A fall from there could be fatal. Not only was the height a serious risk, but also there was a great deal of metal and concrete debris below them.

Jeremy started to take a step. As he stood, Helen also began to move with him. As Jeremy began to step with his right foot, a metal rod moved directly in front of his ankle, causing him to bark his shin and to fall forward.

"Owww," he yelled.

Helen reached for him with her left hand to try to break his fall. As she was stretched out in her lunge to help him, something shoved her hard from her right.

She lost her balance and fell to her left, right at the edge of the walkway. Years ago, a railing would have been there, but it had long since rusted away and fallen to the ground itself.

Helen felt herself sliding off the walkway and yelled, "Jeremy! Help!"

Jeremy forced himself around.

He saw Helen holding on to the walkway with both hands and her body dangling below.

Jeremy moved directly in front of her and grabbed both of her arms. "Hang on, Helen, and pull up. I won't let go."

Helen got up to her elbows, with Jeremy gripping her arms in a hold that was much tighter and stronger than she would have expected. She scrambled onto the walkway and slumped onto her back and gasped for air as Sam and Roosevelt rushed over to them.

"Are you both ok?" Roosevelt asked.

Sam knelt by Helen, who was resting on her back and breathing hard. "Helen, are you alright? You hurt at all?"

Roosevelt turned to Jeremy, who was also sitting and breathing hard. "How are you, Jeremy?" Roosevelt asked.

"I'm good…just look to Helen."

Roosevelt nodded and moved to her. Sam was still with her, and he asked again, "Are you ok?"

"I'm fine, just winded. But I wouldn't be here, if it weren't for Jeremy." She looked at him and smiled, and he blushed.

"Jerry, you're a fucking hero, and I ain't busting on you. I mean it." Sam looked at Jeremy with deep respect.

"Jeremy, I concur with Samuel, though not with his choice of language."

They decided to collect their equipment and break for the night. "We have plenty to examine, and we will be back to deal with this," Helen said.

"That's right. Whoever you are, we're coming back." Jeremy was still angry.

"Oh yeah, we're coming back, motherfucker. 'Cause now it's personal." Sam stared back at the ruins and raged inside.

Chapter 43

July 30, The Present

"Ms. Murray? Can we talk with you?" That was what the email had said. Helen was surprised that two of her students had contacted her. It was summer, and even the best students usually wanted to be away from the high school and their teachers. So, she was intrigued that these 2, in particular, had contacted her by her school email. It seemed odd because they were only part of the group that she called "The Three Musketeers." They all seemed to be joined at the hip and never seemed to go anywhere without the others.

These were kids who hadn't yet found their way. They were not the best students, and they often got into trouble, but Helen thought she had detected real talent and thoughtfulness in them that could one day emerge. She contacted them and said they could meet at the Bethberg coffee shop at lunch time to talk. While Helen liked these kids, she was smart enough to know that she should meet with them only in a public place. And she couldn't ignore them, because they sounded like they might be in some kind of trouble. When it came to her students, Helen would do anything she could to help them.

Taylor Szabo, a goth girl, had serious writing talent, but she needed to learn to focus. Helen thought her poetry, while still mainly of the teenaged angsty kind, still had powerful images, and that the girl had potential if she would learn to apply herself.

The girl also wanted to write a novel about mystical creatures. "Not vampires, or stuff like that, but I want to make up a whole new world," she had told Helen one day when they conferenced about her studies. Helen encouraged her to focus both on her studies and her writing.

"With your talent, you can get a degree from college, and then maybe go to a graduate school with an M.F.A. program in writing. Helen hoped that the girl took her advice about reading and writing every day.

Jason Baumgardner, an overweight boy of 16, was deeply shy. He was skilled with computers and loved roleplaying fantasy games, but he had no other friends besides the other two musketeers. He was bright, but he didn't seem to care about any classes outside of computers. Helen had also met with him several times, and she was working on putting together an internship with a local company that was a high-tech startup in the area. This company was specializing in designing new software, including computer games. Helen believed if Jason could see what his future might be if he stayed in school and focused, then he might be able to succeed.

The last of the trio was Jimmie Lansing, an African-American boy, whom Helen was sure was gay, but she didn't think he knew, or he was completely closeted. In this little city, that would not have been surprising, even today. He was a talented musician but seemed afraid to admit to it. Helen wasn't sure why, but she knew like the other two, he was very intelligent. Helen had encouraged him not only to play in the school band and orchestra but also to try singing his songs at the open mike night at this coffee shop.

She worried about the three of them. When they were together, they were happy, and they were going to hangout during the summer, and maybe listen to Helen's advice. Maybe.

It was Jason who had emailed her, on her school address. It was clear something was wrong, and they didn't know what to do. He practically begged her to meet, so she couldn't refuse.

When Helen arrived at the coffee shop around lunchtime, Taylor and Jason were sitting there, both radiating worry and fear. She went to them and told them to sit still. Then she ordered a coffee and sat with them.

She saw that both had been crying. What the hell is going on? she thought.

"Ms. Murray, I don't know what to do. . ." Jason trailed off and looked down.

"Oh God, oh God," was all Taylor was saying.

"Ok, kids, look. You have to tell me what is going on here." Helen spoke to them in her calm but stern voice. She was starting to get worried that something bad had happened.

They both looked at each other and tried to stop crying.

Helen waited. She sensed that they were liked scared deer now. If she were to push them to talk, they might startle and leave, and something was clearly wrong now.

Taylor finally spoke up. She was the leader of the group, so it didn't surprise Helen. "Ms. Murray, Jimmie is in trouble, and we don't ... know...what...to...do!" As soon as she got the words out, the girl started crying again.

Jason looked over at Helen. He also had tears running down his cheeks.

Helen reached over and took one of their hands in hers. "Look, you two. Whatever is going on, no matter how serious it might be, you have to tell me. You called me. You want me to help. Now, let me help you."

Taylor wiped her smudged eyes. "We decided we wanted to have some spooky fun, more than the goofy online or board games, so we decided. . ."

"To have a séance." Jason completed her sentence the way the three of them often did. It was sometimes as if they were all truly connected in a way she did not understand.

"Okay, that seems harmless enough." But Helen already had chills. She had witnessed enough with the battle with Maledicus and then other investigations to know there was far more in existence than most people ever imagined. *What had these kids gotten themselves into?* she wondered but did not ask aloud.

"Yeah, we thought so too. It would just be a big goof, you know? I mean, I like to dress up in the Goth clothing and let people think I am all weird and into this stuff, but I really don't believe in it. At least . . ."

"We didn't. Before." Jason was struggling to speak without crying.

She looked at both of them. This wasn't going to be good. "Ok, go on now. You know you can trust me."

They did. The kids in their school all knew Ms. Murray was a person of her word. They all thought she was weird, but in a cool way, and that was quite a compliment from teenagers.

"So, the other night...Last Tuesday, the three of us went to the old Iron Mills...you know, on the outside of town."

The feeling of dread increased as Helen heard this. Her skin felt like it was actually tightening.

"It's a real pit there…but we brought flashlights and things…didn't want to fall in anywhere. I wasn't a boy scout for nothing." For a moment, Jason almost looked like he might have when he was ten years old. "We also looked around to see if there was any cars there. Didn't want to run into any shady types there. You know, too many go there to party."

"But not us. We may be weird, but we aren't partiers." Taylor looked at Helen as if she were terrified that the teacher might think something like that of her. Her veneer of toughness was completely dissipated.

At that moment, both Taylor and Jason looked like scared little kids.

"I believe you, Taylor. Don't worry."

"So, Me and Jimmie and Taylor scoped the place out. Decided the spot on the far west was the best place to go. Looked really deserted and all, I don't know, creepy there. You know?"

Helen nodded. That was the place were something had attacked her.

"So, we set up our stuff, and a Ouija board, but it's just a stupid game, you know?"

"We really didn't think anything would happen. But Jimmie was really into it. He had dressed all in black, complete with a hooded cape…like he was some kind of black Dracula or something." Taylor sniggered at the image. Then she remembered what had happened and immediately teared up again.

"We, you know, had candles out and sat down around the board. We said stupid incantations…we made them up on the spot. Just dumb stuff," Jason added.

"Then Jimmie, he ordered any spirit to appear," Taylor said in a very quiet voice. "We all laughed. It seemed so ridiculous. I mean, none of us believed any of this stuff, and it isn't like we're, I don't know, Satanists, or anything."

"It got so cold then." Jason looked at Helen. "You know I love nerdy stuff like watching the Weather Station. Other kids laugh at me. I like that station more than HBO or Showtime and stuff, but it was like a cold front had come through, but just there."

"But Jimmie wouldn't stop. It was like he was acting or something, and he loves being the center of attention." Taylor was now speaking softly.

"Yeah, he kept saying shit, like…oops, sorry, ma'am, um, stuff" Jason's face turned bright red.

"It's ok, Jason. Don't worry. No detentions here for language, and I have heard far worse."

"Stuff, like – appear to me! Then, come to me, O spirits of the night! I command you, in the name of the Three Musketeers!" Taylor shook her head. "Why did we have to go? It was so stupid."

"It was funny then," Jason added. "But now, it just seems…dumb."

Helen sipped her coffee and waited for them to continue.

"Then there was this guy there, but not there too. I don't know how to explain it!" Jason hated not having rational explanations for anything.

"But he was there, and he was really scary. Bad scary. He looked wrong, you know? Like he was. . ." Taylor shivered as she recalled what she saw.

"In the wrong time. That's it! He looked like someone out of one of your history lessons. Dressed in black, but in old-time clothes." Jason was pleased to remember that.

"Then, he said, 'you called me, sinners, and I am here!'" Taylor shook a little. Jason held her in an awkward hug.

"He said—all sinners must be punished," Jason said. "Then, and this is the worst—he said this negro sodomite will be punished tomorrow night."

Helen leaned forward. "Did you guys try to get away, to run? Please tell me you did."

"I was so scared I could barely move, Ms. Murray. Then, he reached out to Jimmie. . ." Taylor could barely be heard now.

"And it was just...they weren't there anymore. Like a magic trick, only it was no trick, you know?"

"They were both just gone. Ms. Murray, what are we gonna do?"

"This is what you will do. You will go home and wait for me to contact you. Some friends of mine and I will look into this. If we cannot find anything, then you will go to the police. Understand?"

They shook their heads.

"Promise me you won't go back there." She knew she should probably contact the police now, but she also knew something bad was there, and they wouldn't be able to do anything to help Jimmie.

Maybe the IPS could.

Chapter 44

July 30, The Present

Sam's mouth hung open, almost as wide as his eyes. It was as if the past had suddenly made a detour and found its way onto the highway of the present. Martha had walked into the diner.

Roosevelt and Jeremy saw the way Sam was looking at this woman, and they both wondered what the story was, but they had the sense not to joke about it.

At that moment, Sam didn't even remember that his friends were with him; all he could see was the woman who suddenly saw him and smiled the warm, wide smile that had captured his heart so many years ago.

He stood up and waved to her.

Moving with confidence and grace, Martha approached the booth.

Sam stepped out of the booth, and they stood before each other. Martha held out her hands, and Sam took them in his. "Hello, Martha," he said and smiled.

"Hello, Sam." Her voice was warm. Then they moved naturally into each other's arms and kissed.

Roosevelt and Jeremy were stunned. Jeremy almost blurted out, "Forget that other woman." But he had the good sense not to say it.

Instead, after they broke their clinch and realized others were around, Roosevelt simply said, "Samuel, are you going to introduce us to your lovely friend?"

Sam turned to them, and holding her hand, said, "Rosy, Jery, this is Martha, a very dear friend, and Martha, these are my closest friends, Roosevelt and Jeremy."

Martha shook both of their hands with a firm grip. "I am very pleased to meet you. Any friends of Sam are friends of mine."

"Please sit down. We were just getting ready to leave." Jeremy stood to let Roosevelt out.

"Oh no. I appreciate that offer, gentlemen. But I could not intrude on your meal."

As she said that, Sam glanced over at them with a pleading-let-me-have-some-private-time-with-her look on his face.

"No, you are certainly not intruding. We were finished with our meal and getting ready to leave anyway. Besides, we do this a couple of times a week." Roosevelt bowed slightly to her.

"My friend is telling the truth. Please sit and enjoy your time with Sam." Jeremy also gave a small bow.

"My, my. Sam, your friends are gentlemen. I am pleased to see that."

Sam blushed a very deep red. "Yes, they certainly are."

After they left, Sam and Martha sat in the same booth across from each other.

Chapter 45

July 30, The Present

Michael Flannery was feeling pressure from the other members of the board. They were beginning to worry that this plan to develop the old steel ruins in Bethberg were taking far too long, and that they should start to look for other possible places.

Ordinarily, Michael would have agreed with them and tried to make a decision based solely on objective measurements and information, but he wanted this project. This would be the one that would make him the most powerful man in their consortium. If it failed, then he was not sure he could maintain his grips on the organization.

Damn those old fuckers, he thought. *I need that report. Fuck, if this were the old days, I would just send some guys to make them cooperate. But I am trying to drag us into the 21st Century and not use such tactics, unless absolutely necessary. Especially not against a bunch of old guys. I would be laughed at if it came out.*

Still the worry chewed at him, and he would need some kind of answers soon.

Chapter 46

July 30, The Present

"Ok, guys, what do we do now?" Jeremy asked the other members of the IPS as they gathered at his apartment.

"Whatever we decide must be done as a group. This affects not only us, but others as well." Roosevelt was thinking about the little girl Helena and that Helen was her only living relative.

"Don't you go there, Roosevelt. I'm a member of this group, and I think I already proved that I can investigate and fight as well as any of you." Helen's eyes lit with the fire of the warrior, and her mouth tightened. To make her point she held out the palms of her hands, which still carried the scars from the burns she suffered when wielding the silver cane against the Roman statue through which Maledicus manifested his power on Earth and the realm of the living.

Roosevelt bowed slightly to her. "I am very sorry, Helen. I never meant to suggest that I questioned your courage or ability."

"And yes," Jeremy added. "You wielded this cane," he said holding up the heavy silver wolf's head cane based on the one used by Claude Rains in The Wolfman to kill the werewolf. "Better than anyone, except perhaps my David."

"Yeah, our Jerry's right on that, Helen. You stood and fought while I was blubbering in a corner."

Sam winced at the memory. He hated the idea that he had been reduced to being a coward.

They went silent as they sat around Jeremy's modest kitchen table.

"No one here questions either your courage or anyone else's. That was a horror show of the worst kind, and Sam, you are one of the bravest men I have ever known. Do not ever forget that.

Jeremy said, "Let's get this going, shall we? Does anyone need anything else?" He had put out refreshments on his modest dining room table. This house was not anything like the grand one he had owned with David.

When he sold the Victorian home that he and David had owned, he had told Roosevelt, "I neither need nor desire the grand table that David and I used for hosting dinner parties, not since David died. That's part of his memory. A simple table like this serves my needs."

"I understand completely." Roosevelt understood the demands of grief.

"Helen, I am sorry I offended you. I know your valor." Roosevelt's dead wife, Sarah, would have chastised him if he did not acknowledge Helen's courage.

Helen smiled. "And I'm sorry, Roosevelt." She reached out and took his hand. "I am just sensitive about being seen as weak because I am female. I know you three do not do that."

"Don't worry, Helen. None of us is ever going to think that," Sam added. "And I bet you got no problems keeping the knuckleheads in your high school class in line."

"No, I don't."

They all laughed.

Sam stood and poured himself more coffee. It was excellent, made from beans roasted at the

Bethberg Coffeehouse. "It is the best coffee house in the area," Roosevelt, a self-appointed connoisseur of coffee and coffee houses, had pronounced. Jeremy also always purchased his coffee beans there, but his tea came from the tearoom in downtown Bethberg, where he used to go to have visits with Sarah. They had become like brother and sister. "So, let's get back to the original point. What are we going to do?"

Sam hid his anger the best he could, but he was trying to control two volcanic buildups of rage within, for the monster who had ordered the killing of his son, and towards whatever or whoever it was that had attacked Jeremy and Helen. Nobody goes after my friends. Nobody, he thought, but he kept that to himself.

"Well," Jeremy said. "We have reviewed the evidence—Helen and I—so let's begin by seeing what we found."

"Then, we can analyze it," Helen added.

"All good. And then we come to a plan of action." Sam spoke in his cop voice. "Let's go to it then." Sam was tapping his fingers against his right leg, a sign Roosevelt knew of his friend's impatience.

"Right." Jeremy had both the video and audio evidence ready to show on a laptop computer with a large 19 inch screen. "Let's guy with the visual evidence first, guys."

"The first piece doesn't show much." Helen pointed to a section of the screen where a faint haze seemed to materialize near Roosevelt.

"The only reason we didn't dismiss it immediately was because it happened during Sam's and Roosevelt's questioning. The haze lasted for only two seconds, then it simply vanished."

"Yeah, I don't think that shows much, so what's next?" Sam was definitely impatient.

"Ok, this was towards the end of Helen's and my EVP session." Jeremy's face hardened as he played it.

The screen showed Helen and Jeremy walking slowly along the upper catwalk, with Jeremy in the lead.

As they walked, a piece of metal, a rod of some kind, moved from its original position about perpendicular to the slightly curved wall to directly in the path of Jeremy's ankle.

The front of his ankle hit it directly; he tripped, he went sprawling forward.

As he did, Helen reached to try to catch him, stretching out as far as she could.

Then, in an odd, almost jerky motion, she seemed to stumble to her left and started to fall off the walk.

She yelled and grabbed hold to the metal as best she could, but she was dangling over the 30 foot fall. All watching knew that would have killed her.

Jeremy righted himself, and faster than it seemed likely for a man of his age, scooted to her and gripped both of her arms. He held her so hard that she later had bruises from his hands.

As he held and pulled, she was able to scramble back up onto the walkway.

Helen stopped the visual.

"Son-of-a-bitch," Roosevelt said.

"Yeah, Rosy." Sam said. "That was fucking intentional."

"It's a good thing we had a camera set in that direction, or we might not have seen what happened." Jeremy spoke in a muted voice.

"Yeah, shit. And it's a doubly good thing you are as strong as you are, Jerry, and you are as powerful and nimble as you are, Helen, or you would have fallen to the ground . . ." Sam looked away as he started to tear up.

"That fall," Roosevelt said. "was at least 30 feet, onto metal and debris. That would most certainly have been fatal."

"But I didn't go over. Also, I didn't trip. When Jeremy went down and I reached for him, I felt something shove me hard."

"We believe you, Helen," Roosevelt added. "The evidence clearly shows that, and we would believe you anyway, evidence or not."

"Thank you. I appreciate that. And I didn't know Jeremy was so strong." She smiled, and he blushed deep red.

"But what fucking matters is that someone or something tried to kill you. Do all of you understand that? There is a fucking murderer there."

"Sam, we do." Jeremy glanced at him.

"Let us proceed with the audio evidence if that is the last of the video." Like Sam, Roosevelt was seething, but he was better able to control his outward visage.

"Yeah, that's it with the visual. Ok, guys. Here is the first EVP. It happened when Sam and Roosevelt were asking if anyone was there."

Jeremy hit "play," and they listened.

"Is anyone there?" They heard Roosevelt's calm voice, then a pause.

Then, "I am here, sinner."

"There was nothing more during that EVP session, but that was clear, more clear than in most EVPs we have captured." Jeremy said.

Helen was fascinated by its implications. "He or it called you sinner."

"Yes," Roosevelt said. "What are we to make of that?"

"Sounds like a fucking religious nut to me." Sam shook his head in disgust. "Met enough of those while I was a cop. Can't stomach fucking hypocrites."

Jeremy shuddered. "I hate those kinds. They are usually the worst bigots and the worst to condemn others for desires they are repressing."

"But that's not all we have, even though it would be plenty," Helen said as she gave Jeremy a reassuring look.

"This one," Jeremy continued. "happened when Helen and I were up on the catwalk, or whatever you would call it in a factory. We went up there to check out what seemed to be the sound of a voice. But I assure you, guys, that we were very slow and careful in our movements. So, we stopped to do the EVP session. I asked if anyone was there and if they wanted anything."

Helen played the EVP. "I want justice."

"That was right before the metal tripped me, and something shoved Helen."

"So now, we've seen the evidence. What do we think it means?" Sam drummed his fingers on the table and frowned. He was eager to attack whatever was there, but he knew he had to wait.

"We certainly cannot report to the casino people that it is safe to move forward," Roosevelt said waving his hand like he was dismissing an errant student. "But I truly do not care about them and their plans."

"Neither do I, Roosevelt." Jeremy was shaken by what almost happened to Helen. He had grown to love her as a sister and Helena as a niece. He couldn't bear the idea of harm coming to either. He would die to prevent that.

"Helen and I have to do just a bit more research, so we understand what it is we are dealing with and what to do about it, how to deal with it." Roosevelt enjoyed sharing the historical research with Helen, and he knew they were looking for something evil.

"I have another piece of information that is pertinent," Helen said, and she filled them in on her conversation with the high school students.

"Yeah, you two will do the recon we need. But do we agree, whatever this fucking thing is, we take it out? Especially with what Helen told us, if we are to have a chance at helping that youngster, then we have to act."

"I agree with Sam," Jeremy said. "That place attracts too many people, too many kids, and I don't want anyone else getting hurt there." He looked at Helen.

"I'm in," was all she said.

"As am I." Roosevelt spoke with calm fury.

"And me. Soon, fucker, we'll be coming for you," Sam said.

Chapter 47

August 4, The Present

"I can't do it. I'm sorry, Roosevelt, but I can't." Martin looked down at the table, where Jeremy, Roosevelt, and he were sitting. They were gathered in the kitchen at Martin's apartment.

Roosevelt nodded and said nothing. He wanted Martin's help, but he could not try to persuade someone to go into battle once more against an entity, especially someone who had lost a person close to them to Maledicus.

"Martin, are you sure? There is a teenager at risk." Jeremy tried to keep his voice even, but he was worried about the youngster, and he had grown to be impatient with cowardice, especially since he had conquered his own fears.

They had come to Martin in the hope that he would try to do another cleansing ritual. It had not been successful in their previous battle against the demon Maledicus, but they thought it was still worth the effort. Perhaps, they reasoned, it would have more effect this time.

"Jeremy, you have to understand. That thing, Maledicus, killed Branwyn. She was my closest friend, and it killed her. Now I can't stop dreaming about it. I can barely even function in my normal life."

Jeremy began to say something, but Roosevelt held up a hand to stop him. "Martin, it is not your fault, and you should not feel ashamed of how you feel. What you are experiencing is similar to what many soldiers have felt after being in battle." Roosevelt reached into his wallet and took out a card. "Please consider calling this counselor. She is very good, and she has helped me."

Tears began to form in Martin's eyes. "I'm so sorry. I wish I could help, but I can't." Before they stood to leave, he spoke again. "But I can give you the things I use to do a blessing. It doesn't really matter who does the ritual, as long as they believe in it. And I know you two understand the reality of the supernatural." Martin stood and went to get his carrying bag.

Roosevelt and Jeremy looked at each other and waited.

When he returned, Martin said, "This might help." He handed them his blessing paraphernalia.

After they left, Martin sat as his table and held his head in his hands. Then he cried.

Chapter 48

July 30, The Present

"Ok," Helen said. "So, now we know who is haunting that spot in the old factory. Ebeneezer Schwarznacht...wow, what a name."

Roosevelt, Helen, and Jeremy were meeting at Jeremy's apartment. They were sitting at Jeremy's antique oak table and having tea and coffee as they discussed what to do.

"Do you know what it means?" Roosevelt asked. They both looked at him.

"Sorry, German is not one of my languages," Helen replied.

"Dark night. It means dark night." Roosevelt looked at all of them. "I am not joking about the name, and I understand how it sounds."

"Wow, guys, that is as ominous as Maledicus." Jeremy shuddered at the memory. "I certainly hope we are not going into anything like that again."

"I agree with you, Jeremy. I, too, hope, not nearly as dangerous or hard to eliminate as that bastard." Roosevelt shook his head at the memories of that battle they had shared.

"Yeah, guys, but there is one big difference here." Jeremy shook his head and sipped his tea.

"Yes, we need to talk about the glaring gorilla in the room." Helen's face saddened as she spoke. "We're missing one of our team."

"Samuel must need more time alone. I thought after our initial reconnaissance of the site, he would be here, but whatever he needs we must allow him. I have more respect for him than for almost anyone else in the world, except for the two of you. And I know he is in great turmoil."

"I understand, Roosevelt." Helen stood and looked at him. "I just wish it wasn't happening now. This ghost, or spirit, or thing, Schwarznacht, is dangerous, and we know it."

"Yeah, it is. We have collected evidence of quite a few deaths, but we still don't know what we should do to stop it." Jeremy was concerned about the investigation, but more about his friend. "Roosevelt, I thought Sam was getting better and with us on this."

"So, did I, but I think we will just have to proceed as if Sam will not be with us on this case. Are we all good with it?"

"I am not sure about good, but yes, I do understand," Jeremy answered.

"But afterwards, we have to try to help Sam," Helen said. "But we do have to stop it. Too many evil things are happening. Do we all agree?"

They all nodded.

"Look, battles have been fought many times with depleted armies, but they still fought and often won." Roosevelt looked subdued.

Helen laughed. "Now, Roosevelt. That was, I have to say, really encouraging!"

"It just doesn't feel right though. It just doesn't. I mean, guys, how do we do this without Sam? I mean, Sam, is our strength. You know what I mean?" Jeremy looked glum, almost as bad as when David died. "Sam is our tough guy."

"Jeremy, you proved yourself to be very tough in our battle with the demon. You should trust in yourself now."

"Roosevelt's right, Jeremy. I trust in you. You have proven yourself many times. Helena wouldn't be here now if it wasn't for you."

Jeremy blushed. "Well, you are more of a warrior than I am."

"We are all warriors, and it is time to fight this thing, or we stop now. That is our choice." Roosevelt stood and said, "I am going to the fight Schwarznacht."

"I'm in. Too many people are being hurt." Helen's face was set and determined. Not too long ago, the story of several teenagers being killed at the site convinced her that she had to do battle. When children were in danger, she became fierce.

"Yeah, guys, I'm in too." Jeremy still wished Sam would be there. He felt better when the whole group was together.

"I wish we had more to go into battle with. We will try to perform a cleansing ritual and convince the ghost to move on." I have already spoken with Martin, but he has no interest in confronting anything like Maledicus again."

"So, he won't help us?" Jeremy was startled. He thought for sure that Martin would help out again.

"We shouldn't judge him, Jeremy," Roosevelt said.

"No, we shouldn't," Helen agreed. "But it would still have been helpful if he were with us."

"He did say, however, that he would lend us his books and equipment to use if we want to. What do you think?"

"I'll get them and learn it." Jeremy spoke in a determined voice.

"Good man, Jeremy," Helen said.

"And if that doesn't work, Roosevelt?" Jeremy was still unsure. He wanted a more set and detailed plan, but he would follow Roosevelt and Helen into anything, even death.

And it might come to that.

"This thing tried to kill me, to throw me off the catwalk, which means it has presence in our world, somehow. The demon Maledicus used that little fucking statue to manifest, so maybe, just maybe, it is using something to create its power." Helen stood and started to pace back and forth, the way she did when she was trying to work out some kind of intellectual puzzle. "Perhaps, if there is something it is using to gain access to our world, we can try to destroy it. I think that is the best possible solution. There has to be an answer."

"Let's hope we figure it out soon." Jeremy looked over at Helen and tried to smile, but as they continued to discuss this situation, he grew less and less confident. They had, indeed, been able to defeat Maledicus, but that had come at a terrible cost, with the death of Patrick, and they had their entire group together for that battle. This time, they were depleted. And Jeremy would have felt much better about their attempts if Sam were there.

Roosevelt did not want to tell them how worried he was, not only about the outcome of their attempts to remove the spirit but also about Sam. He had never seen Sam this depressed and withdrawn before, and he hoped Sam would recover soon.

But he was not sure.

Chapter 49

July 31, The Present

Early one morning, at 5:45, to be exact, the ground shook in the northern region above the Lehigh Valley, Pennsylvania. No one expected this to occur, but no one was really startled by it either, at least no one who was human.

The wild deer in the area as well as the black bears and the horses on several farms knew it was coming about an hour or so before it hit. They acted worried, and some tried to find cover, but human beings were simply startled by it.

As earthquakes go, this wasn't much. Compared to many devastating events around the world, this one didn't garner much attention outside of the immediate region. It was low on the Richter scale—about 3.5, but since such events were not common in the eastern region of Pennsylvania, it got some notice there. The weather stations at the local TV station covered it like a major event. It was centered on a fault, a minor one that ran about 20 feet from the western end of the ruins of the steel factory.

Several years earlier, a much bigger quake had occurred in Reading, PA, but this was small in comparison. If it had not been for the almost exceptional nature of the event, it would have been ignored.

There was a loud explosive boom that was heard for miles, and in Bethberg, there was about five seconds of shaking, with minimal damage.

Police and fire engines responded to the event, but when they arrived, all that was found was a relatively small split in the ground in the western section of the ruins. No real damage was reported in the surrounding area.

A few people had some cracks in their walls, and a few reported some broken windows and dishes from falling to the floor, but that was the extent of the damage.

No one had been injured in the earthquake, and there was much relief because of that.

This was simply an unusual event, one that made the day's evening news cast, and then it was quickly forgotten.

But it had impact.

And seismologists were predicting more earthquakes were likely.

Chapter 50

July 31, The Present

Something had changed. Since claiming this spot during his death, Schwartznacht had remained as a presence, watching and becoming infuriated at the desecration of this sacred site of his gallows.

His anger would build slowly to a point, where, like an active volcano, he would erupt and manifest into the world of the living, but always for frustratingly short periods. He would do what he could to punish any sinners he found in his locale. He wasn't sure how he had gained this ability, but he was certain that it was a holy gift that came with the responsibility to serve God, to cleanse the world of as many sinners and abominations as he could, sending them directly to hellfire to burn forever.

Afterwards, his presence in the earthly world would slowly fade, and he moved into one of great loneliness, one in which he seemed to be able to move, but only in a murkiness limited by the dimensions of the original gallows. Time meant nothing. As he receded into this world, he had nothing with which to measure the passing of hours and days. The waiting to remerge might have been six hours, six days, or even sixty years. It was all interminable to him.

Then he would begin to feel stronger, and the process would repeat, over and over.

But recently, something had happened. But when—he wasn't sure.

A great sound had crashed and reverberated through the dimness. As the noise exploded, it was as if a light had shown into the darkness. Something had shifted. He saw before him a revelation.

The main pole of his beloved gallows had appeared before him. It was as if it had been unaffected by all the years in the ground. He reached out and could touch it. He could feel the solidity of the wood, and through contacting it, Schwarznacht also grew stronger.

Once this contact was made, and he manifested into the earthly realm and after punishing sinners, he did not recede deep into the other world. Instead, he moved enough into it to be invisible to the living, but he could now watch them as they invaded the sacred area. *This is God's plan for me,* he thought. *I am his vessel, and his is pouring his wrath into me!*

Indeed, Schwarznacht and the wood of the gallows were now intertwined, almost like a battery powering a generator. Not only did the gallows give him strength, but also it filled Schwarznacht with growing strength. They were like a continual electric spiritual circuit.

Scwarznacht could see somehow that the earth above the gallows had weakened. It would not take much for the wood to break through and emerge. And when it did, he understood that he would have strength of which he had never dreamed, and he would ensure that his gallows of God would stand forever—as a testament to his righteousness, as a monument to the holiness of his task.

It will be soon, O Lord. They terrible vengeance will be felt by the unworthy sinners once more and forever. In your name. Amen.

Schwarznacht felt invigorated, almost as if he had a true body again. He had been able to venture out of the earth before and manifest into a physical form on occasion, but each time had been for a short duration. Each time, after he appeared, he felt his energy ebb soon after appearing. His visits to the world above were short, although recently he had been able to stay longer than before. And the last time he was the most powerful he had been.

Not only was Schwarznacht able to stay above ground longer, but he had been able to do something he had never been able to do before.

He had been able to carry out executions before, but never had he been able to bring one of the heathen unbelieving sinners back with him. This visit to the world above, he was able to capture that sodomite and return with him. He bound him and placed him in captivity in a cave, where he would await his coming execution. He was pleased that he would have the opportunity to do this one completely correctly.

Schwarznacht measured the size and weight of the condemned one. He would have the proper length and drop prepared for the soon-to-be-execution.

Chapter 51

July 31, The Present

Sam couldn't believe that he had seen Martha again. After they had split up and he had gone into the Marines immediately upon graduating from high school, she had left his life, he thought forever.

She had, he had heard while serving in Vietnam from a friend back in Bethberg, been accepted into Stanford University in California on a full scholarship to study physics, a rare feat, especially for a black woman. He filled with pride when he heard that. She would be very important one day.

But he also knew that meant they would be apart forever. He was a mere grunt in the Marines, only slogging in country duty, and she was going to become a scientist. Their worlds were separated by far more than the color of their skins.

And in those bad old days, skin color was more than enough.

Today, perhaps, could be different.

"I was a coward," Sam said to Martha and looked down, unable to hold her direct gaze. He still was embarrassed, after all those years. "That's what I was—I was young and a coward. It's not an excuse, not at all."

"Sam," she said and reached across the end booth in which they sat at the Bethberg Diner.

She took his hands in hers and looked at him and smiled—the same gentle smile he had loved as a young man. "We were both scared kids. Don't you know that?"

Sam paused before answering. "Yeah, I do, Martha. But you were always smarter and stronger than me. I think I must have been afraid of everything. I didn't understand how good we were together and how much that meant."

Martha smiled a wide smile, but her eyes were sad. "We were good, weren't we?" She smiled, more brightly and winked at him. He always liked when she did that. Even though he was looking at a beautiful woman of 69, he felt, briefly, like he was the 18 year old boy he had been, just on the cusp of adulthood. He then thought of some of their dates and blushed.

"Why now, my Sam, I always loved making you blush. Your face is lovely then."

"Me? Lovely?" He looked at her, then he laughed. "Martha, I've been called many things in my life—pig, ugly, but never lovely."

"Well, the people who called you that didn't see the sweet, sensitive young man I knew. The sweet, sensitive man you still are."

Sam laughed and waved his hand like he was trying to brush aside the compliment. He blushed again. Then he leaned back and patted his wide stomach. "I'm certainly a much bigger guy than I used to be."

"Oh, that is just the effect of age, Sam. It happens to all of us—I'm certainly not the girl I used to be. Having three kids will do that to you."

"Well, Martha. . ." Sam hesitated and took a swallow of coffee. Then, "May I say something? I don't want to say anything wrong."

"Certainly, you may." Martha reached across and placed her hand on top of his again. "I can't imagine you saying anything that would bother me."

"Well, I hope I don't. What I wanted to tell you is that you are even more beautiful now than before when we were just kids."

"Oh, Sam. Don't be silly. I'm an old lady." Still, a smile formed on her face, and her eyes shined as she gazed at him.

"I mean it, Martha. When you're young, you think you're so... I don't know handsome or beautiful, but you don't realize you're simply unformed. But, age builds beauty by the way we live, like a painting that a Master worked on over many years. It transforms from its beginnings as a clear, empty canvas to a detailed, beautiful, and defined piece of art. And Martha, you are like such a painting."

Martha looked and him and smiled. "Sam, that was the most beautiful, perhaps the loveliest thing, anyone has ever said to me."

Sam also smiled.

"You know, Sam. I've thought very much about those days. I worried about you when you went to Vietnam. And I checked up on you."

"You did? But you went to college in California. I assumed you simply put us behind you."

Martha laughed and sipped her tea. "Yes, but it wasn't the stone ages, although my grandkids seem to think so. And sometimes, it seems like it was the dark ages. I called friends I knew from Bethberg on the phone and wrote to others."

"I never knew."

"I thought it was better that way. We had made a break, and I didn't want to cause you any pain.

Martha smiled a sad smile. "You had enough to deal with being over there."

"Yeah, I was all wrapped up being a Marine in the war."

"I imagined that. And I was so relieved when I found out you made it back home safely."

Sam was amazed. He had never considered that she would keep track of him the way he did of her.

"And I was so proud of you, Martha, to know you graduated with honors, Summa Cum Laude, with a degree in Physics from Stanford University."

"Why, Sam. You were doing the same thing!" She laughed and gently slapped his hand.

"Yep, I suppose great minds think alike."

"Uh-huh. . ."

"And I was even prouder when you went to Princeton and got your Ph.D. there. It couldn't have been easy in those days, as an African-American woman."

"Noooo. It sure wasn't. I had some serious battles to fight."

"But you succeeded, as I knew you would."

Chapter 52

August 1, The Present

Max sat in his makeshift office and smiled. He was happy with the direction of his immediate plans, but he also had much larger goals to put in motion once this vengeance was complete against his old adversary Sam Sadlowski.

And that, he was certain, would happen soon. He was putting that machine's transmission into gear, and it would soon run over Sadlowski and crush him with its tread.

He poured himself a shot of rye. "To your death, fucker," he said and shot it down. Then he poured another.

After finishing the good detective, he would begin expanding his reach through the distribution of drugs— heroin, other opioids, and meth. He wasn't going to worry about pot. He would let that to the smaller dealers. Pot had had its day, and Max considered it to be small time now. One day in conversation with one of the other RiotRiders, he said, "They're going to fucking legalize pot, and then they will regulate and tax that shit. So, it ain't going to be any use even for money laundering. So fuck that."

But drugs would not be the entirety of his planned empire. He also wanted a stake in prostitution, gambling, and loan-sharking, old standbys that always offered easy ways to make a substantial amount of money. That was a prospect Max liked very much.

In order to accomplish his goals, he would have to eliminate any competition, at least at the lower end to begin, so he could claim a portion of the northeastern part of Pennsylvania, from above Wilkes-Barre/Scranton to the Lehigh Valley as his turf.

But he would remain behind the scenes, like a man manipulating others without being noticed. He liked that idea, at least in terms of the illegal activity. But he did like the idea of being seen by the public as an important person. He wanted both.

He was now in his 40s, and Max wanted to live in a large suburban house and have a hot trophy wife to show off and give him kids.

He smiled at the thought of the future. *I'll even start a charity. How is that for fucking with them? That'll keep all the pigs and feds guessing. I'll look legitimate to everyone else.*

Then, I'll even begin to use my full name again and be proud of it: Maximillian Herbert Esel. And all those fuckers will cheer for me when I give money to their charities. I'll dress in a fucking tux and look good.

And I'll have power.

Chapter 53

August 1, The Present

At midnight, most of the patients in the Bethberg Hospital Hospice, a facility about two blocks from the main hospital, in a quiet wooded area, were sleeping, and all was quiet except for the occasional blip of a medical monitor. A small staff of nurses and aides worked the evening shift, and all the patients were resting or sleeping.

Outside the building three men, dressed in black, including head masks, slowly approached the facility and watched carefully. They saw that a police car would slowly drive by about every 60 minutes, because almost nothing ever happened in terms of crime at this place. Instead, it was a place of rest and peaceful death.

The Bethberg Hospital Hospice had an established reputation of providing excellent end-of-life care. The staff was dedicated and professional and committed to giving the best care they could for the patients and counseling and understanding for the family and loved ones. The hospice had been in existence for almost 30 years and had one of the finest ratings for palliative care in the country.

This was a place of calm and quiet, and nothing was allowed to interrupt the staff's efficient and compassionate care for their patients. It was always quiet and peaceful there.

It would not be serene this night.

The men, who were waiting outside, knew from prior checking of the place only two people would be on duty at the moment, a nurse and an aide. They should provide no difficulty. They would be easy to overcome.

The men waited. They knew the aide would go to the back door and stand outside to smoke a cigarette at about 12:10, and she always kept the door unlocked. They had done their surveillance, and they knew what to expect.

They saw her step from inside the building and light up her cigarette. As she exhaled her smoke and held the cigarette in her left hand, one man emerged from waiting just behind the garbage pails, grabbed her from behind, clamped one hand over her mouth to keep her from screaming, and then injected her in the neck and held her until her struggling stopped.

He then pulled her to behind the garbage pails, gagged her, and tied her with plastic bands. He signaled to the other two men.

The three men quickly entered the building. The nurse was sitting at her desk and looked up in surprise to see guns pointed at her.

"Don't move at all, bitch." The intruder's tone was clear, and so was the threat, but this was someone not easily intimidated. Jeanne Toner had made a career of being a nurse, first in the army where she served both in field and standard hospitals, and she had assisted with terrible wounds suffered by soldiers and civilians. She had served 20 years, retired, and then moved into working for the hospice.

She had cared for dying soldiers, and now she tended to the elderly and ill in their last days, and she did her best to help them be in as much comfort and as little pain as possible.

Jeanne had also been a physical fitness fanatic, training in martial arts most of her life, and now, in her mid-40s, was a 6th degree black belt in Okinawan style karate.

Jeanne neither frightened nor intimidated easily.

When she saw the intruders, the first thing she thought of was that they were going to try to steal drugs. What other reason she quickly had wondered could they possibly be there for? *Well, that certainly was not going to happen, not on my watch,* she thought.

While one of the men stood next to her, the other two went into the patients' section. Now she was deeply concerned. They should have been trying to find the drugs, if this were truly a robbery. They should have asked her about where the drugs were kept. This definitely was something unusual.

She looked up at the man next to her and saw him briefly look into the other room.

She quickly made two decisions: that she would not cooperate with them and that she would do anything she had to in order to protect her patients.

Jeanne saw him look away from her for a moment. Without hesitation, she reached up grabbed him by the wrist and twisted the gun away as she rose. Then she hit with a knife hand strike to his throat, a killing technique she learned from her training. She crashed the edge of her palm in a hard sudden thrust to his throat.

Choking for air, he gasped and went down hard, crashing against a cabinet and knocking it over.

In the quiet of the night, it sounded like an explosion.

"What the fuck was that?" The two other men turned and rushed back into the room.

They saw the nurse scrambling on the ground for the fallen fellow's gun, with him on the ground holding his throat and breathing in very shallow gasps.

The first one aimed his gun and fired three rounds rapidly. All of the bullets slammed into the nurse, in her chest and top of her head. The effect was devastating and immediate.

"Fuck, man. You killed her." This one was worried. "That wasn't in the plan. We were supposed to follow the plan!"

"No fucking shit, man. Look at what she did. She would've shot us. Was that in the fucking plan? Would that have helped?"

"Fuck, fuck, fuck. We're in deep shit here."

"Now get your shit together, and take care of this. But we got to cover ourselves and quickly. Get him and shove him in the van. Do that now!"

He helped the fallen man up, and half-carried and half-dragged him to the van and threw him in the back, then he returned to the room.

"Now, fast. Let's grab the girl."

"Man, this is a fuckup," the first one said.

Soon, they had Maria strapped to a bed in an old, unmarked van.

Chapter 54

August 1, The Present

"Almost fucking ready. Soon, the bastard will be mine."
Max sat at the improvised desk in a room above a garage
on the outskirts of Bethberg. Only one half a mile from
the steel factory, it had served as a perfect place for his
operation, at least for now. The man who owned and ran
the small garage owed him a favor—his son was doing
time for selling meth, and Max, knowing he was from the
same hometown, protected him, and let his father know.
Now, his father would do anything for Max.

But soon, he would have an office for his operations
fit for a king. He just had to finish this particular
operation first.

Max was speaking with his lieutenant. Simple Smith was
his street name—he was called that because, as a child,
he was very quiet, and people thought he was stupid. But
he wasn't, only very introverted. He would rather listen
to others talk than say much himself, but it did not mean
that he was not intelligent. Still, it caused problems for
him, and he was often a target of bullies because they
thought he was dumb.

Much had changed, though, since Smith was young.
He wasn't picked on anymore. He had learned when he
was a young teenager how to fight, and he developed a
reputation for being vicious. When he fought, he not only

defeated his opponents, but he made sure they were left with injuries.

This soon kept would-be tormentors from bothering him.

He also learned that he had a talent for buying and selling, not in a pushy way, but with a quiet confidence. Had he chosen to go to college and earned a business degree, he might have been able to move successfully up the corporate ladder, but Smith had no desire to wear a coat and tie, and he hated the concept of being controlled and forced into a timid conformity.

Instead of looking for a legal nine-to-five job, he thrived, instead, on the street, primarily in the realm of procuring and moving drugs and weapons.

Now, when he talked, others listened. As Max's second-in-command, people on the street knew he was very dangerous, both on his own but also as a weapon in Max's holster. He was excellent at organizing, planning, and keep records. And he was loyal and devoted to Max. Max had seen something in him that no one else had, and he would never forget that.

For this plan, they would have six other guys, whom Smith had checked out, in addition to him and Max. Eight men in total would be plenty to surround that old fucker, Sadlowski. They would get him in a circle by luring him to the old steel ruins, and when Max gave the signal, finish him. This was Max's show, after all. It was something he knew his boss had obsessed about for many years, and this would end it. First, Sadlowski's son was killed about ten years ago, then his partner's daughter would be used as bait, and then Sadlowski would be finished.

Smith would be happy, because then they could return to what he considered far more important—expanding their meth and heroin network. Huge money was waiting to be made, and he was looking forward to it. *Fuck this life of hiding out,* he thought. *I want more.*

Soon they would be wealthy and powerful. Then Smith would take vengeance on those who had mocked him. *I remember all of them. They'll pay.*

They knew they could get Sadlowski to show up. He would have two incentives—to save the daughter of his former partner and to take his own revenge for the death of his son.

He would come alone. Smith had let him know that if he brought anyone or told the cops, they would kill the girl immediately. They had taken the girl from the hospital, and they had let Sam speak to her briefly, only enough to let him for sure that they had her. Sam, being the boy scout he was, would do exactly as they said. Then they kill him, then the girl. She would have no further use to them.

It would happen tonight.

Chapter 55

August 1, The Present

Sam had received the letter dropped in his mailbox—hand delivered, with no postage on it. He opened it. In a scrawled handwriting, he read:

We have your buddy's daughter Maria. You want her to be returned alive, come tomorrow night to the old steel mill. Go to the eastern end. COME ALONE! NO COPS! NO FRIENDS!
OR THE GIRL DIES. Be there at midnight.
Sam crumbled the paper and threw it to the floor.
He would be there.
He had no choice.
But he would be prepared.

Chapter 56

August 1, The Present

"Dad, please forgive me. I'm so sorry." Sam was back in his original home and sitting at the dinner table. He had come into the room to talk with his son.

It was early in the morning, and Sam was wondering why his boy, who always seemed to have trouble going to bed early and getting up early for school, was sitting there.

Sam got a cup of coffee and sat down with him.

"So, what's up, Josh?"

Josh looked at Sam with a strange, almost distant gaze, as if he were looking at him from across some great distance.

"Pop, I'm so sorry."

"Why, Josh? What are you sorry for?"

As they spoke, Josh's face changed. It lost color and Sam could see that Josh wasn't breathing.

"Josh! You have to breathe! C'mon, breathe for me."

Josh was slouched over in the driver's seat in the old car, and fumes had filled the garage.

"Josh! Josh!" Sam could feel panic setting in. He had to get to his boy, but he felt like he was moving through mud up to his neck.

"I'm so sorry, Pop." Sam could see that Josh was already dead, but he kept repeating this anyway.

Sam screamed, and they were back at the table. It was after Josh's funeral. Sam was dressed in his black suit, and Josh in his blue sports coat.

It was after everyone had left, and they were alone.

"Pop, I'm sorry. I should have come to you for help. I know that."

"Josh, I would've done anything to help you. Anything."

"Pop, I know that. But now, I have to ask you to do something else."

"Anything, Josh. Just tell me."

"Help Maria, Pop. You're the only one who can save her. I tried to, but it didn't work.
You've got to help her."

"You did help her, Josh. I know what you did and why you did it. You were braver than any man I had served with in Vietnam or on the force. Braver than I am."

"Pop, Max has her again. I didn't save her."

"Yes, you did Josh. You did. Never forget that. I am the one who failed, not you."

As he said those words, he saw Josh starting to fade away, beginning to recede and change.

Then he was walking to Josh in his coffin at the wake. His beautiful son, his precious boy, the hope of his life, the light in his soul was dead. What else was left?

Sam reached out and laid his hand on Josh's crossed hands, the ones he had held when Josh was a little boy, the ones he had bandaged when they were skinned from falling off his bike, the ones that held a baseball bat and hit singles and doubles with ease and grace, the ones he hoped would one day give a woman a ring and marry.

Now they were cold and hard, all the life gone from them. Just as he felt his soul had been drained away.

Josh opened his eyes and looked at his grieving father. "Please forgive me, Pop. I'm sorry. I'm sorry."

"No, Josh, forgive me for failing you."

"But promise me, Pop. Promise me that you will help Maria now."

"I will, Josh. I promise you."

Sam's eyes opened slowly, and for a few seconds, he was still in the dream. Then he realized what had happened and where he was.

First Sam cried.

After he stopped sobbing, Sam knew what he had to do.

CHAPTER 57

August 2, The Present

All the threads of Sam's past seemed to be weaving together to complete the tapestry of his life. Josh's death, Maria's illness, his detective work with his homicide partner Steven, his fighting along with Roosevelt in the Vietnam War, his battle against Maledicus with the IPS, and his life-long love for Martha, all seemed to be intertwining at this particular juncture in his life.

The dream had shaken Sam badly. No matter how many times he dreamt about Josh, he always woke with a feeling of deep sorrow and guilt. No matter how many times he had reasoned the circumstances through, he always returned to the same conclusion: he should have been able to do something to help his on. *I should have seen it coming. I was his Pop. I should've seen it.*

And now he knew why. Now he knew what had happened to his son. Now he knew who had killed him, as if Max had pulled the trigger himself.

Now Sam was certain of what he should do.

Sam had never been a hesitant man. He was not one who procrastinated or put off unpleasant tasks. But he hated what he had to do now, and that was to lie to Roosevelt.

Roosevelt was the one person Sam had respected the most in life. He was a brother in arms, having served in the same Marine Corps Unit in the Vietnam War.

Moreover, Roosevelt had been a granite port during the torrent that was Sam's existence at the time of Josh's death. Roosevelt had stood by him, and Sam knew that Roosevelt would give his life to help Sam if it were needed.

That was the problem.

Sam couldn't bear the idea of anything happening to Roosevelt or to Jeremy or Helen, because he knew that they, too, would stand by him. Sam had grown to respect all of them almost as much as he did Roosevelt. They had, after all, proved themselves in the battle against Maledicus.

And the idea of anything bad happening to Helen was the worst of all. Not only was she an extraordinary person, but also, she was now Helena's "mother." Sam would not let anything happen, if he could help it that would take Helen away from Helena. He would rather lie to them and incur their wrath and distrust rather than put them in harm's way with Max.

Besides, the meetings were on different nights: his rendezvous with Max was tonight, Friday night, and the IPS would investigate on Saturday. If all went well, he would surprise them by showing up on Saturday. If not, well . . .

Sam had made his decision, but he couldn't tell the others why. He hated doing that, but that was the way it had to be. He couldn't place Roosevelt's, Helen's, and Jeremy's life in danger for a battle he had to fight. But there was one person who could help.

Sam picked up his phone and made a call.

Chapter 58

August 2, The Present

"Fuck you, Rosy," Sam growled. "I ain't going." Sam moved away from Roosevelt and sat on the opposite side of his kitchen table. Sam looked like he hadn't slept in a while. His clothes were filthy, and he needed a shave.

Sam had not answered his phone, despite several calls from Helen, Jeremy, and Roosevelt, so he decided that the time had come to pay a visit in person, alone, to his old friend.

Roosevelt had gone to Sam's door and kept ringing the bell. He knew Sam was there. He had seen movement, and he could be just as stubborn as Sam. Finally, Sam opened the door, scowled, and then walked away.

Roosevelt followed him.

Roosevelt looked at his friend in surprise. This was the angriest he had seen Sam since Vietnam. "Samuel, I do not understand why you are so upset, but we need you. We need you at our attempt to get rid of this ghost. This was all talked about before. You were there, and we need you."

They were talking at Sam's house. Roosevelt had refused to take Sam's ignoring of his phone calls as a final answer. Something was wrong, badly wrong, and he wanted to know what it was.

"Samuel, stop acting like an ass. We need you, and I have never known you to abandon your responsibilities."

"What the fuck do you know about my responsibilities, man?" Sam was standing across from Roosevelt in his small kitchen. He slammed his fist down on the counter. "I've fucked up way too many times, Rosy. You don't know about most of how I have. It's all on me, Rosy, on me. And I can't help you now."

Roosevelt stared at him and did not look away. "I have known you for many years, since we were just young men. You, along with Jeremy and Father Bruno, are the best men I have ever known. You are not a fuckup. And if I heard anyone else say that about you, they would have to fight me, even now, at my age. If you think I am going to let you get away with something like this, talking about yourself like this, you are completely wrong."

"Goddamnit. What the fuck do I have to do to get rid of you, old man?"

"I really do not know the answer to your question. But you are starting to piss me off, Samuel."

"Really, Rosy? Well, I'm already good and pissed off. Who the fuck do you think you are to keep checking up on me? I ain't no kid, and I sure as hell don't need your fucking help."

Roosevelt could feel the anger rising in him, but he tried to control it. He did not come here to have a fight with his old friend. He could see this was nothing like anything he had expected. He could tell Samuel was hiding something, but the stubborn fellow would not budge. Roosevelt controlled himself and attempted to soften his tone. "Just tell me what is wrong. That is all I want to know."

Sam looked at Roosevelt and almost answered, but then he stopped himself.

No matter what happened, no matter how pissed off at him Roosevelt got, he wasn't going to let him know what was going on. He knew that ghost they were investigating presented danger, but that was nothing compared to the threat of Max. *If that son of a bitch learned about my friends, they would all be in danger. I can't let that happen.*

Sam wanted Roosevelt out of this place. He had to get ready for his meeting, and he didn't want his friend to know about it. While both meetings were to occur at the mill, they would be on separate ends of the facility, and it was so large, they should not have any inkling that the other was occurring. And they would be on different nights. At least, that is what Sam hoped for.

"Nothing is wrong, man. Not a fucking thing, except for you being here. Don't you understand a fucking word I'm saying? Get the fuck out of here. Now!"

"Fuck you too, Samuel. Fuck you." Roosevelt spoke softly, then he turned and left.

Sam looked at Roosevelt as he left and thought, *I'm really sorry, Rosy, but I had to do that.*

Chapter 59

August 3, The Present

The IPS, or at least the present members, had decided. They were going to try to rid the steel mill ruins of this spirit that was threatening people. They had been undecided for a while because of their distaste for investigating for the investors, but the circumstances had changed.

Since three of Helen's students had confided in her what had happened to them when they went on an adventure at the mill, they had decided to act to rid the area of this malevolent ghost. None of them could stand the idea of the thing threatening the innocent. The circumstances had altered. Now, it was no longer simply an investigation, although one with risk. Once again, they were going to do battle with some kind of supernatural entity, but without one of their warriors present.

And they couldn't wait until Saturday as they had planned. With the youngster's life at risk, The I.P.S. would go tonight, on Friday.

It was Helen's ferocity that led them into battle. She couldn't stand the idea that one of her students had been captured by this ghost or whatever he was. That youngster might still be alive, and if he was, then she would do whatever she could to fight to rescue him.

Roosevelt and Jeremy were startled by her intensity. She reminded them of some kind of Celtic Queen exhorting them into battle.

"Are you with me or not? I'm going to fight for this kid…Are you? I can never, never, let an innocent be hurt if there is something I can do about it."

The only problem with their plan was that Sam was nowhere to be found, and he wasn't answering his cell phone.

"We cannot wait any longer. We will simply have to trust that Samuel is okay." But Roosevelt was clearly worried about his friend. Roosevelt had not told them about his visit to Samuel. He kept his concern to himself. He had known Samuel for many years, decades, but since the death of Samuel's son, this has been the most depressed he had seen him. He was angry with Samuel, but that would not keep Roosevelt from helping his old friend. But first, they had a more urgent matter.

They had a responsibility, and Roosevelt never shirked what he saw as his duty.

Jeremy and Helen were also worried about Sam, but all they could do for him now was to be there if he chose to talk to them. They also were compelled to try to deal with this ghost, if that was what it was.

"We are with you, always. Let's go kick this executioner's butt and rescue that kid."

"Well spoken, Jeremy. It is time for battle." Roosevelt felt almost like he had when he was in combat in Vietnam.

They loaded their van with all their equipment, plus a few other items.

"I wish we had someone with us who could try blessing this place," Jeremy had said.

"I understand," Roosevelt replied. "But it didn't work very well last time."

"And Martin will not help, not with what happened last time," Helen said. "But we can still try the blessing itself. I paid attention, and I believe I can lead an attempt at a cleansing. It might work, or it might be futile, but we may as well give it a try."

"I agree with you, Helen. We should use everything we can in our arsenal against this Schwarznacht." Roosevelt had taken on the bearing of a Marine Corps officer. As he spoke, he missed his nephew Patrick with a deep gash to his psyche. His nephew would have been able to lead them. Roosevelt never told anyone that he felt guilty over his nephew's death. *Why should an old man have survived that battle,* he thought. *Why should a vibrant young man like Patrick perish when an old man like me simply continues on? But, Semper Fi, Patrick. Semper Fi.*

"And I hesitate to ask anyone else to do this with us. We really are unsure of what to expect," Helen added. That uncertainty, however, was not enough to keep her from trying to protect her students and other kids who might be victimized by this spirit.

"I wish though, we had more time to prepare," Jeremy said.

"Sometimes, Jeremy, in the course of battle, you simply have to improvise," Roosevelt had said as they were packing their equipment earlier. He had seen that Jeremy was bothered by the way they were doing it. "I wish, also, that we had more time to figure out exactly what to do, but I do not think that this boy has much time himself."

"Roosevelt, I do understand. I'm just scared here."

"Jeremy, so am I."

"As am I," added Helen.

"Still," Jeremy said in a quiet, firm tone. "Let's go fight this being."

With that, they finished packing.

About ten minutes later, they were packed and driving. After another ten minutes, they arrived at the steel mill on the outskirts of the town.

Chapter 60

August 5, The Present

"There's someplace I have to go tonight, and no, you can't go with me." Steven tried to be as firm as he possibly could be. He needed his wife to listen to him, not that he had any control over her. But he hoped that just this once, she would do as he asked.

They were in the living room of their modest split-level suburban home, and Steven was acting as if he were on a top secret investigation, but Monica knew there were no more of those for her husband. He was on desk duty until he retired in two more months. Then he would put his badge and gun aside, and they would simply try to enjoy their lives the best they could, even with what they had to face.

Monica ignored Steven's declaration. "Do you know where our baby is, Steven?" Monica looked directly at her husband. She could read his face with the knowledge of having been married 28 years. She loved him more than she had loved anyone, except for her daughter, Maria—that girl owned her heart. But she was also no one's pushover. She was a strong woman, and she had always been his partner and not his doormat.

Steven looked down and to the right before answering. "I don't know," he said.

"That is a bald-faced lie, Steven, and you know I can't stand it when you don't tell me the truth." She could see deep anguish in his eyes. She knew he was trying to protect her.

"Do you think I'm some kind of delicate flower that wilts with bad news?"

She was not a large woman; many considered her dainty with a 5'1" frame and a ballet dancer's body, but inside was a good heart and a core of steel.

Her eyes flashed now, and she glared at him. "You know me better than that, mister!"

And Steven knew he was in deep trouble when she referred to him as "mister." It was as bad as when he was in trouble as a child and his mother addressed him by his full name. But he would not budge, no matter how angry his wife might get.

"I know you do, but I have something to do, and you are not coming with me. That's final."

Monica glared at him, feeling even more anger rising. But she knew this was not the time for a fight, not if she wanted to know what was going on. She controlled herself, making her face look calm, and though it was a great effort, she was a woman of enormous self-control and inner strength.

"Fine," she snapped, after releasing a long breath. "But you'd better be careful, Steven, and you'd better come home with Maria."

"I will," was all he said. As he got to the front door, he stopped. "I love you." With that, he went outside and got into his car.

Monica waited.

She knew she couldn't simply tail him. He was a detective for far too long not to notice being followed. But she always paid attention.

He had been looking online for articles about the old steel ruins on the outskirts of town. When she had asked about it, he had answered that some damned casino was trying to come to town. That just didn't sound right. Steven was a good man, always faithful, and provided a comfortable living for his family, but he loved to go to Atlantic City and play blackjack there once or twice a year, and he occasionally visited the casino in Bethlehem, PA. You would certainly think he would be in favor of a such a place coming to Bethberg.

Plus, he had that look in his eyes that he got whenever he had an important lead on a case. That convinced her of what to do.

Monica went to the gun safe, took out her gun, a Beretta semi-automatic, loaded it with a full clip, and went to her car.

Now was the time to see what was happening. If it involved her daughter, then she would be there also.

Chapter 61

August 5, The Present

The members of the IPS arrived at the western end of the steel mill, and they looked grim. They had done battle the previous year with the demon Maledicus, and while they had been victorious, they had suffered a terrible cost for their efforts. Roosevelt's nephew, Patrick, a battle hardened Marine, had died in the conflict. Still, they had fought to save a child then, and they were fighting to save a teenager now. Their faces were set and determined. They looked like they were ready to go to war.

But they also felt depleted. Not having Sam with them was a blow to their strength. And they had no one to take his place. They all felt the sting of Sam's absence. And he was not the only one who would not be helping.

While Martin declined to be there, he did offer suggestions and the use of some of his paraphernalia so that the IPS could attempt a cleansing of the area themselves. Roosevelt and Jeremy took the equipment with their thanks.

The IPS arrived at the western end of the old mill at about 6 P.M. They wanted to have light to be able to set up their equipment. It was still summer, so they would have plenty of daytime to work with.

"Looks like we are going to have to deal with some bad weather also." Helen had been keeping a watch on the forecasts, and she hoped they were wrong.

A massive summer storm, including lightning and thunder was likely to hit. Normally, that would mean staying away from a place like this, filled with old steel structures, but a boy's life was in danger.

They had prepared for such an eventuality—extra tarps for the equipment, ponchos, and a small generator, and extra gasoline if needed. They were all wearing waterproof boots also. They had agreed that if they did not find anything tonight, the boy would be reported to the police as missing, but they thought this was the best chance of getting him back. If they failed, the civil authorities would be unlikely to save the teenager.

"Okay guys, we have our stuff set up. I have the control table in the van, just in case the weather does get bad. The cameras are up, and I hope we are ready to do this." Jeremy didn't like the lack of real planning. They were doing things too quickly. He liked order and careful preparation, but he was willing to compromise his preferences for the sake of saving the youth.

When all the equipment was arranged, paying special attention to the digital recorders, because they hoped to capture some recording which might help them find the boy, Jeremy began the cleansing.

"One of us has to take over for Martin, so I'll do it." Jeremy hadn't asked to do it, and they simply nodded their agreement.

As he began, Helen and Roosevelt walked with him. He gave them sage to hold, and they carried large flashlights to illuminate the path. No one wanted anyone to be hurt, especially by falling. They moved slowly and stepped carefully as Jeremy began.

"I'll begin with 'The Lord's Prayer,' because that is what Martin did," Jeremy said and glanced at them.

He opened the Bible and read:
"Our Father, who art in heaven,
Hallowed be Thy name.
Thy Kingdom come,
Thy will be done,
On earth as it is in heaven. . ."

As Jeremy read, they felt a sudden drop in temperature, which could just mean an oncoming storm, but the decline in the heat was fast. The sky also darkened, as clouds began to move over.

Jeremy continued,
"Give us this day our daily bread.
And forgive us our trespasses,
As we forgive those who trespass against us.
And lead us not into temptation,
But deliver us from evil.
For Thine is the kingdom, the power and the glory, for ever and ever.
Amen"

Helen and Roosevelt replied, "Amen."

"Sinners!" The voice was soft, but it could still be heard. They all stopped and listened.

"Are you ok, Jeremy?"

"Yes, but that was strange. Something is here." He looked around then shook his head and continued. "Let's go, guys, to the next piece—I'm feeling, let's just say, a bit weirded out. Maybe this will help:

"The Lord is my shepherd;
I shall not want.
He maketh me to lie down in green pastures;
He leadeth me beside the still waters.
He restoreth my soul;
He leadeth me in the paths of righteousness for his name's sake.

Yea, though I walk through the valley of the shadow of death,

I will fear no evil. . ."

"Sinners must be punished!" This time, the voice was clear.

"Seems like we've heard something like this before, and we are here to deal with you!" Helen was now getting angry. Her eyes lit with anger.

"Helen, keep calm, but ready." Roosevelt looked and sounded like the Marine Corps officer he had been many years before.

Helen looked at him and nodded.

Jeremy continued,

"I will fear no EVIL: for thou art with me; thy rod and thy staff they comfort me.

Thou preparest a table before me in the presence of mine enemies;

Thou annointest my head with oil; my cup runneth over.

Surely goodness and mercy shall follow me all the days of my life

And I will dwell in the house of the Lord forever."

When he completed the Psalm, they stopped and listened. They couldn't hear any more voices, but a small wind picked up.

"Well, this seems to be having some kind of effect. Let's go on." Helen spoke quietly and led the way, moving to the area where she had been pushed. "We are moving onto the remains of a catwalk, and there is a big drop to a pit below." She pointed to the fall. "Please be very careful."

Jeremy replaced the Bible into the satchel, then he took out more sage and a tablet.

"Martin suggested the ample use of this stuff, so let's try it." With that, Jeremy handed it to Roosevelt and Helen and then lit more sage. "I am going to combine several incantations intended to remove spirits."

Jeremy fumbled with the notes for a moment. He realized that they were upside down. He smiled an embarrassed grin, then he righted the papers.

"Okay, here we go," Jeremy said. "If spirits or demons threaten anyone in this place, I Fight Fire with Fire, Wind with Wind, Earth with Earth, and Fire with Fire. We expel them to the void, nullify their abilities, remove their curses, and purify this place—completely! To all that would harm others, to unclean spirits, we command you to begone from here! You are cast out!"

The wind started to pick up more, and flashes of lightning illuminated the sky in the distance.

Chapter 62

August 5, The Present

Sam couldn't quite believe that bastard Max was back, but what the hell. It was like a movie monster, like Dracula in the old Hammer movies—he just kept coming back. Well, this time, maybe Sam had the wooden stake needed to put an end to this creature.

He was certainly going to try to drive the proverbial stake through this vampire's heart.

Sam wanted to stand over Max's corpse and know the man who had murdered his son was dead.

But this situation was worse than he thought. That asshole Max had Maria. That couldn't be allowed to stand. She was his goddaughter, and he loved her as if she were his own daughter.

Beyond that, the poor girl was in terrible shape; she was dying, and now this degradation, to be ripped from her hospice was worse than anyone should have to endure. Sam hadn't been a very good godfather to her. He was sure of that, no matter what Steven said, but he could take care of this, and get her back, away from that scumbag Max.

Sam felt his mood changing. The deep darkness he had been in wasn't gone, but it was being altered. Now, instead of despair, he felt anger, slow, burning rage, like an iron nugget that had been heated to a white-hot core of steel. For several weeks he had been stuck in a pit of self-loathing, and it was still there, but with the anger, he could feel a change coming.

He dressed in black, like in the old days, including black work boots and loose fitting trousers. He had a gun, a 9mm Berretta in a shoulder holster, a blackjack on his belt, and a .38 Smith and Wesson revolver in an ankle holster. If there were to be any trouble, and he considered that possibility to be very likely, then he would be prepared.

He would be there tonight like they had said, and they were probably watching him, so they would see he was traveling alone. But that didn't mean he wouldn't have backup. He was too well trained to do that game. He also would not use his home phone or regular cell. He didn't know what capacity they had, but he had an older burner phone that he kept for such situations.

He punched in a number... "I'm going there now."

Chapter 63

August 5, The Present

Jeremy, Helen, and Roosevelt looked around at the darkening sky. Clearly, a major storm was coming. The clouds had formed above them, blanketing the sky with ominous darkness. Flashes of lightning could be seen in the distance.

Helen stopped them and pointed at the clouds. "Time to put on the ponchos."

They put their equipment down, quickly donned them, and put the hoods up. The ponchos weren't perfect raingear, but they would help. If it stormed, they would have a minimum of protection. Then they picked up their gear, for which they carried extra plastic to cover the valuable equipment and continued.

Jeremy resumed. He wouldn't be satisfied until he ran the entirety of the cleansing. He wasn't Martin, and he didn't have experience doing this kind of thing, but he was committed to their work, and he believed in the rightness of their cause. Jeremy hoped that would be sufficient to have an effect with the rite.

"This is the last piece he included," Jeremy said. "I hope it works. I read it over before we came here, and I wanted to end the blessing with it because of its power." Jeremy stood erect and spoke in a loud and ringing voice:

"I pray to the Goddess and God, to all the spirits of good,

Bless this dwelling and those who abide here,

Give protection to your servants,

Lend us your power so that we may dispel anything negative or evil herein.

Spirits of the Wood,

Spirits of the Wind

Spirits of the Earth,

Spirits of the Air,

Spirits of the Water

Bless us with your power and bless this house with your power, protect all who live here.

Spirits of evil, begone!

Spirits and unnatural creatures, begone!

Leave this place, and let the good in!

Leave this place and let the Goddess and the Horned God in!

We compel you in their names to leave!

You are unwelcome here!

Begone! Begone! Begone!"

When he finished, Jeremy had to catch his breath. He had tried to put all the power and projection into his voice that he could.

"Jeremy, are you okay?" Helen looked at his flushed face and was concerned about his physical condition.

He nodded his head yes. Then he caught his breath. "I'm fine. Just haven't tried to project like that in a very long time. Last time I did that, I was in a high school play."

"So, Jeremy, just last year." Roosevelt looked at him and smiled.

"Yeah, Rosy," Jeremy said and laughed.

Then a peal of thunder rang out, stopping their joking. But no lightning appeared.

They went silent.

"Did it help?" Helen asked.

They stopped and looked around. No one could tell if the blessing had any effect or not. All they were sure of was that the clouds had become even more ominous. They had become denser in the sky, and they had darkened with an odd color on the edges.

"I'm not sure I like the look of those clouds. This might get bad very quickly." Helen stood looking past the ruins of the western wall of the factory.

"Why, they just look like storm clouds to me." Jeremy looked at Helen.

"Do you see that greenish tinge around the ends of the clouds?"

"Yes, I do," Roosevelt answered. "Is it significant?"

"It might be. We need to keep an eye on those clouds. Right now, it suggests the possible formation of a funnel."

"A tornado? What did we get ourselves into this time?" Jeremy laughed but could not hide his worry.

"As long as there is no rotation, we'll be fine." Helen, despite her assurances, looked concerned.

Chapter 64

August 5, The Present

Sam knew he had to perform this rescue, even though he also realized this might be the last day of his life. Sam had faced danger before, especially when he served in Vietnam, and he realized that every day in country was a day he might die. And he was able to do that as a young man, when he had his whole life ahead of him.

Now, Sam knew he was reaching the end. How much longer he had was something he could not know, but he definitely was on the last few laps of his life's car race. The finish line would soon be in sight. And he was ready for it.

Fuck it, he thought. *We all have to go sometime.*

He had parked about half a mile from the ruins. He pulled his Camaro into a spot on the eastern end of the ruins, one he remembered from using it for stakeouts when he was on the Bethberg Police Force. He drove the last quarter of a mile with his lights off. He knew the road well, and he did not want to take any chances that he might be seen.

He turned the car off and got out as quietly as he could. Satisfied that his car was hidden behind trees, he moved forward with extreme caution.

I hope this works. I don't care if I die, but I want to get Maria back safely, Max thought. *I have to make sure I do this correctly. I can't fuck this up.*

Sam walked carefully, judging his footing by the occasional moonlight that peeked briefly from the cloud cover. He had a flashlight, but he wasn't going to use it unless it was necessary.

Sam had been in this area enough times in the past that he knew his way. One of his skills in life had always been with directions. He almost never got lost, and if he had been somewhere one time, he usually remembered it in detail. This was not a skill that applied to all aspects of his life, mainly it worked with directions.

Max's guys had told him to be at the eastern end, near the old offices, so he was headed there now. He moved slowly and carefully, just in case he was being watched, which he assumed was happening.

I'm sure they see me. If not, they are even dumber than I think they are.

He saw the old trailer that used to house offices for the steel factory. *Time to go in.*

Chapter 65

August 5, The Present

"Sinners! You are all sinners. And all sinners must be punished!" The voice was loud and resonated even above the noise of the oncoming storm.

Jeremy looked at the others. "I'm not sure this is working."

"I think you may be correct, Jeremy. We may have to try something else." Roosevelt was worried though. He really was not sure what they could do. Against Maledicus they had a real plan, and they also had their full contingent plus Patrick. Still, we have to do the best we can.

The wind increased, and the clouds were starting a slow rotation in the sky. "Look at that—it looks like a funnel cloud might be forming." Jeremy pointed to the cloud. "This could get bad here. What do you think we should do?"

"If it were not for the missing boy, I would say to try again tomorrow, but let us see what we can do." Roosevelt hated the idea of abandoning their attempts to find the teen they were certain that Scwarznacht had taken.

"I'm not going anywhere. I want to find Jimmie. He needs our help." Helen was determined to find her student.

A flash of lightning seemed to split the sky open as it went across over their heads. Like a bomb exploding, the sound of the thunder followed almost immediately after the bolt. They all ducked down instinctively and covered their heads.

"Holy shit," Jeremy muttered. "That was fucking crazy."

"Language, Jeremy." Helen looked at him with her stern teacher expression.

He started to mumble an apology, and she laughed. "I'm messing with you, don't worry."

Jeremy smiled a crooked little grin.

They all moved farther into the ruins. "Keep alert for anything that looks unusual. Use all the equipment we have. We have to do our best to find this young man." Roosevelt was, once again, assuming his leadership positon.

"Look!" Roosevelt pointed to the ground below them, about 20 feet from the wall and the walkway on which they stood.

Helen and Jeremy stopped talking and saw what Roosevelt was looking at. They were all astounded. For a moment, not one of them could speak.

The ground had split open, like an overripe melon that had burst from the inside. The rupture spanned about twenty feet, and dirt, rocks, and debris had been thrown out of the fissure.

But there was something else, beyond the split in the ground that had captured their gazes. A long piece of pole was pointing out of it. They could see at the top of it another piece of wood attached to it, and a rope with a noose hanging from it. It looked aged and somewhat rotten, but it also seemed to be holding together.

"Oh my God, that isn't possible." Jeremy stood there and stared at it.

"I am afraid, Jeremy, that given what we have already experienced, anything seems to be possible." Roosevelt did not want to believe, though, what he was seeing. It was like watching a movie, but this was really happening.

A sound came out of the fissure, like that of an old wooden ship that had struck an iceberg. It was loud and prolonged, and as it was heard, something else began to move.

The wood righted itself and moved out of the sliced open muddy ground. As they watched in awe, the wood materialized completely. It was attached to a long base that somehow arose undamaged from the earth, like an oversized insect emerging from a tiny cocoon. Soon it was some old-fashioned wooden gallows, upright and ready for use.

"I think we are going to need more than those blessings," Jeremy said.

As he spoke, mist formed on the platform of the gallows, and they saw the outline of a man come into focus.

"Let's get down from here, so we can get closer," Helen said in a soft voice.

"I agree but be careful." Roosevelt felt like battle would soon break out.

As they moved off the walkway onto the ground, the mist dissipated, and they could clearly see the image of a man with long, ragged brown hair in a ponytail, thin and wearing dark clothing from the 1800s.

As they watched, they saw, seemingly from nowhere, as a skinny African-American teenager, terrified and tied with his hands behind him, appeared on the platform of the gallows.

"That's Jimmie!" Helen shouted and pointed at the teenaged boy.

Chapter 66

August 5, The Present

Sam entered the area where he been instructed to go, and he waited. He was standing in front of the old, deteriorating trailers that had once served as offices in the mill. He could see lights on inside them, so someone had managed to get power hooked up in there, and they didn't seem to care that he could observe this, and it didn't comfort him in any way.

They clearly did not expect Sam to leave here alive.

Sam had never dealt with anyone or anything in quite this way while on the force, and being exposed felt wrong, even though he really didn't care what happened to him. When he was a police detective, they had rules and protocol, and that did not include being completely vulnerable, but he was no longer a police detective. And he would do whatever he had to.

"Well, well, I have to say, I didn't think you would have the balls to show up, Sammie," Max said as he exited from the office trailer and stood in front of Sam. He held two guns pointed straight out. Max looked much like Sam remembered him, only older, but still looking like something out of a barroom brawl. He projected an attitude of a rabid raccoon that had emerged from a dumpster, mean and dangerous.

"You don't really think I'm afraid of you, asshole, do you?" Sam felt no fear, only anger—rage that was building inside him.   He knew what Max had done. And he would have his vengeance.

But he had to control himself, or he had no chance of succeeding.

Max smiled. "Well, no, I didn't. But a guy can hope, can't he?" Max walked towards Sam and continued to hold the two guns pointed straight at him. But he didn't get closer to Sam than about eight feet. Max knew that if he stood too close to Sam, then the former detective would have the potential opportunity to try to take the guns away, and he would not let that happen. No, he was enjoying this moment far too much.

Max had waited years for this time, and he wasn't going to rush it. He wanted to savor every bit of it as if he were slowly eating a porterhouse steak. He wanted to feel the anguish and fear coming out of Sadlowski. That fucker had ruined his family, first putting his father in prison and then shooting his brother. Now, Max was going to finish what he had started with the killing of Sadlowski's son.

"So, I'm here, Max. Where is Maria? This is between you and me, no one else." Sam didn't flinch at the guns facing him. "Let's stop fucking around. Let's do this."

"Well now, Sammy. You don't get to decide who or what I should be concerned with. Or when we do something. I'm in charge here. Think of this as my little version of you being in prison, like I was, and now, this time, I'm your guard. And I think I caught you trying to escape. And you know what happens to prisoners who try to get out." Max was enjoying this.

Sam simply glared at him.

Max smiled. He figured he had Sadlowski exactly where he wanted him. "She's here. The little bitch is here. Don't worry about her. You're the one I care about, asshole."

"Well, you got me, Max. You got me. But you're still nothing but a fucking coward. Afraid to face me without your guns, aren't you?"

As they spoke, lightning crashed across the sky.

"Motherfucker! That was close." Max cringed and ducked as the lightning crashed overhead.

For a brief moment, the whole area was illuminated as if they were there at noon instead of at night.

"Afraid of a little lightning, Max?" Sam smiled. "That was nothing compared to Nam. Oh, that's right...your father wasn't there, was he? Got himself a deferment. What was it for? Let's see if I remember. . . for some bullshit about flat feet, nope that wasn't it. Yeah, he shot a fucking little toe off his left foot. And that's why he limped a little."

"Fuck you, man. Who gives a shit?" Max glared at Sam hard.

"It shows what a fucking candy-assed coward he was, you miserable son of a bitch. You're the same, just like your old man, and just like your brother. All fucking cowards." Sam could feel his anger growing.

Sam continued to hold his hands up, as he was sure Max wanted. But his arms had begun to ache a bit.

"I'll show you who's a coward, you fucker. But first, before we go any further, get rid of your gun, Sammie...very slowly."

Sam reached into his coat and removed his Beretta from its holster, held it out by the end of the grip and dropped it to the ground.

"Good boy, but your other piece too. No pig goes to a meet without his ankle piece."

Sam shrugged. "Well, you got me there." He knelt and pulled up his left pant leg, where his snub-nosed .38 Smith & Wesson revolver was holstered. He also placed that one on the ground and then stood.

"Now, that's being a good boy, Sammie."

"Glad to see you're satisfied. Can I put my hands down now?"

"Sure, Sammie, but you stay right where you are." Max signaled to the trailer, and two more men came out. They were also holding guns, one a very large pistol and the other an Uzi. Quite a bit of firepower.

"So, what now, Max? Are you going to let the girl go?"

"You know I can't do that, Sammie. But look on the bright side. She was dying anyway, so I'll be doing her a favor and make it happen sooner. You know, less suffering that way."

"Yeah, you're a regular good Samaritan, fuckhead. But still a coward. Always was. Always will be."

"Maybe, Sammie. But I'll still be alive when we leave tonight. You'll be in a fucking bodybag."

Sam shrugged. "We all have to go sometime."

Max smiled. "And this is your time."

Chapter 67

August 5, The Present

"Please, help me." Jimmie's plea sounded like it was coming from a much younger child than a teenager. The look on his face said that he had seen too much, and his sanity was receding. He might have been a boy of sixteen, but in the grip of Schwarznacht, he looked like a frightened child of six who had just found out that the monster under the bed was real.

"This sodomite, this nigra, this abomination has desecrated this holy spot, and for that he must be punished!" Schwarznacht hated all who were not white, and he intended to use this teenager as an example of his judgement. He wanted to help the Lord remove such as this interloper from the world. He believed he was God's instrument of retribution. "This is the time of regeneration. I have waited too long, and now this sacred place of punishment will thrive again!"

"He is a crazy as an outhouse possum," Roosevelt said.

Helen looked at him. "I like that simile. It's weird, but I like it. Plus, he's a bigoted asshole."

"C'mon, let's rescue that kid." Jeremy hated what he saw, and he intended to stop this assault now. He had enough of supernatural creatures that threatened children. Was there no end to such horror? If he had anything to do with it, then Jeremy would put an end to it. He held

David's wolf's head cane in his right hand like a club and charged forward, but Roosevelt ran ahead of him.

"No! No one must interfere with this sacred task!" Schwarznacht bellowed at them, his voice filling the area as if he were preaching to his terrified flock.

Roosevelt had started to scramble up the platform on the old steps to the side. Schwarznacht simply looked at the steps, and they shattered under Roosevelt. The old wood of the gallows fell apart under Roosevelt, and he slammed onto the ground. He screamed as his left leg snapped on impact with a large piece of rusted metal on the ground.

"Be gone, sinner! I will deal with you later, after I carry out the execution of this sodomite."

"Rosy!" Jeremy yelled.

Helen ran forward and pulled Roosevelt back. She grunted with her exertion, and he tried not to scream as pain filled his body. She grabbed him under his arms and locked her arms around him. Then she tugged him with all her strength. As Helen pulled Roosevelt, his broken leg bounced on the ground. He screamed and almost passed out from the agony.

"No one can interfere with the execution. It must take place. This is the justice of the Lord! I sentence this sinner to spend the rest of eternity burning in hellfire for his abominations!"

"Please help me," was all Jimmie could say. Tears were now cascading down his cheeks, and his body was shaking with convulsions.

"We have to do something. That fucking loon will kill him." Helen was angry and desperate to find a way to attack the executioner.

She placed Roosevelt on the ground a fair distance from the gallows, and they both looked at the sight of the executioner.

"We can't get to him. I do not know how, but he has resurrected that gallows, and he seems to be able to keep us away from it." Roosevelt was frustrated. There had to be an answer, but they did not seem to have any weapons to use.

"We'd better find a way soon." Helen was watching the gallows.

Schwarznacht dragged the crying teen to under the noose and forced him to stand. "You will do as I say, and you will face the wrath of God. You will be punished for your sins. And then I say unto you, that you three will also feel the wrath of God. You are nothing, but useless sinners, corrupt abominations, and God has placed you into my hands, and I will cut the cord of your life and send you falling into the flames of hell!"

"Really, is that the best you have, asshole? Plagiarizing 'Sinners in the Hands of an Angry God' by Jonathan Edwards? You are not only a hypocrite, but you are also a thief. That wasn't your sermon; you're a pathetic excuse for a preacher! If you were my student, I would fail you for stealing those words!" Helen keep yelling at Schwarznacht, hoping to find some time for them to make a way to Jimmie. She was trying to keep him distracted, at least for a few minutes.

Jeremy lost patience and ran to the platform, but as he reached it, a bolt of lightning crashed from the sky, and hit nearby. Helen saw Jeremy's body flung ten feet from the impact of the strike. He then fell like a broken scarecrow.

"No!" was all Helen could say.

"It is ordained. God demands his justice!" The executioner fit the noose around the teen's neck.

Chapter 68

August 5, The Present

"Time to die, Sammie."

"Maybe it is, and maybe it isn't, asshole." Sam simply looked at him, and Max looked puzzled. Why wasn't this pig afraid and begging for his life? He had planned everything, and even more than simply killing Sam, he wanted to make him grovel. Max wanted to see him on the ground on his knees and begging for his life. Max wanted Sam to know that the power of life and death rested in him. And after he let Sam beg for a while and think he might be spared, then he would kill him. Then Max would put a bullet right through his head. And he would laugh when Sadlowski fell to the ground.

Max stepped forward slightly. "Beg for your life, Sammie. Beg, and maybe I'll decide to let you live, to let you know that I spared your miserable existence."

"No, Max. I don't think so. In fact, maybe you should be the one begging for his life."

Max looked at Sam with scorn. He had had enough.

As he decided to kill Sam, he heard another voice out of the darkness say, "You should really think about dropping your weapons." Steven stepped forward holding a pistol in one hand, and a sawed-off shotgun in the other.

"Well, well, Sammie...not quite as stupid as I thought you were."

Max looked at Steven and laughed. "Got to give it to you. You got balls, but, you see, the thing is, we still got you outgunned." He signaled, and five others came out of the trailer...all armed.

"Do you think I wouldn't be prepared for anything, Sammie?"

The newest additions stood in a semi-circle. Altogether, there were six facing Sam and two against Steven. All were ready for a fight.

But neither Sam nor Steven were going to go away quietly. They were also ready for battle.

The shooting began.

Chapter 69

August 5, The Present

Helen was horrified by the sight of Jeremy sprawled on the ground, but she couldn't stop trying to save the boy.

"Thus, shall all sinners be punished, and the filth of the world shall be cleansed by God's holy fire!" Schwarznacht stood facing out from the gallows, as if he were addressing his flock at his church. He was filled with power and righteousness—he could feel his strength increasing, and those people trying to stop him where only insignificants insects to be crushed. *Let them try to oppose me, and they will feel God's anger!*

Helen ran to Jeremy and saw him open his eyes. His face was covered in dirt from where he fell, and his clothes were torn, but he had no broken bones. "I'm fine. I hurt like hell, but it's nothing like when we fought Maledicus. Help me up, and let's get this self-righteous son of a bitch!"

Helen braced herself and helped Jeremy to his feet. She looked over at Roosevelt who was immobilized with his shattered leg. He sat up though and said, "Go and get that child. Save him. I will see if I can do something to distract him."

They nodded at Roosevelt, and he took out from his coat pocket his .45 Colt Peacemaker and began firing it towards the top of the gallows where the rope to the noose was hung. His shots rang out like cannon fire.

Helen and Jeremy moved to the remains of the steps to the gallows, which now hung precariously. The lightning seemed to have damaged the wood. Still, Helen and then Jeremy scrambled up, buoyed by the fear for Jimmie and the anger towards Scharznacht racing through them.

They ran to where Jimmie was standing with the noose around his neck. When Scharznacht pulled the lever, the floor would drop away, and Jimmie would fall to his death.

They had to get this right the first time. There would be no second chance.

Jeremy put his arms around the trembling teenager, locking him in a tight bear hug. Jeremy then spread his legs on either side of the trap door to hold the boy if the trap door opened. *I hope I'm strong enough to do this. Please let me be.*

Jimmie didn't seem to be able to see anything that was happening. His eyes were vacant, and his head was lolling to one side.

Schwarznacht turned to look at them. "I am delighted you could join me in this sacred place." The executioner laughed. "Now I will have more infidels to eliminate. I sentence the accursed sodomite to death by hanging!"

Chapter 70

August 5, The Present

Now it was eight against two, and those were terrible odds, Sam thought. *Although, not as bad as what Henry V faced in the battle of Agincourt against the French Army. Just can't seem to stay away from Shakespeare...thanks Roosevelt.* Even now, Sam could feel the influence of his closest friend, Roosevelt and his discussions of Shakespeare.

Sam was standing near a pile of steel rubble, and he leapt behind it as the shooting began. His sudden movement drew the fire of the others. Bullets from many weapons were thudding into the pile of steel, some ripping through, dangerously close to him. One sent a piece of shrapnel against his head, ripping open a four inch long cut on the side of his scalp.

"I think I got the asshole," one of Max's men called out.

It was the distraction Steven needed. Standing next to a very large oak tree, he opened fire with his Sig Sauer and quickly took out two of Max's men. They went down without a sound. His shooting skills were still as good as when he earned the Bethberg Police Marksman Award.

Steven quickly moved behind the tree to have cover.

"What the fuck?" Max yelled and pointed at the tree. "Get that motherfucker!"

Two men advanced on Steven, one firing an Uzi, the other a pump action .10-gauge shotgun.

The noise was deafening, and the firepower overwhelming. If something didn't happen soon, they would probably be able to get to and take out Steven.

As they moved forward shooting, a lightning flash sliced across the sky and briefly lit the area as if it were daylight. And the sound of thunder boomed like a bomb exploding in their area. For a moment the advancing men hesitated and crouched slightly.

It was enough.

Sam could see their advance from his position. He reached for his other ankle gun, on his right leg. *Didn't think Max was smart enough to check for two hidden guns,* Sam thought. He also pulled out of his pants pocket a two-shot antique derringer. *Had to come prepared. Can never have enough firepower against assholes like these.*

Sam had a perfect line on the two advancing to Steven. He aimed his other .38 Smith & Wesson snub nosed revolver and fired four shots, two per man in rapid order.

"Fucking shit!" Max roared, as he watched two more of his men drop to the ground.

Now, it's just four, Sam thought. *The odds are getting better.*

Steven aimed around the tree to shoot, but one of Max's soldiers fired first, and Steven fell, clutching his right leg.

Sam fired his last two bullets from the revolver at that man, but he missed.

Sam only had his derringer left. *I got a big problem. Four of them, and only two bullets.*

Plus his head was hurting badly from the cut and the noise. Sam's head felt as if he were back in 'Nam and bombs were exploding near him, only the pain was from the inside of his skull. He wanted to moan, but something instinctive kept him quiet. Dried blood coated the side of his face.

Sam held the derringer ready to use, and he could hear the sound of steps coming towards him.

Chapter 71

August 5, The Present

"I sentence the sodomite to death by hanging!" Schwarznacht pulled the lever, and the trapdoor fell open under Jimmie. The noise sounded like an explosion, and Jeremy felt the vibrations go through his body, as gravity tried to claim the youngster. Jeremy strained against the unconscious teen's weight. He felt his muscles straining almost to the breaking point like a rubber band stretched too far.

No! I can't drop him, Jeremy thought. *Please, let me do this.*

Somehow Jeremy held onto the boy, keeping him from falling through, but it was deadweight now, and Jeremy didn't know how long he could last. He could feel his fingers beginning to lose their grip.

"Helen, help me. I can't hold him for long."

"Anything you try do will not work, sinners!"

"Let's see if you are solid, since you were able to pull the lever," Roosevelt said to himself. He squeezed the trigger emptying the remaining bullets into Schwarznacht.

Schwarznacht screamed in pain as the bullets ripped through him. *How could this infidel hurt me? How is this possible?*

Roosevelt did not expect the bullets to be able to kill something that was already dead, but he had reasoned that if Schwarznacht could affect this physical world, then the laws of physics should apply to him also, at least during the time he was manifested. It was worth the try.

Schwarznacht screeched in pain, then he whirled to face Roosevelt. "I will be certain that I keep the most painful execution for you, offending nonbeliever!"

"You spawn of hell, I am sure God has something planned for you, and I would not count on ending up in heaven."

As Roosevelt was engaging Schwarznacht, Helen was on the other side of the boy from Jeremy and pulling on the rope with one hand. She had a knife out, one with a four inch blade and was cutting furiously on the rope above the kid's neck.

"Helen, hurry, I'm losing my grip. I can't hold him much longer."

"Just a little more, Jeremy. Hold on!" Helen's small, razor sharp knife was slowly working through the thick, hemp rope.

With a last cut, Helen's blade slashed through the rope. She grabbed hold of the boy, and she and Jeremy rolled him off the gallows. Jimmie dropped with a thud, but he was better down there on the ground than up on this platform of death.

"NOOOO!" Schwarznacht looked both angry and surprised. "But this changes nothing, sinners. Watch!"

He pointed at the rope, and it was reforming, as if it were some kind of vine that grew rapidly. Within seconds four more nooses had appeared. "There will be one for all three of you, abominations! I will dispose of you, and then make the sodomite meet his scheduled appointment!"

"It might be time to think about getting out of here," Jeremy said to Helen and Roosevelt.

As Jeremy spoke, a powerful hand grabbed him, and another took Helen by the throat.

Chapter 72

August 5, The Present

A tan minivan pulled up next to Steven's car and parked. *Damnit,* Monica thought. *I knew he was going to do something like this. Can't be married to a man as long as I have and not know what he was going to do.*

She knew he was going to try to find their daughter on his own, but she had other plans.

Steven isn't going to do this alone. We'll both fight for Maria. We're in this together, and we both live or die for our baby girl.

She heard the shooting and yelling. Monica took the pistol from her purse and got out of the car.

She moved toward the shooting quickly and quietly. She moved with the natural grace of the track star she had been in high school and college. And she handled the gun with confidence; after all, her father, a retired Army colonel, had taught her to shoot when she was ten years old.

She had quickly become an expert shot, and she had no fear of using a weapon if needed. She had no emotional attachment to guns—they were simply tools for protecting her family. And now she intended to do just that. *No one threatens or harms my family without paying,* she thought.

She reached a row of trees and saw Steven laying behind one and bleeding badly. He looked like he was awake but in deep pain. He held a shotgun in front of him, but he was shaking badly. She could tell he was in serious trouble.

Monica saw one man move to the right of the tree and one to the left. They were going to use a pincer formation to finish her husband. If they reached him, he would have no chance of survival against them. He might have been able to get one of them, but the other would surely kill her husband.

That will not stand, she thought.

Neither man saw the small African-American woman standing in the classic pistol shooting stance. Before they could get to Steven, she fired at the closer man, the one coming from behind him.

She shot twice and hit him two times, her bullets ripping into his chest and through his heart. He went down in a heap — dead.

The fall of his fellow distracted the other man just enough for Steven to point the shotgun in his general direction and fire.

The blast removed most of the man's face.

Sam saw what had happened. *Son of a bitch!* he thought. *The cavalry has arrived. Down to two. Monica, you truly are an angel from heaven.*

At that moment Sam heard Josh's voice, "And you are my hero, Pop. Please save Maria."

"I plan on it, son."

At this point, Max could see his entire plan had gone to hell. He signaled to his last man to go to the trailer. Now, he had to go into survival technique. He had to do whatever he could to escape and plan to come after that fucker Sadlowski another time.

Sam aimed his derringer and fired once. He hit the man who was retreating to the trailer directly in the chest.

Max was stunned as he saw his last soldier dead on the ground.

Just Max left, Sam thought.

Sam stood and pointed the derringer.

Max laughed. "What the fuck is that little toy, Sammie? It don't beat my piece."

"Really, little man? Mine does," Monica said. "Now drop your gun or die, you bastard."

Coming from Monica, Sam thought that was quite a burst of profanity.

Max couldn't believe it. All his men were dead, and he had two guns pointed at him. The bitch clearly knew what she was doing, and now Sam was advancing on him.

"You think I give a shit if you've got your gun, Max? I only need one bullet to put you in the ground. Just one. So shoot me, I don't give a fuck, but I'll shoot you."

"Fuck you, Sammie."

"No. Fuck you, Max. You killed my son. You killed Josh. And you threatened Maria."

They both pulled their triggers.

But Sam fired first. His bullet landed in the center of Max's forehead. As it did, Max's hand jerked, and his shots went wide.

"Maria!" Monica yelled.

"In there," Sam said and pointed to the trailer. Sam ran to Steven and used his belt as a tourniquet to stop the bleeding. Steven had lost a great deal of blood, but Sam believed he could save his friend if he could get him quickly to a hospital.

Monica came out carrying her terrified daughter. As she did, the ground began to shake.

"Get Steven and get out of here!"

Sam turned to go to the other side of the ruins when he heard Josh's voice again — use fire, Pop. Use fire. Help the others. They are here now fighting the ghost of the executioner. They need you, Pop. They'll die without you.

Chapter 73

August 5, The Present

Sam heard Josh's voice, and he knew what he had to do. Something had changed, and the IPS moved their investigation up one day. He hadn't expected them to reschedule their efforts, but Sam knew he had to help them.

Instead of running towards the western end, where he knew Roosevelt, Jeremy, and Helen would be, Sam hurried back to his car. It would be faster. He jumped in and slammed the accelerator to the floor, and his vintage Camaro roared onto the road, like a low-flying airplane. The car flung gravel and spun out of the parking lot as if he were in a chase scene in an action movie.

He handled the car perfectly as he careened to the western part of the ruins. He saw the IPS van and slammed the brakes, stopping the Camaro with a screech next to the van. As he stood next to the car, Sam observed the IPS, an unconscious teenaged boy, and what looked like a battle was going on.

Sam saw some large and decrepit looking gallows not far ahead, with Roosevelt on the ground holding a broken leg, trying to move, a body of a teen-aged boy lying near him, and Jeremy and Helen on the gallows struggling with what looked like an executioner out of the history books. He held them both and was dragging them to nooses. They were struggling with all their might, but they clearly could not break his grip.

"Helen! Jeremy! I'm coming," Sam yelled, but they couldn't hear him.

The sound of Josh's voice kept repeating in his mind, Fire, Pop, Use fire!

Sam ran to the IPS van. *Please be there, please be there,* he thought.

Sure enough, there it was—two five-gallon containers of gasoline that they always carried in case they needed to use their generator. *Thank you, Jeremy. I swear, I'll never bust on you again for being so organized.*

Sam disconnected the large gas cans from the straps that held them in place and hefted one by each hand. He let out a large grunt as he lifted them. *Damn. I definitely have to get to the gym more often. Should be able to handle these with no problem. Feels like I'm carrying a hundred pounds in each arm.*

Sam held onto the cans and ran with them to the gallows as fast as he could.

Sam's heart was pounding, and he was sweating profusely with blood running down his face. His arms were aching, and he felt like he might fall over, but he continued.

It was like being in a dream where he felt like he was trying to run through mud and getting nowhere.

Somehow, Sam found the strength to continue, and he moved forward.

He looked up and saw Schwarznacht laughing at him. "Here comes another infidel waiting to be executed. Look, he is running to my grasp. But you will have to wait until I dispose of these other sinners!"

Sam stopped at the gallows. "I can't wait, pal!"

Sam set the cans down and opened both of them.

As he started splashing gasoline over the base of the gallows, he heard the executioner cry out, "Stop, sinner!

You are not allowed to desecrate this sacred place. I have God's business to do."

"Well, you don't look like no kind of angel to me, just another asshole. And those are my friends you got there. Let them go now, freak, or I torch your setup!" He had finished covering much of the base of the gallows with gasoline. As Sam emptied one can, he threw it aside and poured the gasoline from the other around it.

"No! You cannot harm this spot. This is holy ground. You will be destroyed! God will send his holy punishment and strike you down!"

"We'll see about that, crazy motherfucker!" Sam took out his lighter and flicked the flame on.

"NOOOOOOOOOOO!" Schwartnacht dropped Helen and Jeremy and swept both arms forward.

As the executioner did this, wind seemingly from behind him, struck forward like that of a gale. The gust howled like an ancient banshee screaming in the night.

Sam's lighter flew backwards out of his hands, and the force of the wind knocked him to the ground.

Chapter 74

August 5, The Present

As Schwartznacht roared, two things happened: the sky lit up with several lightning strikes, as if bombs were cascading around the ruins. Some of the lightning went sideways. Some crashed to the ground nearby. The sky seemed to alternate between light of day and dark of night as though they were in some supernatural ball room with a paranormal strobe light.

Simultaneously, the ground began to rumble. As the strikes hit nearby, the fault that ran under the western end of the ruins also began to move. The gallows shook, and one end collapsed to the ground, forming a steep ramp. Helen and Jeremy rolled off. She helped him up, and they staggered forward. As they rose, they looked for the unconscious teenager and moved towards him where he fell on the ground.

"Into the van! Now!" Sam ran forward and saw Rosy crawling. He raced to his old friend, who shouted, "No, get the boy first!"

"Rosy, don't worry. Helen and Jeremy have him. It's you I need to get away from here."

Sam saw a piece of steel about five feet long, from an old railing. He grabbed it and helped Roosevelt stand. "Use this as a crutch."

"Sam," Roosevelt shouted. "They do not have the boy. Schwarznacht is blocking their way." As the executioner was occupied with trying to keep Helen and Jeremy away from his condemned prisoner, Sam saw his chance.

He hurried behind the turned execution and ran to the fallen teen. He felt his neck. Still alive.

Sam knelt to pick up the boy.

As Sam hefted the youngster and put him in the classic firefighter's carry, Schwartznacht appeared directly in front of Sam, blocking his way. "You can't have him. I must have the sinner to exterminate."

"Samuel, run with the boy! I am your backup! Ignore him."

Roosevelt had seen what Sam had been attempting. He pulled his own lighter out, flicked it on, and threw the flame into the fuel, igniting the trail of gasoline.

It only took a few seconds for most of the gallows to begin to burn. The gasoline ignited the wood, the winds fed oxygen to the fire, and an inferno burst into being.

Sam staggered forward, with the boy slung over his right shoulder. He moved to Roosevelt and let him hold onto his right arm. Together, they moved to the van. When Jeremy and Helen saw them, they ran forward and helped everyone into it.

"Drive, as fast as you can!" Jeremy could see the ground splitting open.

Sam pounded the gas pedal. The van lurched forward. It didn't have the pickup of his beloved Camaro, but it would have to do.

Schwarznacht screamed as his gallows burned. As the structure began to collapse, it was engulfed in flames, like a large bonfire, but with no celebration of high school kids around it.

As it burned, another quake shook the ground—it started with a massive boom that could be heard for miles, and tremors that could be felt as far away as Reading, PA.

The fault ran deep in the earth, and this quake reached the depth of the natural gas pool. The gallows was now collapsing and falling into the widening fault.

Schwarznacht felt his power leaving him, and he felt himself growing smaller and weaker. The split in the ground went the distance of the ruins, and a large hole opened swallowing everything, including the crumbling ashes of the gallows.

The entire length of the ruins, running from one end to the other, was crumbling into the ground.

A piece of flaming pole broke off the gallows and careened into the edge of the natural gas.

More explosions bellowed, and an inferno burst out of the earth. Flames erupted out of the hole in the ground sending giant tongues of bright red high into the sky. Smoke and filthy ground, like that from decaying graveyards, was flung upward and swirled together like a diseased torrent. The smoke rose like the beginnings of a small mushroom cloud.

Schwarznacht was frantic. He tried to stop the blaze, but he was impotent to halt the carnage. His form began to flame as he tried to extinguish the blaze.

He howled in torment, and his body began to fade in and out of existence.

As more and more of the gallows burned to ashes, he became less and less material. He was fading away.

As they cleared the area, Helen yelled, "You have to see this!"

Sam pulled the van over and looked back, along with the others.

It was like someone had ignited a small atomic bomb, but without the radiation. A cloud of debris raised into the sky about 100 feet over the ruins. They thought they could hear a loud scream, but it might have been steel grinding against other pieces of metal.

"Let's get out of here, now. I don't think staying here is a very good idea, guys." Jeremy spoke in a low voice, but Sam nodded and hit the gas hard.

Behind them, the earth opened like it had been split in a running seam under the ruins. This fissure went the entire span of the old mill. A final sheet of flame burst from deep within the earth, and more black smoke billowed into the sky. It reached so high that the stars and the moon were temporarily hidden from the ground, leaving only a carpet of darkness over the ruins.

Everything that had been at the site was swallowed by the giant fissure, as if a large shark was swallowing a school of small fish in its open maw. Old steel, cars, and corpses all fell into the wide pit and were incinerated by the flames, like the fires of Gehenna itself were bursting forth.

Schwarznacht gave one more scream into the night. It was a howl that created a cacophony, like a discordant symphony played by devils and demons on hellish instruments. As the screaming ceased, Schwarznacht simply vanished out of the air, burnt away from this world.

Then the earth and debris uprooted by the explosion fell back to the ground as the split in the land sealed back together, leaving only a wide scar as if a giant sword had carved through the entire area, and it left no trace of the old steel ruins behind.

All that remained was a misshapen field of dirt that covered what had been the steel mill ruins only minutes before.

Chapter 75

August 5 — August 29, The Present

It didn't take long for emergency vehicles to respond to the explosion at the site, but all they found was debris. No indication of anyone having been there could be found. Sam's Camaro and the cars that brought Max and his crew had been swallowed, along with the corpses of the fallen men.

Satisfied that no one needed tending, the emergency responders rapidly dispersed to a series of other calls resulting from the unusual thunderstorm and sudden earthquake. Luckily, no one was injured, and only minor property damage occurred.

While an investigation took place, nothing came of it. With neither an apparent crime nor victims to associate with it, the authorities quickly moved on to other matters.

Earthquake investigators were, however, fascinated by the oddity of the seismic event, which seemed to be highly localized in a unique way. It would give scientists from local institutions of higher education material for study for years to come.

The IPS went straight to the Bethberg Hospital where Roosevelt's broken leg was set, and Jimmie was admitted for observation.

Helen altered the truth of what happened because she knew no one would believe her.

She simply reported that Jimmie's friends had contacted her, and they had come upon him because Sam, the former cop, suggested likely places where teens might go. He was tested for drug usage but was completely clean. After several days, he seemed to be fine, although he was disoriented and had no memory of what had happened.

"That is probably a blessing for Jimmie," Helen had said. "He doesn't need to have to deal with that trauma on top of the stress he went through."

Jimmie's friends were overjoyed that he was okay, and they also decided that speaking of this matter would be in no one's best interest. Besides, who would believe them anyway? They would all be seen as delusional. Letting people think it was just the unfortunate result of wild teenagers getting into trouble was fine with them. They would soon be yesterday's story.

And Helen would continue to keep an eye on them.

Roosevelt simply reported, at the hospital, that he fell after losing his balance. The doctors who treated him saw only an elderly man prone to accidents.

Max was declared a fugitive from the law, because he was officially listed as having broken his parole. Sam and Steven knew he would never be found.

Steven recovered from his wound after reporting that he had been shot by unknown assailants, and his fellow officers were relieved that he would survive. Perhaps, his Captain had suggested to him that after recovery, it might be time to think about retirement. With his wound treated and completely bandaged, Steven checked out of the hospital. He had important matters to attend to.

Maria was returned to the hospice, and she lived three more weeks with her parents by her side for every minute, at least once Steven was able to leave the hospital. Monica and Steven slept there, ate there, and showered there. Sam and the IPS visited, but when the time came, Maria passed quietly in her sleep. Steven and Monica both cried and held each other.

Roosevelt, Helen, and Jeremy attended Maria's funeral as a group. Sam sat near Steven and Monica. At the wake, Sam placed a picture of Josh and Maria into her casket. "Thank you, Pop," he heard Josh say to him.

Chapter 76

September 1, The Present

Helen, Jeremy, and Roosevelt were sitting at the table in Sam's kitchen drinking coffee and tea. Sam had also put out bagels, biscotti, donuts, and cream cheese and jam. "Not quite what we can get at the diner," Sam had said. "But it will have to do."

"Well, actually, Sammie. It's pretty good," Jeremy said as strawberry jam over on half of a toasted pumpernickel bagel.

"Indeed, it is." Helen bit into a chocolate biscotti and smiled.

Roosevelt looked at his friend and sipped his coffee. "Samuel, this is not like you. Why did you insist on meeting here?"

Sam grinned. "Because Rosy, I have something to show you. Please follow me down the hallway." He stopped for a moment and looked back. "Rosy, please be careful, and don't fall again, old man."

Sam laughed at the annoyed look on his friend's face.

"Samuel, I am certain I can negotiate the battlefield of your hallway." Roosevelt stood and used two crutches to walk with. It would be at least another month or so before his broken leg was healed.

Normally, Sam's hallway was laden with a variety of things piled up—books, boxes, and tools found their way to one side or the other.

But because he knew Roosevelt would have to go down the passageway, he completely cleared everything, and the hallway was safe for walking.

Sam led them to the door at the end of the hallway and opened it. As they walked through to that room, they were stunned.

They had entered Sam's painting studio, a place they did not know existed, a sanctuary he had shared with no one. "I wanted you three to be the first to know that I am painting again. No more hiding from the world, especially not from my closest friends."

"Sam," Helen said and smiled a huge grin. "This is wonderful! I'm so happy you're doing this." Helen hugged Sam tight.

Jeremy and then Roosevelt did the same.

After Roosevelt's hug, Sam said, "I have one more thing to show you." Sam walked to a painting on an easel that was covered with a sheet.

Sam stood to one side and pulled the covering away. It was a portrait of Josh as a teenager, based on a photograph Sam had taken of him on their last fishing trip. Josh was smiling, his blond hair unruly in the wind, and his blue eyes sparkled.

"That's amazing," Jeremy said in a soft voice.

"It's beautiful." Helen's eyes sparkled with tears.

"Samuel," Roosevelt said. "This is the very image of Josh. I remember that day, because you both stopped in the diner after fishing, and I happened to be there. No one, and remember, Samuel, that I know art and painting very well, no one could have done a better job. This is your son."

Sam smiled and continued to beam as he stood next to the painting. Tears ran down his broad face. "That's my boy."

Chapter 77

September 9, The Present

Two weeks after Maria's funeral, Sam and Martha sat in a corner booth at Taylor's Hotel. It was an older bar, that once had been a dive, but the new owners did a complete renovation, including restoring its walls to the way it had been when built in the late 1700s, so that now it was an upscale bar and restaurant. The lathe between some of the granite stones could still be seen, and they featured a wide variety of excellent beers on tap and both basic bar food and upscale cuisine. It had several rooms, and Sam had reserved a small table in one of the side enclaves.

This room had been prepared to his specifications, including a dozen red roses placed into a vase on their table.

He had picked up Martha, in a 2006 Ford Mustang he had purchased to replace his lost beloved '66 Camaro that had been swallowed in the earthquake. He knew he would grow to love this car as much as the previous one. It had as he had told Roosevelt after purchasing it, "plenty of kick."

Sam was dressed in a new and tailored three piece suit—"I like the old-fashioned look of the vest," he had said when having it altered to fit him.

Martha wore a modest red dress and a scarf around her shoulders. When Sam saw her, he thought, *She is the most beautiful woman in the world.*

They had been seated and ordered their meals, and they were sipping glasses of white wine. Sam had also requested a favor from the owner, Stan, a fellow he knew and had helped in the past with a problem with his son. Sam didn't break any laws in doing this favor, but he did facilitate helping the kid enter a good long-term rehab for drug addiction issues. Stan smiled at Sam's request and played Motown over the sound system when they went to their table.

When the Platters began singing "Heavenly Shades of Night Are Falling," Sam stood and asked Martha to dance with him. They stood, easily went into each other's arms, and slowly moved with the gentle rhythm of the music.

As the song ended, they looked at one another, and they kissed.

"I won't be a coward again," Sam said.

Coming in 2019
From Charles F. French

Evil Lives After:
The Investigative Paranormal Society
Book 3

Prologue

Visual Delights was a new and successful art gallery in the downtown of Bethberg, PA. Bethberg was making a determined push to build a series of art galleries in the town to compete with the success some of the other nearby communities, such as Jim Thorpe, PA, Easton, PA, and Bethlehem, PA had with creating this environment.

The gallery existed in a part of what had been a bank for decades from the end of the 19th into the first part of the 20th Century. The bank failed in the Great Depression, and the building, which was ornate and granite, was purchased and became, at first, an illegal speakeasy. For several years, during the 1930s, the building also served as a meeting place for local Nazis and white power groups who wanted to keep the USA out of any European war. When World War Two began and patriotism filled the majority of the country, the local Nazis stopped meeting at the nightclub and went into hiding, like cockroaches afraid of being seen in the light.

After prohibition was lifted, the owners simply changed the speakeasy to being, a legal nightclub, a playground for the local wealthy crowd.

The nightclub was successful into the early 1960s until the mysterious death of a young woman in the basement of the building.

She was found on the floor in a situation "of distress" as the reporting went at the time. No further details were ever released. A police investigation was inconclusive, but rumors spread quickly about the girl being a mistress of a local business magnate and a possible unwanted pregnancy. Nothing could be determined, but the resulting scandal drove the local crowd away, and the nightclub went bankrupt.

The building was then vacant for many years, until recently a consortium of investors, interested in trying to create a local art scene, purchased the property and renovated the building. It was divided into several sections for stores, the smallest of which was now the gallery Visual Delights.

The town leaders were pleased so far with the increased business and tourism that was coming into the community, and they saw this building, its stores, and the gallery as a welcome addition to the small city. They wanted Bethberg to be seen as a place welcoming to upcoming artists who might one day have their work displayed in Manhattan.

Terry Swenson, a woman in her late 20s, with a M.A. in Art History from Villanova University, was curating the upcoming exhibit of paintings from local painters, all of whom had been judged to be of very high quality and might be able to impress buyers from the New York City. This show would open on the event the town called "Third Friday" in which local galleries and stores on that date in each month stayed open into the evening, served wine and snacks, and encouraged patrons to walk around the downtown. Bethberg had been holding this event for several years, with increasing success. The next installment would be in just two days, so Swenson wanted everything to be correct.

The gallery had three rooms, the largest of which also featured a raised stage with 4 steps to reach it. The very best of the local painters would have their work featured in this prominent area.

Terry stepped back and examined the three paintings on display—one an abstract with a play of colors and shapes; one a stunning landscape of the outside of town, almost harkening to the much earlier Hudson Valley school of painters; and one a mixed media of household items, featuring built up 3d images on top of the painting.

She jotted down some notes on her tablet and turned to go down the steps to the adjacent room. She had much to do to continue preparing for the opening of the art show.

But first, Terry needed to go into the basement for more supplies. As she walked, she felt a hand grab her ankle, and she fell down the steps.